FLOR DE MUERTOS BOOK 3

VINDICTIVE BLOOD

JOCELYNE SOTO

I had one job and one job only.

Bring down the most notorious drug lord known to man.

Dead or alive, that was it.

As I worked the case more and more, the lines started getting blurred. I made enemies where I wasn't supposed to and friends in places that would get me killed.

Then I met her, at a bar in Midtown Manhattan of all places. She became the one thing in my life that was a constant, the one thing that made the dark hole I was in as bright as could be. She was younger but that didn't matter to either of us. I was starting to see a future with her. That is until I heard her cries of despair for her father.

That man I'm supposed to take down?

That man is the father of the woman I love.

A federal agent falling for a kingpin's daughter never ends well.

CONTENTS

Author's Note	ix
Prologue	1
Chapter 1	3
Chapter 2	14
Chapter 3	23
Chapter 4	34
Chapter 5	44
Chapter 6	57
Chapter 7	67
Chapter 8	80
Chapter 9	90
Chapter 10	100
Chapter 11	107
Chapter 12	117
Chapter 13	127
Chapter 14	136
Chapter 15	143
Chapter 16	152
Chapter 17	160
Chapter 18	169
Chapter 19	181
Chapter 20	192
Chapter 21	205
Chapter 22	211
Chapter 23	223
Chapter 24	234
Chapter 25	244
Chapter 26	251

Chapter 27	259
Chapter 28	268
Chapter 29	274
Chapter 30	285
Chapter 31	292
Chapter 32	298
Chapter 33	308
Chapter 34	317
Chapter 35	326
Chapter 36	335
Chapter 37	346
Epilogue	357
Playlist	367
Acknowledgments	369
Books by Jocelyne Soto	371
About the Author	373
Join My Reader Group	375
Newsletter	377

Do not break. You are strong and are able to get through anything and everything imaginable.

AUTHOR'S NOTE

This story contains on page violence, gun violence and death by gun. If this is something that you are not comfortable reading, please do not continue.
If you would like more information about the content warnings related to this book, please visit my website for more information.
Thank you.

NATHANIEL

I'VE BEEN TOLD my whole life that revenge is a dangerous game.

One that you can't necessarily come back from.

If it's something that you truly are invested in, that you take as seriously as you do staying alive, then it will take over every last bit of you.

You will become a new person, losing the person that you once were, forever. There will be no chance that you will ever get them back.

Revenge is a deadly sin and there is never an end in sight. Especially if you've made it a lifelong mission.

You may think at times that the end is closer than you thought possible, but then you have to reevaluate everything. That's when you realize that you are nowhere near where you want to be.

This all started with a friendship, then the money came and lines got blurred. That is until it all escalated to a burning car with a body inside and a man dead.

And it will continue to escalate until the one person that started all of this is taken down.

Until the person that called for the execution is behind bars or better yet, dead.

For years, I've been trying to accomplish this. I've been trying to take down the man that decided it was his choice when my father died.

For years, I've been working tirelessly to make that happen.

Everything that I have done in my life has been to make sure I was the one that did it.

I did my research.

I know the history.

I became the agent.

I made sure that I did everything that I could so that I would succeed in my mission.

My whole life has centered around one thing and one thing only.

Take down Ronaldo Morales, the most feared man in Mexico.

The drug lord.

The kingpin.

The head of the Muertos Cartel.

It's been years, but the time has finally come.

Ronaldo Morales will meet his demise and it will be at my hand.

It's time that Ronaldo pays for his sins.

CAMILA

WHEN IT COMES TO LIFE, I always expect the worst.

I guess it was the way that I was brought up that made me like that, to doubt anything good that has ever come my way. All because there have been dark moments that have come and ruined it right after.

Because I tend to expect the worst in most scenarios, I tend to try not to get my hopes up for any little thing.

There is absolutely no reason for hopes to be up if a black hole is going to open in front of me and suck me in.

There have been too many occasions in my life where this has happened. Maybe not necessarily a black hole, but there has been death. Lots of death.

And all of that is because of my father.

Don't go there, Camila. Do not go there.

Thinking about my father is not going to get me anywhere, so I'm going to lock it up and put it in the back of my mind. At least, for now.

I have more important things to do. Like not getting my

hopes up about the interview I just left. The interview that could possibly change the whole trajectory of my life.

I just need to keep my hopes in check just in case I don't get in, because in all the honesty that I have, I will be fucking devastated if I don't.

If you must know, I'm currently in New York City for an interview for a spot at NYU and their prestigious art department. For the past year, I've been working on my art degree at a community college in San Antonio, Texas.

The farthest that my father would let me go. Which raises a few eyebrows since my sister was able to go to Austin, which is another hour and a half drive north, but that's irrelevant, I guess.

San Antonio was nice and it was a great place to get my feet out in the real world, but it wasn't for me. I probably would have stayed there and finished my degree, but given the actions of my father, I wanted out.

Here I go thinking about him again.

My father is a cartel drug lord, and throughout my life I've heard of all the despicable things he has done in his line of work but never seen them firsthand.

I experienced what it's like to have all the money in the world and get everything that I ask for, thanks to the cartel.

But I never experienced the actual inner workings and how dark that world actually was until this year.

Until my father forced my older sister to marry the son of another cartel boss to gain money and power. For the first time in my life, I saw how little my father cares about his children, how everything that makes him even bigger and powerful is what takes precedence.

This man that I held up on a pedestal, that I saw as someone that could do no wrong, proved to me in just a short amount of time that all he cared about was himself.

For the first time in my life, I was scared of him. If he could practically sell off my sister for money and personal gain, what would happen to me? Would I be sent to another country in exchange for better coke?

That was always a dark thought that came creeping in when I least expected it.

It was at the wedding of my sister that I saw who my father really was. Saw the monster that he had become. He was good at hiding it, from not letting his real self show. But that day, that day it all just came out.

I was dragged out of the church by him, away from the protection of my brother and sister. Away from people that actually loved me.

That night was also the first time that my father laid a hand on me. As soon as we were in the comfort of his estate and inside his four walls, he swung back and struck me on the cheek, repeatedly. All while he was yelling at me that I needed to respect him, that I needed to do my daughterly duty and do what I was told. I lost count of how many times he struck me, but it was enough to bring tears into my eyes and for my face to swell.

My father slapping me is something that I have yet to mention to my siblings.

My cheek was red and started to bruise in the days that followed, and that's when I decided that I wanted out.

No, I needed out.

So, I started packing. I was going to run away, but then

I overheard my father talking about how my brother, Leonardo, was going to be coming to the estate.

That day I applied heavy makeup to my face to cover up the bruising and I was planning to sneak away with him.

That is until my sister Isabella, came into my room and told me that I was going to be leaving with her and that she had lined up something for me in New York.

If I wanted it.

Did I want to leave my father's estate in Mexico for an opportunity in New York that wasn't a sure thing?

Fuck yes.

So, I grabbed all the bags that I packed and walked out of that estate at my sister's side. Not one mention at the amount of make-up that I was wearing.

Now three weeks later, I'm out of my father's grasp, for now, the bruising on my face almost non-existent and in New York for my interview with NYU.

I think the interview itself went well. I just have a hard time when someone is looking at my work with a critical eye. It's as if I know they will find something wrong with it and criticize the fuck out of it and tell me that I don't know what I'm doing.

Painting and drawing are two things that I hold near and dear to my heart. It's something that I did with my mother almost daily before she died.

With Isabella, she made dresses or anything that had to do with sewing. With Leo, actually I don't know what she did with Leo, I just remember that he used to complain a lot about doing whatever it was.

With me, she used to paint. I may have been under the age of five, but I still remember having her there teaching me how to hold a pencil and a brush and all the different mediums we used to do with them.

Now painting has become a passion of mine even fifteen years after her death.

Fingers crossed that the head of the art department really like my stuff and offers me a spot.

Otherwise, I don't know what I would do if they don't.

Do I go back to San Pedro, Mexico, to my father's estate with my tail between my legs and pretend like nothing happened?

Do I find another program? Maybe one that is even farther away from him?

I don't know,

but for now, I need a drink.

Something to get my head out of the possible impending doom, because when something good happens bad is only a few feet away.

I continue walking down the sidewalk of the busy New York City street, until a small pub-like restaurant comes into view.

The sign on the window announcing the best burger on this side of Manhattan is enticing enough for me to walk in.

The place isn't empty but it's not exactly popping either, but it's enough people to make me think that this place is actually good.

Instead of finding a table, I head straight to the bar and make myself comfortable on one of the stools.

"Can I get you something to drink?" the female bartender asks, placing a small napkin in front of me.

"Can I get a shot of whatever tequila you think is best and a Pacifico?"

"Sure. Can I see an ID?" she asks, an eyebrow raised and a smirk playing at her lips.

You're not in Mexico anymore, Camila.

Right.

"Sorry, I guess my mind is still in Mexico. I'm not twenty-one. Can I get a club soda with lemon instead?"

She gives me a smile. "Sure."

Right away, a glass lands on the napkin and she fills it with the club soda before putting in a couple slices of lemon.

"Thank you."

"No problem." She gives me a nod and starts to walk away.

"Wait, do you have chicken strips?" I stop her.

I need some sort of comfort food so that I don't start to spiral in my thoughts and chicken strips are a staple, no matter how old you are. If this place served Mexican food, then I would be eating a whole different meal.

She looks over at the space next to me, possibly at a patron that just arrived before she gives me a small smile and nods.

"I do."

"Can I put an order in? With ranch. And a side of garlic fries if you have them?"

Now she is fighting not to let out a laugh. "Sure, anything else?"

"Boneless buffalo wings, with more ranch."

The laugh that the bartender was trying to hold in, finally escapes and she gives me a nod.

"I'll put that in for you," she says before turning to the person that just walked up. "I'll be right with you, Nate."

"Take your time," the Nate guy answers.

Holy shit.

My focus instantly leaves the bartender retrieving and is hyperaware of the strange man next to me.

That voice.

All he said was three words and I so badly want to turn to see if the face matches the voice. Because damn. I want to pull out my phone and record it, so I can hear it every single time I fall asleep. Okay maybe that's a little much, but still, no one should get this hot and bothered over three simple words. Yes, three simple words made me squirm just a bit.

Don't turn, Camila. Do not turn.

Too late.

I turn slightly as if I were looking at the door to see who just came in. Of course my eyes don't play along, so they position themselves on the floor by the man's feet and travel up to his face.

Where I make direct contact with a smirk and the bluest eyes that I have ever seen staring back at me.

A blue that looks like ice meeting a dark ocean. Hair that is blond but looks like a lighter shade of brown.

A man that could very much be any woman's wet dream.

My wet dream.

Fuck.

Abort mission.

Abort mission!

I feel a slight blush creep up my cheeks as I rapidly turn to face the giant wall of liquor in front of me.

I try to look anywhere but the gorgeous man that is next to me.

And when I say gorgeous, I mean this man is fucking gorgeous. Like out of this world. I don't even know how to explain it.

And yes, I do mean 'man', because the person standing a few feet away from me has nothing boyish about him. He must be a good ten years older than me.

I continue to look at the wall as I hear the stool next to me dragging against the floor.

Oh my god, is he pulling it out? Is he going to sit next to me while I wait for my chicken strips like a child?

It doesn't help that the second he sits down, the bartender comes back with my three plates and my immense amounts of ranch.

I guess this gorgeous man is about to witness me stuff my face. Now would be a good time for that black hole to open and suck me in.

I concentrate on the food while the bartender makes googly eyes at my new barstool neighbor.

"What can I get you, Nate?" the bartender crosses her arms and places them right under her boobs and leans forward until both me and Nate are looking down her shirt.

I'm all for flaunting what you have, but don't do it in

front of my chicken strips. They shouldn't be subjected to that, but I must admit, this girl's chest is something to be envious about.

"I'll have the same thing as my companion, extra ranch and all."

If I wasn't looking at him in the mirror, I would have missed the nod he threw my way.

"Sure," the bartender gives him a sweet smile. "Anything else?"

"Club soda with lemon."

Okay, this guy is either trying to get my attention, or my meal made him want his own. Honestly, if I heard that there were chicken strips involved, I would do the same.

"Coming right up."

She makes his drink like she did mine and goes to put in his order.

As soon as we are somewhat alone, I have to go and open my mouth.

"She wants you to fuck her," I say to my neighbor as soon as the bartender steps foot into the kitchen. My words causing him to spit out the drink of club soda he was about to swallow down.

"Jesus." He coughs, reaching for the napkins in front of him to wipe up the mess.

"Sorry." The feeling of club soda up his nose must burn.

"Are you really?" He raises an eyebrow at me, while he wipes his mouth, a hint of teasing on his voice.

"For the comment, no. For causing you to snort up your drink, absolutely."

He continues to wipe up his mess but given the smile he's wearing he finds what just happened at least a little funny.

"I'll take that apology then."

The bartender comes back with his food and this time she doesn't hang around. She just places the plates down and goes to the other side of the bar.

"Are you really going to eat chicken strips?" I ask when I see him grab a piece and dip it in the ranch.

"What's wrong with chicken strips?" He looks at me as he takes a huge bite of the chicken drenched in ranch. I smile a little when I see the ranch all over his mouth.

"Nothing, chicken strips are a staple. Just figured a man like you would much rather eat a burger or big juicy steak."

"A man like me, huh?" Another bite. This time of a wing.

Why the hell am I so entranced by him eating?

"Uh-huh." I divert my attention to my own food, trying very hard to not turn back to my neighbor.

"Well, I can tell you right now that the type of man that you think I am and the actual one, are very different."

I dip my wing into the ranch and after my garlic fries are covered in ketchup, I finally turn back to him.

"Maybe you should tell me about the actual man then." I stuff the wing into my mouth.

It's as I'm chewing that I realize the words that I spoke.

Shit.

I really need to control the crap I say.

My neighbor, Nate, I mean, laughs a little as I keep looking at him.

"Well, since I'm sharing a meal with you, I would think that's fair."

Nate shifts his body toward me and extends a hand.

"Let's start with names. I'm Nate."

I give him a smile and without thinking I place my hand in his.

"I'm Cam—" I stop. Should I really give him my real name? Sure, it's just first names that we are exchanging, but I don't know who this guy is. For all I know he could take my first name and find out everything about my family. All it can take is a few clicks and all the family secrets are out in the open. So, I swallow down and plant a smile on my face. "I'm Cami."

"Nice to meet you, Cami."

"Nice to meet you, Nate."

Even if it's for a few minutes, I want to be Cami and not Camila, the drug lord's daughter. I don't want to be the girl that is trying to escape her father and only be the girl that is scared that she isn't going to get into her dream school.

And what better way to do that than to pretend to be someone that isn't held down by her family's actions?

Being Cami for a little bit is a good way to start.

2

NATHANIEL

Do I have better things to do than sit at a bar talking to a pretty girl?

Fuck yeah, I do. Currently my desk has files stacked up so high that I won't see the bottom of it until a year from now.

Would I rather be here and forget about work while I talk to this girl? Again, fuck yeah, I do.

I don't make it a personal mission of mine to strike up conversations with random women, but there was something about this one that intrigued me.

Maybe it was the way that she stood out in this dingy bar and the way she told everyone here that she didn't belong without saying much.

Or maybe it had to do with the fact that I haven't interacted with a woman in months.

That is true.

I've been so lost in my work that the only women that I have interacted with has been Nikki the bartender and the ones that I work with.

Doing what I do, it doesn't leave a whole lot of time for socialization.

There are other things that take priority.

But right now, I want to forget about the files on my desk, the ones about murderers and drug trafficking and enjoy a random lunch with a strange woman.

"Now that the names are out of the way, are you going to tell me about the man you really are?" I watch Cami as she grabs two of her fries and puts them in her mouth.

Her eyes are bright, even with the chocolate brown color of them, there's a twinkle in them that you don't see in many women.

I give her a smirk. "What do you want to know?" My eyes stay on her as I grab a piece of chicken and pop it into my mouth.

As I chew, I see her eyes land on the lower region of my face and she watches the motions of my jaw. I keep watching and start to become captivated when she licks her own lips at the action.

She shakes her head before she answers. "What's a guy wearing such an expensive suit like yours doing in a bar like this eating chicken strips?"

Well, damn.

She's right, the suit that is currently adorning my body is way too expensive to be touching the sticky vinyl that I'm currently sitting on.

Do I care?

I'm sure my head would be full of gray hairs if I did.

In my line of work, I have to wear suits often. Mostly

for the office, but it's still often enough for me to think that I needed to invest in a few good pieces.

They may look as simple to the ordinary eye, but I guess there are people like Cami here, that can tell when a Tom Ford suit is in their vicinity.

"My work is close by, and like the sign on the window says, they have the best burger this side of Manhattan. I come here when I actually have time to grab a bite to eat."

It's not very often, but it does happen.

"Are you a lawyer?" Her eyebrows bunch up like being a lawyer is a bad thing.

I shake my head. "Detective."

More like a special agent, but detective simplifies things.

I work for the Drug Enforcement Agency, better known as the DEA. We work to enforce every drug law that this country has. Every piece of my job is ass deep in the illegal drug trade that happens against the United States of America.

Gangs. Mafia, Cartel. We handle them all.

In a simpler context, my job takes down the criminals that smuggle illegal substances into this country and distribute them.

At least I try to. There is one drug lord that I've been trying to take down for years, and I have yet to do it.

Soon.

Soon the bastard will be behind bars.

I just have to keep my fingers crossed that I see it happen.

Shaking out of that headspace, I concentrate on Cami, who is looking at me with pursed lips.

"Don't have a thing for detectives?" I jokingly throw out.

It wouldn't be the first time that a woman didn't appreciate my choice of career.

Cami shakes her head. "Never met one. I was always told to believe that when it comes to cops, I shouldn't trust them."

Well, that's not encouraging at all.

"Do I look like a man that you shouldn't trust?" I ask her, looking her straight in the eye.

Throughout my thirteen years in law enforcement, I have done my fair share of things that could be questionable. I've done a handful of those things in just the last year, but I'm not dirty, and I don't plan on becoming it.

Anyone that comes to me for anything, can trust me with their life and hold me to my word. No matter how shady they might be.

Again, Cami shakes her head. "Even with a few minutes of conversation, I can tell that you are trustworthy."

I nod, accepting her statement.

We eat for a few minutes in silence, but every once in a while, we look up at each other and give the other a small smile.

As I finish my wings, I turn back to her, breaking the silence between us.

"Tell me, Cami, how long have you lived in New York?"

She wipes her mouth and faces me head-on. "I don't.

I'm currently living in Austin, Texas, at the moment. I'm just here for an interview at NYU."

I would never expect Texas to come from her mouth, especially since she doesn't speak with a southern accent. There is some sort of accent that wants to peek out when she speaks a few words. But spending years on the east coast, especially New York City, you get used to hearing accents when people speak.

I nod. "NYU is a good school. Is it for a graduate program? A job?"

Cami shakes her head. "No, it's to finish my undergrad. I'm only entering my second year."

Shit. She looks young. I just didn't think that she was *that* young.

"How old are you?" My curiosity got the best of me.

"I'm twenty. I turn twenty-one next April, which is why I'm currently sitting in a bar drinking a club soda." She waves to the glass in front of her before she turns back to me. "How old are you?"

Apparently, a lot older than her.

"I'm thirty-four," I say, giving her a tight smile.

"Really? I thought that maybe you were younger." She gives me a smirk. It's a small gesture, but the way her eyes brighten a bit with it, has me readjusting a little.

Fuck.

She's only twenty, you pervert.

I clear my throat and try to concentrate on something else.

"What's making you want to move from Texas all the way over here?" I take another drink of my club soda, diverting the conversation. Anything to stop myself from thinking about her smirk and what else her mouth can do.

Like wrapping themselves around my cock.

Cami looks at me and for a quick second and I think I see fear swimming in her eyes, but it disappears just as fast.

"I need a change, and my sister thought that coming to a different state and starting at a new school would be good for me. With a few connections, she was able to get me an interview at NYU. Now hopefully I'm able to get in."

The way she says the words tells me that there is something more to it. It's like she silently saying that she wants to get in to escape whatever her life is back in Texas.

"I'm sure you'll get in," I offer.

"You don't even know what program I interviewed for, your well wishes might be for nothing." Cami shrugs.

She a pessimist, is she?

"Okay, then tell me. Tell me what program you applied for?" I turn to show her that she has my full attention, which causes her to give me another small smile.

"You really want to know?"

I nod. "I really want to know."

She nods, but instead of saying anything, she reaches for her bag and takes out a folder. I watch as she lays it in front of us and opens it. The folder is a portfolio, an art one at that.

The second my eyes meet the pages, I see an onslaught of different colors and different line thicknesses. The only way that I describe what I'm seeing is beautiful.

"Shit. You did this?" I ask Cami. I'm sure my face is filled with surprise.

She nods and all I can do is continue to be in awe.

"Wow," I say as I go through the pages of the portfolio. Every single page brings a new design. Drawings, paintings, everything looks amazing. They are printed on picture paper, and I can't help but wonder how everything looks like in person.

"Everything looks absolutely beautiful and amazing," I say when I reach the last page, which is a picture of a portrait drawing she did.

In the picture there is what looks like a painting of a woman, with sugar skull makeup on her face. There is something about this woman that reminds me of something, but I can't pinpoint of what exactly.

"You really think so?" Cami's surprised tone is what takes my concentration away from the painting in front of me.

Forgetting about the picture, I turn to her and give her a smile.

"Absolutely. You will definitely get that spot at NYU. They would be crazy not to take you." I close the portfolio and slide it back to her.

I'm not bullshitting her. She may be only twenty, but this girl has some major talent. I know if I was some sort of art connoisseur I would buy her paintings. They are that good.

"Thank you." She blushes slightly, moving a strand of hair behind her ear.

As I watch her, I get the feeling that maybe she doesn't feel as confident with her paintings as she wants to be.

"Do you not think that you are good enough for that spot?"

She is silent for a few minutes before she responds.

"I want to think that I am. But there's a small part of me that tells me that I never will be and that I won't get accepted and I'll just end up back under my father's roof."

The way she shrugs it off, tells me that this really bothers her but that she wishes it didn't.

When I first walked in here today, I didn't think that I would find the girl with the gray hair so intriguing.

We started off this conversation by her wanting to know about me and the type of man that I am. Yet as the conversation continues, all I want to do is get to know her more and forget about everything else for the day.

Which gives me an idea.

I check the time on my watch, which causes Cami to let out a groan.

"Oh my god. I'm so sorry. I'm taking up all your time and you probably have things to do, like being a cop in New York City. Like that isn't a busy job." She stuffs her mouth with some of her fries before she takes her portfolio and puts it back in her bag.

She's getting ready to leave.

I reach out and place a hand on her forearm, stopping her.

"I was checking my watch to see the time because I got an idea." I try to give her a reassuring smile.

"You don't have to go back to work?" Her eyebrows raise in confusion.

"Well, I do, but um…" What do I say? That she should follow a stranger out of this bar and to this secret place he wants to take her to? It's not really a secret since she probably goes there often, but she doesn't know that. "Seeing your paintings sprung an idea."

It was more along the lines of seeing her lack of confidence, but I don't say that.

"An idea?" Again she raises her eyebrows.

I can't help but laugh a little. "Yeah, an idea."

Getting up from the stool, I reach for my wallet and put enough money on the bar to cover both our tabs, which causes Cami to look even more confused.

"What type of idea?" She's hesitant as she should be. I may look trustworthy like she said, but I'm still a stranger. She shouldn't trust me with anything that easily.

"One that would consist of you going with me somewhere. If you are up for it, of course."

I'm leaving this all to her. I'm not going to drag this girl out of this bar with me.

Cami thinks on it for a long minute, even taking her bottom lip between her teeth in contemplation, before she nods.

"Okay. I'll go along with your idea."

I smile

For the cold-hearted man that everyone accuses me of being, I've been letting out a lot of smiles when it comes to this woman.

"Excellent. Let's go."

3

CAMILA

IF LEO WERE with me right at this moment, he would tell me that I am crazy for agreeing to go anywhere with a complete stranger.

I'm sure that he would lecture me until his face was red and threaten to put a security detail on me.

You know, protective older brother shit.

But since I'm the rebel of the family, what with my beautiful brown hair artificially dyed gray, I would have shrugged at him and gone anyway.

Why? I have no idea.

I've spent a total of maybe forty minutes with this detective and now I'm walking beside him down a New York street.

You don't even know for sure that he is a detective.

I don't, and I should be worried, even if it is just a little, but for some reason I'm not.

There is something about this Nate guy that tells me that I can trust him. Maybe it's the fact that I know he's a detective or how he presents himself or something else entirely, but there is just something about him that is speaking to me.

We continue to walk down the busy street neither of us saying a word, that is until he pulls up to a stop in front of a store.

An art supply store.

"What are we doing here?" I ask as I follow him in.

Right away, I'm hit with a strong whiff of all the supplies and I feel like I'm in my safe space.

A space I can lose myself in for hours.

Seriously, why did he bring me here?

Mr. Detective doesn't answer me. We just walk through the store and I continue to look at the man that is guiding me. As much as I want to go down the aisles and grab some supplies to take back to my hotel room, I don't. Instead, I'm becoming a little wary.

And that feeling becomes stronger when we reach the aisle with all the canvas.

I stay at the end of it, and I watch him come to a stop at the middle and he extends his arm.

"Choose one." He gives me a smile, one that I'm starting to like, and I can feel both my eyebrows raise to my hairline. Something that I've been doing since I met him earlier.

"You want me to choose a canvas?" I look from him to the canvas surrounding us. What in the world is happening?

"Yeah, I want to see you paint."

Not what I expected him to say.

What did you expect?

I don't know, maybe to help him buy art supplies for a local kids' club? I definitely didn't expect him to say that he wanted to see me paint.

"Are you okay? It's the middle of your workday and you want me to show you how I paint?" Is that a normal thing to do?

Nate nods. "Yeah, I'm okay. Do I have more pressing things to do? Sure, but they can wait."

How can a man in his midthirties be so spontaneous?

"Why are you doing this?"

There has to be a reason why he brought me to an art supply store, and why he wants to watch me paint?

It that even a thing?

Who meets someone at a bar, sees their art portfolio and decides I need to see this individual paint in real life?

Nate gives me a small smile before he starts to make his way to me, stopping when he's a few feet away from me.

"You're a talented person. I just saw a few of your pieces and I was already in awe. And as I heard you speak about you only thinking that you are good enough and not really believing it, I got the idea for this. For you to show me your skills and see for yourself that you are, that you are good enough. And what better way for someone to tell you that than a complete stranger?"

Who is this man?

Normal people would just say that you are good by looking at your portfolio. They sure wouldn't offer to see you paint to prove it.

It's sweet though.

It's thoughtful that this stranger man wants to prove that to me that I am good and worthy of that spot at NYU.

Something that I'm sure my father doesn't even think I'm capable of.

I look at the man standing in front of me, realizing that he is definitely not the man that I first perceived him to be.

I lean up and place a kiss on his cheek, which takes him a little bit by surprise.

As soon as my lips meet his skin, there is a hit of electricity that travels between the two of us and I want to savor it, but I just met this man. So, I don't.

"Thank you." I give a smile when I lean back.

He looks down at me with wonder in his eyes before he gives me a small smile in return.

"You're welcome."

"So, where will this painting take place?"

We can't very well paint in the middle of this store or go back to the bar now, can we?

"Um." He stops, thinking about my question. It takes him a few minutes to think about it but finally he answers. "How would you feel about going to my apartment? It's close by or we can find a park somewhere? Whatever you're comfortable with."

He sounds nervous at his suggestion. He even runs his hand through his hair, and he cringes a little.

Whatever I'm comfortable with. That's the statement that sticks to me like glue.

When it comes to drawing or painting, I like doing it in a secluded place, never in public for everyone to see. I guess it's my way of keeping everything I do for myself.

A park somewhere, wont be secluded.

Am I contemplating going back to his place?

Yes, yes, I am.

I can hear Leo now. He is going to blow his head off when he finds out that I did this. Even if my companion is a cop. The man has a lot of shit going on through that head of his.

But what he doesn't know, won't kill him, right?

"We could go to your place." I give him a smile and I'm awarded with one back.

For the next half hour, I pick out everything I'm going to need for this little painting date, while Nate follows behind me and holds all our materials.

Is it a date though?

He's just trying to prove to me that I'm good. That I'm good enough to get into NYU. He's just doing something that my brother and sister or even Santos would do.

Right?

I don't know, but in my head, I'm calling it a date, solely because I need to distract myself even more from my interview.

Soon we are paying, I tried to offer my credit card, but Nate just waved it away, and walking out of the store with everything we need for painting.

Yes, I said we. I'm making this guy paint with me.

With all the stuff in tow, we make our way to his apartment. I suggested we get a cab or an Uber, but he said it wasn't that far walking. It wasn't, but still why walk when you can take a car that gets you there faster?

I guess if I do end up going to NYU I should get used to walking.

When we make it to his building, I'm in awe. The building itself looks like an architect's dream, and once I stepped inside, it made my jaw drop.

That is nothing compared to when we make it inside the apartment.

Seeing New York City apartments in pictures and on TV show is nothing like seeing it in real life. I didn't know places like this actually existed.

"I'm sorry, but is that the Empire State Building?" I ask as soon as I step foot into the living room.

The place has floor to ceiling windows that span from wall to wall. It's has a perfect view of the New York skyline.

"It is."

He says as he walks deeper into the apartment, putting down our supplies on the counter separating the kitchen from the living room.

"Here I thought that cops didn't earn a whole lot of money," I say. My line of sight is not moving from the view. It's a spectacular one.

Definitely not one that you would get back in Texas. Or one that you would want to take your eyes off of.

"I never said that I was a cop," he voices when he turns back to face me, a smile playing on his lips.

That comment finally breaks my appraisal of the view.

"You said you were a detective." Oh my god. Did he just say that to lure me to his apartment? So that I could trust him and not run away screaming?

Maybe I should have listened to what Leo told me

when I was twelve and never trust anyone with a badge. Or someone who says they have one, like in this situation.

"I am, but I don't work with the NYPD."

"Then where do you work?" It's an okay question to ask, given the fact that I am in this man's apartment!

My question just causes him to laugh, "How about we don't talk about my work, and we talk about what we are going to be painting?"

I guess work is a sore subject. He must see some grim things. Or handles things that he rather not bring into his home.

But either way, I nod, dropping the topic of his work and concentrating on something else.

What are we going to paint?

"Do you know how to draw at all?" I walk over to where he set the supplies down and start prepping everything.

"Do doodles on paperwork count?" He comes over to where I am and starts helping me.

"Of course, they do." I turn to him with a smile on my face, but when I do, I'm met with a whole lot of broad chest and shoulders. I wasn't expecting him to be so close to me, because I practically slammed myself into him.

For a quick second I become disoriented, but he is able to stabilize me with his hands.

His strong hands that are currently gripping my upper arms.

"You okay?"

I nod my head a little too quickly. "Yup, totally fine."

I try my hardest to not show just how feeling his grip on me is affecting me. Clearing my throat and turn my attention back to the art supplies and getting them ready for us.

When I turn back to him, I make sure that I put a few feet between us so that I don't bump into him again.

"Okay, everything is ready. Where do you want to do this?" I ask, not really looking at him.

Instead, I look around the apartment, well of what I can see anyway, and try to see where we can set up.

The place is big. There is a dark sectional in front of the windows which faces the TV that is above the gas fire-place. In the corner, there is a round dinner table that is beautiful and doesn't look very used.

Everything about this apartment screams a man lives here. It's also way too clean, like said man doesn't spend too much time here.

Or maybe when you are older, you stop living like you're in a frat house.

"Let's do it here, since you love the view so much. Let me go get some sheets to put on the floor." He says before he leaves to head down the hall, and I'm left to continue my marveling at his living room.

There aren't a lot of personal touches, just a few pictures on a bookcase that is against the wall, but that's it. There are art pieces that hanging, but they look like something you would buy at a home goods store and the lamps that are on top of the side tables all look generic. My guess is he must have hired someone to decorate for him, no way he did it himself.

Nate comes back to the living room with a few bedsheets in his hands.

Impressive.

I'm sure that my brother didn't have bedsheets or knew what they were until he married his wife last year.

He hands them to me, and I nod.

"This works. But are you sure you're okay with using them for this?" I ask as I start to lay the sheets behind the couch that gives me a perfect view out the windows.

"Yeah, I was going to donate them anyway."

This man is so put together. I love it.

We get situated and are all but ready to start painting when I remember what we're both wearing.

I borrowed a pair of Isabella's cigarette pants and a nice blouse for my interview. If I ruin them, she will have a heart attack, and possibly a whole lecture on how clothes should be treasured.

Isabella es dramática.

And well, Nate is still in his Tom Ford suit. I don't think that he would be very fond of having paint all over it. I know the price tags on those thing and splashing it with paint will not be pretty.

"Maybe we didn't think this all the way through," I say, my eyes dancing from my clothes to his.

He must realize what I'm talking about because he lets out a laugh. A laugh that I wouldn't mind hearing over and over again.

"No, I guess we didn't." He shakes his head, another smile playing at his lips and starts to unravel his tie. "Come on, I'm sure I have something that you can wear."

Like his clothes?

I don't ask. I just follow him down the hall and into a bedroom.

You would have never thought that I just met this man not even two hours ago and now he is offering to let me borrow his clothes.

The second I step foot into the bedroom, I'm hit with the strong manly scent that fits its occupant perfectly.

It's like leather, cotton and vanilla all combined, and it's intoxicating.

I'm so entranced by the scent that I don't notice Nate pulled out a t-shirt and a pair of basketball shorts and is handing them to me.

"I'm sorry?" I ask, shaking my head, because he clearly said something.

He gives me a smirk. "I said that you can use the bathroom to change."

I turn when he points over my shoulder to the door that must lead to the bathroom.

"Right." I take the clothes from him and quickly make my way over to the bathroom, closing the door behind me.

The bathroom is gorgeous just like the rest of this place, but I don't spend too much time gushing over it. I'm in Nate's bedroom, and I need to get out of here quickly before his scent makes me act like a crazy person.

I quickly discard my blouse and replace it with the one he handed me, which lands at mid-thigh, and quickly move to remove my pants.

I stop when I unzip them.

"Fuck," I whisper.

These pants were a little tight on me and showed a

serious panty line, so this morning I made the executive decision to go panty-less.

Now I'm screwed. I'm going to wear a strange man's basketball shorts without any panties.

I really am going to become a crazy person.

"Fuck it, he won't know."

I pull down my pants and quickly replace them with the shorts.

Shaking my head, I fold my clothes and quickly situate myself before I open the bathroom door.

As quickly as I situated myself, I stop just as fast.

Why?

Why am I currently standing in the bathroom doorway with my mouth hanging open?

Well, it may have to do with the fact that there is a shirtless Nate standing a few feet away from me, looking mouthwatering. His back is facing me and there are so many defined muscles that I just want to explore. My eyes travel from his shoulders, down to the waistband of his slacks.

My perusal causing me to lick my lips at the sight.

Never have I found a man that was in his thirties so damn attractive.

Until now.

I may not survive this painting session.

Fuck me.

4

NATHANIEL

You, Madden, are a very stupid man.

I would say that is a very correct assumption at the moment. Especially since Cami is only a few feet to my left, dressed in one of my old Yankee T-shirts and a pair of my basketball shorts.

When I came up with my plan for her to show me her painting skills, I didn't really think the whole thing through.

I didn't think that I would be bringing her back to my place, and I sure as hell didn't think that she would be wearing my clothes.

Now I'm in my apartment with a strange woman that is nearly fifteen years younger than me, watching as she holds a paintbrush.

Watching her create something with the supplies that we got at the store and her wearing my clothes, is throwing me off.

It's as if something primal is brewing inside of me. Something I want to act on.

Like I said, I'm a very stupid man.

"So, you're from Texas and yet I don't hear a southern accent." I say, dragging my own brush across the canvas in front of me, trying to look anywhere but the beautiful woman wearing my clothes.

"Didn't really live in Texas until I went to college. I'm from a border town, and crossed over to the US for school, the accent wasn't something that I picked up." She answers, concentrating on her work.

I just nod, not mentioning how I spent a large chunk of time going to different border towns trying to find a certain drug lord.

Shaking my head, I go back to my painting. Watching the paint brush move across the canvas, though, isn't helping divert my attention away from Cami.

"How did you get into painting?" I ask, breaking the silence that was building between us and moving my mind away from wanting to strip her of my clothes.

Cami is silent for a few minutes, just concentrating on what she is drawing on her canvas. For a second I think she didn't hear my question, but then she finally speaks.

"It was something that I did with my mom before she died. I may have only been five when she passed away, but painting with her has been something that I remember clear as day."

"You paint for your mother?" I ask.

She shrugs. "I paint because I love it. It's just an added bonus to be able to paint for her."

I watch her as she continues to drag her brush over the canvas.

Listening to her say how she got into painting, makes me think of why I became an agent.

Like her, my father died when I was young, except I don't remember anything about him. That luxury was taken away from me since he was killed when I was two.

The reason I decided to work in law enforcement was because I wanted to bring down the bad people of this world. Another reason had to do with the man I never got to really know. My father was an FBI agent when he died, and a part of me wanted to make him proud of my career choice.

"I lost my father when I was young too, much younger than you were actually. Never got to really know him, but like your mother, he's an added bonus to doing something that I love."

Cami turns face me, a small hint of sadness in her eyes.

"I guess we are both cut from the same cloth in a way. We both lost a parent and we both do something that connects us with them."

She's right.

Never did I think that I would meet someone that I shared that type of connection with, yet here I am. With a strange woman in my apartment, sharing a connection that only one that has lost a parent shares.

I give her a small smile and turn back to my own canvas, dropping the conversation all together.

Talking about dead parents brings on a somber type of mood.

For the next fifteen minutes or so, we paint on our respective canvases without saying a word. The only sound that fills the room are those of our brush strokes.

Cami's being a hundred percent more methodical than mine of course. After a few more minutes, I look over at her painting before looking back to mine.

Mine is a dark blob and hers a fucking masterpiece.

Letting out a small laugh, I finally put my brush down. "Okay, I give up."

"What? Why?" She looks at me with wide eyes, like she's scared that I'm making her stop working on her work of art.

I give her a smile. "Clearly, I'm not good at this."

Waving at my canvas and then hers, I try to show her what I mean.

Her eyes follow my hand and then looks between the two very different paintings that are sitting side by side.

"Yours is nice. I like it." she says, giving me an encouraging nod.

I let out a laugh. "Thanks, but mine is a blob compared to yours."

She must have really liked the view from the apartment, because in a short time, she was able to paint something that resembles it. It's beautiful actually. Even unfinished like it is, it would look nice in my study.

"It's not a blob." Cami puts down her brush and comes over to where I'm standing and inspects my work.

I swear, I know she's only twenty, but having her look at my blob of paint with her artistic eye, makes me want to squirm.

It's like we're in art class and she's the teacher who is about to rip me a new one.

I wonder if maybe that's the way she felt when I looked at her portfolio earlier.

She examines it for about a minute before she grabs the brush that I was holding and starts adding to it.

"My guess is you were trying to make a sunset," she says as she moves the brush before dipping it into black paint.

That's how bad I am at this. I was trying to make a basketball, but sure, a sunset works.

"Yup," I say, as I watch her move the brush against the canvas.

"You need to add a few lines to define it." She looks over her shoulder at me, nodding to come closer as she works on my disaster.

I do.

I step forward and with the height difference between us, her head barely hitting my shoulder, I am able to see exactly what she does.

With the few dark lines that she has added it's already starting to take shape and look like an actual sunset.

"Wow," I say.

Watching her paint her own thing was special, but watching her turn a collection of oranges into something like this is amazing.

"Here. Let me show you how to do it." She reaches for my hand, and I give it to her.

With a few steps forward, my front is to her back and my hand is encased with hers as we paint together.

Her hand guides mine, line after line, until the scenery before us looks almost perfect.

"You really are amazing at this," I say as I continue to watch the blob transform.

Unknowingly, I step closer to Cami, almost not leaving any space between us.

I feel her shrug against my chest. "I've been doing it almost my whole life. It's like second nature."

We continue to paint and as we do that, our bodies get closer to each other. At one point, my hand lands on her hip.

And that's where it currently is, as her hand drags mine against the canvas. My brain must be thinking that there is more to this whole painting thing, because it sends a signal to my thumb to rub against her hipbone.

Cami lets out a small gasp at my action.

"Sorry," I say to her. Stopping the motion of my thumb, but I don't pull back.

I should.

I need to pull back from her but I don't. I just stay rooted in place, not moving an inch away from her.

"It's okay," She says, but she sounds breathless. Like the small motion did something to her.

That thought is confirmed when she leans into me and I feel her ass move slightly against me.

Fuck.

"Cami," I groan, not stepping away from her.

"Yes?" She moves her ass again but this time there is nothing slight about it. This time the way she moves against me is intentional.

"Stop moving," I let out. The way she is moving is causing me to strain behind the pair of sweats I'm wearing. If she continues doing it, I might do something that I could regret.

"Why?" She leans her head against my chest and looks up at me with those big brown eyes of hers.

The way she is fluttering her eyelashes at me is telling me that the stupid man statement from earlier might have a whole lot of truth to it.

"Because you're twenty."

Did I just use her age as an excuse?

"I am." Her voice is like a purr and I'm trying really hard to keep my cock in check, when I feel a hand sliding up my thigh. "And you're thirty-four."

Cami turns to face me after she drops my hand and puts the brush she was holding down. Her arms going around my neck and mine going automatically to her waist, holding her to me.

Stand your ground, Madden. Stand your ground.

"This isn't where I intended for this to go." I look down at her, trying not to move any closer.

I honestly didn't. Whatever is going on right now wasn't even a thought when I suggested it at the bar.

Did I find her attractive? Hell, yeah.

"I know," Cami says, giving me a small smile. "But things go in different directions sometimes and that's okay."

Her hands move to my hair, but I don't take my eyes off her.

I want to lean down and take those plump lips of hers between my teeth and see just how sweet she is.

There hasn't been anyone in months. Cami is the first woman that I've had any interest in a while. Why not see where this little paint date goes? One night can't hurt.

With my eyes still on her, I let my hands travel down to her ass, closing the final gap between us.

Her eyes glisten just a little bit more at my actions.

"Different directions are a good thing sometimes," I say, leaning my face in a little closer to hers.

"Yes, a very good thing." She stands on her tiptoes slightly, our noses touching.

"Are you sure you want it to go in this direction?" I whisper the words against her lips, my fingers digging into the fabric of the basketball shorts she's wearing.

"If it's with you, absolutely," she says, her lips almost touching mine.

Just a little more and I will know what her lips feel like.

"Even if I'm fourteen years older than you?" I dig my nails into her ass, enough to lift her up and have her wrap her legs around me.

"Age is just a number."

It certainly is.

Fuck it.

I break whatever distance there is between us and finally plant my mouth against hers.

A sweet whimper escapes her mouth when I sweep my tongue along her bottom lip and ask for entry.

I devour her mouth as if I were a starving man, and it

sure as shit doesn't help that she is grinding herself against me. Making my cock harder than it was a few minutes ago.

I walk us backward until the back of my legs hit the couch, and I sit us down.

Pulling back slightly, I leave the dance between our mouths and let my mouth travel down her jaw and down to her neck. All the while she grinds her little body against my aching cock.

"You feel so good in my hand," I say against her pulse, and she lets out a small moan. "I wonder what you would feel like without any clothing."

My hands travel from her ass to her thighs, which are exposed by the shorts that she is wearing. I then let them travel through the leg opening, reaching the junction where her thigh meets her pussy. When I reach it, I'm a little surprised. There's no material to move.

She's wearing my shorts without any panties.

Knowing that causes me to let out a groan.

"Maybe you should fuck me, Detective. So that you can find out."

She's straight to the fucking point.

I hum against her skin, my fingers moving through her pussy lips and coating themselves in her wetness. "Is that what you want? For me to fuck you? To fuck this body of yours until you can't take anymore?"

The thought of her under me, squirming and panting out my name, makes me want to rid us of our clothes and take her right here and now.

"Yes. Fuck me, Detective."

With a hand in her hair, I bring her face back to mine and I slam my mouth back onto hers.

I savor everything that she has to give me, realizing that maybe one time may not be enough to satisfy the animalistic feeling I have brewing inside of me.

I pull back just slightly and take her face between my hands. "How long are you in New York for?"

She looks at me a little confused, but she answers anyway. "Until Thursday."

That gives me a day and a half to get rid of the primal feeling this woman brings out of me.

"Perfect."

With that, I devour her mouth in the way I will be devouring every single inch of her.

5

CAMILA

THIS IS NOT how I thought that I would be spending my time in New York.

I thought that for the four days I was here, I would be exploring, going to as many art museums and exhibitions as I could, maybe even some shopping thrown in there. And for the most part, I did that, I just didn't expect to end up in a stranger's bed.

Yet, here I am.

In a stranger's bed, just lying here watching as he pulls on a pair of gray sweatpants.

By the way, who ever thought of the combination of a hot as sin man in gray sweatpants needs a fucking raise.

"Are you going to keep staring?" he asks. His back is towards me, but if I had to guess, the man has a smirk on his face.

I cuddle deeper into the comforter. "Maybe. I kind of like the view. But I think I would like it better if you took off the sweats."

Nate chuckles before he turns back to me, not wasting any time getting on the bed and crawling over to me.

He places a sweet kiss on my lips before he pulls back and gives me a sexy grin. "If I take them off, then the food delivery guy is going to have a heart attack."

Another kiss to the lips before he pulls away, right before the apartment buzzer sounds. Within seconds he walks out of the room and I'm left alone in his bed.

The bed that he has used to worship every single inch of my body.

That is before he did it on the couch with the New York skyline in the background.

I have known this man for only a few hours but he has given me more orgasms in that small amount of time than any other man before. Albeit I have only been with two other men, but still they had nothing on the Detective.

He really knows how to work a woman's body. Maybe it's because he is older and more experienced than me, but he definitely knows where everything is and how to pleasure a woman.

So much so that I think that this time with him will probably ruin me for anyone else. A few hours and I'm already hooked on the man.

It's just one time, Camila. Just one time, then you will head back to Texas, where you will patiently wait for your NYU rejection and move on with your life.

Just one time.

I'm gonna have to keep reminding myself of that.

This thing between Nate and me is only going to be a

one-time thing. After we are done taking from the other, we won't ever see each other again.

A few minutes after Nate leaves the room, he comes back with bags of food. I didn't realize just how hungry I was until I get a whiff of the delicious scents.

I guess that's what happens when you eat bar food for lunch and have a whole lot of sex. You're starving.

"That smells so good." I sit up, the comforter falling to my waist, my chest out for the whole world to see.

"I figured given the meal we had earlier, we were due for something filling. Hopefully you like stake and mashed potatoes." He smirks as he joins me back in bed.

For a slight second his eyes stay on my bare chest, like he is thinking about having something else for dinner, but he shakes his head and goes back to the food.

"I think that anything with potatoes can be categorized as my favorite food," I say, taking the to-go food container he hands me.

Forget delicious. The second I open the container, my mouth legit waters.

"I like a woman that isn't afraid of eating starchy food," Nate muses as he opens his own container.

"Is that really a thing? You've gone out with women that don't eat potatoes?"

I know it's a common thing for a woman to not eat anything that messes up with their diet or may cause them to gain even the slightest weight. I guess to me it was just normal to eat whatever you want.

Being Mexican, it's a little hard to be picky with food when everything is so good.

My sister and I, even Serena, my brother's wife, eat whatever we want. We never think about what mashed potatoes might do to us.

Nate nods. "Dated someone once who would only eat salads. No pasta, no bread, nothing starchy, and would only eat salmon as her protein."

Well shit.

"Only salads?" That does not sound like a happy life. I don't think I would ever be able to do that. What would I do without my tacos? Or worse without enchiladas?

"Yup. After a while, it just became weird. We didn't last very long," he says with a shrug.

"Is dating hard in New York?"

I know it's hard back home, and that's mostly because I keep to myself and don't bring strangers into my inner circle. Especially not with the family business.

I watch as Nate takes a bite of his food before answering. "It is, but it's harder with my schedule. It's so unpredictable and with all the traveling that I do, dating is not ideal."

Make sense.

"Do you make it a mission then to pick up random women at a bar?" I meant it as a joke, there's even a smile on my face as I say it, but for some reason, something shifts.

I thought that he would laugh with me, but instead he puts his fork down and places his container on the nightstand.

Within seconds he takes my food as well and places it with his.

I can feel confusion raising within me as he turns back to me, prowling my way, causing me to lie back down with him on top of me.

"You are the first woman I've been with in months," he states, his icy-blue eyes staring back at me.

"I don't want to believe that," I say, my arms going around his neck, my fingers finding their way to his dirty blond hair.

"Believe it. No one has piqued my interest until you. Not even the bartender." Nate leans down and places his lips on my jaw.

"I must be special then." I tip my head back, giving him more access to my skin.

"You must be." He continues to plant kisses on my jaw and then he moves to my neck before making his way to the top of my chest.

I enjoy the way his mouth feels on me. Everything he does feels different, more prominent and definitely nothing that I have experienced before.

With my hands still in his hair, I push his head down, telling him exactly where I want him to kiss.

Nate lets out a laugh as I feel his hands moving farther down my body.

"You're a greedy little thing, aren't you?" he speaks against my tit before he takes a nipple and sucks on it.

"I'm just trying to get everything I can before I have to head back to Texas," I pant out, loving the way he is paying attention to my chest.

"Trust me, baby girl, I plan to give you everything you want in the time that we have. By the time you step foot on that plane, you're going to be wishing I was going with you."

I already do. Especially with how this man uses his tongue.

"Then you should put some actions behind those words, Detective." I try to push his head lower, but he doesn't budge. Instead, he pulls away from my chest and brings his face closer to mine.

"Are you agreeing to be mine until you leave?" His eyes are intense and by the look alone, I could agree to anything.

"You want to do this until then?"

He gives me a slight nod. "If that is something you are comfortable with."

Am I?

A day in a half spent with a stranger that can give me orgasm after orgasm?

My siblings will have a field day with this.

But I find myself nodding, not caring what they might think. I'm a grown adult.

"Yes, I'm comfortable with it."

A smirk crosses on Nate's face and with a small kiss to the lips, he lowers himself back down. Only this time he doesn't stop at my chest, no, he places kisses all the way to my pussy.

"Let's make you count, shall we?" he says against me, before dragging his tongue along my lips.

"Fuck."

"So fucking delicious. Even better than the food." He

laps at me, his fingers digging into my thighs, holding me in place for him.

Nate presses his face against my pussy some more and then his mouth covers my clit. I pull at his hair, possibly taking out some strands.

"More," I say, wanting more pressure. No, needing more pressure.

My thighs press tighter against his head but when my plea leaves my mouth, Nate grabs my thighs and pushes them farther apart and up. The second that my thighs meet my chest, he devours me like I'm really his last meal.

"Fuck, baby girl," he says, when I let out a moan that fills the room.

He eats at me and when he inserts a finger into me, I can't take it any longer.

"Nate," I pant out, feeling the need to explode on the brink.

"Count, Cami."

With his mouth around my clit and his finger hitting the right spot, I let everything go.

"One."

He doesn't waver, no he continues going, moving his hand faster and his mouth sucking harder. I don't know how it was possible, but even with one orgasm leveling, I feel another one closing in."

"Oh my god. Oh my god," I pant out, my body thrashing, trying to get all the friction to get where I need to get.

"Take what you want, Cami. Take it."

It's his fingers digging into my skin, his mouth on me and his finger moving out of me that hits the tipping point.

Everything is too much and not long after the first orgasm that the other one is able to escape.

"Two," I exhale, black spots clouding my vision.

I'm still not able to catch my breath when Nate climbs my body and aligns himself at my entrance.

"That was such a beautiful sight," he says against my lips. My legs that feel like Jell-O falling on either side of him.

"You sure know how to make a girl feel out of breath," I say before placing my lips against his and tasting my release on his tongue.

"Should we see how high you can count to?" He pulls away slightly, excitement brewing in his eyes.

I'm nodding before he even finishes the question.

"Such a good girl," he says before leaning back fully and reaching for the box of condoms that's on the bedside table.

Once a condom is in place, he sits himself between my legs yet again. I watch as Nate grabs his cock and slides it against my wet folds, coating himself with my wetness.

With his eyes on mine, he slides into me, and he fills me up like nothing else has ever been able to before.

No man.

No toy.

Just him.

Nate takes a few seconds to situate himself and then he starts to move.

He moves until neither one of us can take it anymore.

I count to five.

I'm definitely going to be wishing for him to come home with me.

———————

"I DON'T WANT to get on the plane," I whine when we park at JFK airport and make our way out of the car.

After almost two days of being stuck in this bubble with Nate and a total of seventeen orgasms, it's finally time for me to leave New York and head back to Texas.

The last two days haven't been filled with just sex though. Sure, most of our time was spend getting the most out of each other's bodies but Nate also worked a bit from home, while I finished the paintings that we started. Not only that, but he also took me to Central Park and to walk around the city, and got to know each other a little bit.

It was nice to see the city through his eyes and not from those of a tourist.

And if I'm being honest with myself, these last two days were better than I thought that they would be and definitely better than when I was alone at the beginning of the trip.

It didn't matter that I had just met Nate, there was something about him, about us together that gave me comfort and I will miss it when I'm home.

I think he felt something during our time together because this morning when I said I needed to order an Uber back to my hotel to get my stuff, he offered to drive me instead. Something about wanting every last second together.

Now here we are at the airport parking lot.

"Look at it this way, if you get into NYU, you will be back here in no time," he offers as he takes my luggage out of the trunk of his Range Rover.

"That is if I get in." I pout. Just thinking about it makes me want to break out in hives.

"Hey," he says before closing the trunk and coming over to me, taking my face between his hands. "None of that. You will get in. You are a great artist and the people at NYU will be stupid if they didn't take you. You will be back here and when you do, you have a friend to lean on."

Friend.

Is that what we will be if I come back here?

Calm down, Camila. You're not Leo, who gets married after a drunken weekend.

Ignoring the friend comment, I lean into his touch a little bit.

"Thank you for eating chicken strips with me and for these last two days." I lean up on my tiptoes and press my lips to his slightly.

"You are very welcome," he says, giving me a smile when we pull away from each other.

"Okay, let's do this." I give a curt nod and soon we are making our way to the terminal, hand in hand.

I guess neither one of us wants to leave the small bubble we've been in.

We make it to the terminal in no time, and soon I'm all checked in to my flight and my bag is off to be put on the plane.

"Here is your ticket, Ms. Diaz. You are all set," the desk associate tells me, handing me the small piece of paper.

Ms. Diaz. Not Morales.

Camila M. Diaz is technically my legal name here in the United States. My father had it changed for both me and Isabella, after my mother was killed. According to him, it was a safety measure, and I later found out it was because he wanted to put some of his purchases under our names. That way, the federal government didn't tie them to him.

I don't use Diaz very often, just when it's a mandatory thing.

Like flying.

I could have taken the family private plane, but I wanted to feel a little normal, so that's why I'm flying commercial.

After taking the boarding pass, I make my way back to Nate.

"All set to go." I wave the boarding pass at him, which he takes and examines.

He nods to his left. "You're this way."

I follow him through the terminal until we reach the security gate.

I guess our time together has finally come to an end.

"I guess this is it," I say, not moving my eyes off the security line.

"I guess it is," Nate voices before he places a finger under my chin and turns my face to him. "Don't pout." He leans in and places a chaste kiss on my lips.

"It's a little hard not to." I say when he pulls back.

"I know, but everything will work out and we will meet again."

"How are you so sure?"

He shrugs. "I just am. Here, let me have your number and if you get in, you can let me know."

Nate pulls out his phone and hands it to me.

I enter my number and when I hand the phone back to him, leaving feels all that real.

"You sure you want a child to have your phone number, after all you are a big bad detective."

I say to him, a smile playing at my lips.

He gives me a smirk before he places his hands on my hips and leans into my ear and speaks.

"Sweetheart, I think that you were the one that told me that age was just a number. Besides, the way my cock slammed into your pussy, tells me you're all woman."

The bastard takes my earlobe between his teeth.

Great, now I'm going to be sexually frustrated while I wait for my flight and head home.

"Maybe I should just come back so that you can show me again. I might forget."

He laughs at my statement before he pulls back from me and places yet another kiss on my lips.

I love how affectionate this man is.

"You can come visit me anytime you want."

I give him a smile, but it disappears when a family of five races by us.

It's time to go.

"Okay, I should get in line." I nod toward the security line.

"Let me know about NYU," he says as we walk to the end of the line.

"I will." I lean up and wrap my arms around his neck, holding him tightly, not wanting to let him go. "Thank you."

"Anytime, Cam." He holds me just as tight as I do him, and his face makes it into the crook of my neck.

I can stand here forever.

But I have a plane to catch.

After a few more seconds of holding him, I pull away and give him a smile.

"See you later, Detective." I walk away, giving him a small wave.

"See you later, Camila," he response.

That's the first time he has used my full name, and I like it.

With one final look at the man, I make my way to the security line.

Soon, I'm on a plane back to Austin, feeling like I left a piece of me in New York.

At least I have his number.

6

NATHANIEL

As a federal agent, there is something about office work that I fucking hate. I would rather be out in the field, spending my whole day in a car on a stake out than feeling trapped inside a building. Better yet, feeling trapped inside my office.

That's how I feel right now, trapped. Trapped by the four walls, trapped by this building, trapped by the ever-growing case files that are currently sitting on my desk.

Trapped by it all.

Do I hate my job? No, I don't, but a nice change would be good. Especially when I've been trying to bring down the same drug lord for most of my life.

You were able to get a small change with Cami.

That I was.

Cami served as a very good distraction from everyday life and if she didn't have to go back to Texas, I would still be living in that distraction.

But she did.

And I have some pressing shit to take care of. I don't have a whole lot of time to think about fucking a twenty-year-old again.

But fuck, she felt so good in my arms and wrapped around me. Such a glorious sight when she was coming around my cock and holding me so tight, I thought that she would rip it off.

Then the way she tasted on my tongue and the way she screamed out my name. Every moment, I wanted to savor.

Okay, enough.

Work. I need to concentrate on work and put Cami behind me.

Especially if I won't see her again.

"Well look who decided to finally come into the office." A female's voice diverts my attention from the files in front of me.

Looking up, I see Ava, a fellow agent standing at my door.

Ava has been a DEA agent for about five years. Not as high ranking as I am, but she will get there. She's good and she knows it.

She also happens to be a woman that I may have had sexual relations with in the past. Actually, she was a go to.

Whenever either of us needed to let off some steam, we would reach out to the other and do what we needed to do.

A casual thing in a way, but like I told Cami, it's been a while.

I lean back in my chair before responding to her.

"Working from home every once in a while is good for the soul."

"I would say. You look a lot more relaxed than what you did earlier in the week."

Staying in bed with a certain twenty-year-old, with her pussy or mouth wrapped around your cock would do that to you, I want to state but I keep it to myself.

No need to air out my laundry here at the office, especially with Ava.

"It was much needed. What's up?" I ask her, there's a reason she's here.

"Boss wants to see you. He said that he's looking for an update on one of the cases that you are working on," she says, a knowing smile taking over her face.

One of the cases.

I will bet my whole paycheck that the case in question is the one on the Muertos Cartel.

The Muertos Cartel is the biggest cartel running out of Mexico. They are some of the most ruthless bastards and at the helm of the operations is Ronaldo Morales. He is considered one of the most feared and most dangerous men in the world. The man has moved more drugs and bodies than ever thought imaginable.

Ronaldo is also the man that ordered that my father get taken out.

Dear old dad was working undercover to gain Ronaldo's trust over three decades ago. He gained the man's trust and became an informant to the FBI. Somehow Ronaldo found out this piece of information and called for one of his men to kill him while he was up in Quebec, Canada.

Ever since I found out the truth behind my father's death when I was fifteen, I've been trying everything in my damn power to bring the bastard down.

As you can guess, I haven't succeeded. Not even with the individual from his own inner circle that I have at my disposal.

I nod to Ava. "Tell him I'll be right there."

She just nods but doesn't move an inch.

I inwardly roll my eyes. "Is there something else Agent Hall?" I raise an eyebrow at her.

She continues to look at me. Finally she gives me a smile and steps fully into my office. I watch her as she makes her way over to me and gets situated at the edge of my desk.

"I was wondering if you wanted to get together tonight," she offers in a sweet voice.

I look at her as she sits on my desk, leaning slightly towards me, giving me a knowing smile.

If she had come to me earlier this week, shit even Tuesday morning before I went to the bar, and told me she wanted to meet up, I would have told her yes.

But right now, after spending almost two days with Cami, a woman I barely know, I feel like I need to tell her no.

It just doesn't feel right for some reason.

Which is strange given that Cami and I aren't together and nothing more is going to happen between us.

So, letting out a sigh, I let Ava down. "Sorry, Ava. I'm not up for it tonight. Maybe some other time."

I give her a small smile, pushing my chair back and standing to full height.

"Oh." I can hear the disappointment in her voice. "Okay, yeah that's completely fine." She gives me a smile, but I can see through it and see that it's not in fact completely fine.

With a nod in her direction, I wave for her to walk in front of me and together we leave my office. I head down to our boss's office and Ava turns the corner to head back to hers.

I could have said yes to her offer, but like I said it didn't feel right. I think it had to do with the fact that I was with a woman just yesterday, being with another one not even twenty-four hours later is a douche move.

Shaking the thought of Ava out of my mind, I walk up to my boss's door and knock before entering.

"You wanted to see me?" I ask the special agent in charge, Beck Williams. Dude's a scary motherfucker and runs the whole New York division.

"Yeah, come in." He waves me in without looking up from the file in front of him. I take a seat in one of the chairs facing his desk, making myself comfortable while I wait for him to speak.

This is a process that we do almost on a weekly basis, so I know the drill.

Beck finally closes the file and looks at me with a stern look. The only look that the man can muster. You would think for a man that is only a few years older than me, that he would smile more.

"Anything new on the Muertos case?" he asks the same question that he has been asking for the last year.

I shake my head. "Not since the last time you asked."

Early last year, we almost caught a break in the case. I had gone undercover in Houston and became friendly with one of the cartel soldiers, Adolfo. The man was hungry to spill anything on the cartel and get rid of the kingpin himself.

He told us about runs, some of the dealers, even some of the routes that the Muertos would use to move merchandise. I thought that we were golden.

After talking to him for a few weeks, the DEA had a plan set to infiltrate one of the runs. We were one step closer to getting our hands on Ronaldo. Of course, all that fell to shit when Adolfo disappeared, and the run never happened.

We concluded that Adolfo was found out and he was killed for being a narc.

For weeks after that, I tried to get any lead that I possibly could. Talking to street-level dealers and even going back to Adolfo's men and seeing if they wanted to help.

Every single person that agreed, would wind up disappearing shortly after.

I thought I had caught another break when I got a notification that a certain kingpin's son got married in Las Vegas.

I was able to track down the blushing bride and offer her a chance to talk, but unfortunately, she didn't want to and went on her way.

After that is when this case turned into more shit than it already was. Especially when I agreed to help Leonardo Morales, the kingpin's son and the Muertos' second in command to save his wife.

Lines got blurry.

I should have arrested Leonardo and his man Santiago Reyes right there and then, but I didn't.

The only bright side of all this is that something shifted with Leo because a week later he was calling me telling me he would help me take his father down.

The stipulation, I get to take down his father and only him. I leave the Muertos and the rest of the men out of it.

Fine by me, as long as Ronaldo Morales was behind bars or in a box, I was happy.

But that was months ago. I have yet to get any reputable information to put away Ronaldo.

"We need something to put the bastard away. At the very least, one of his top men," Beck says, sounding a bit frustrated.

Did I mention that I haven't told Beck about my deal with Leo yet? I should, but I'm waiting for the right moment.

"I know, and I'm working on it. There are a few leads that I have going on, but they are going to take time." More like I need Leo to come to me with something that will move things along.

I'm essentially buying the man time.

"Work on it harder. The Muertos have been in control of this drug trade for decades. It's time to finally put them to a stop," Beck says, stabbing his desk with his finger for emphasis.

I nod. "I will try my best to move things along."

I'm pretty sure that I'm talking out of my ass, but hey I have to until I hear something from Leo.

"You're free to go." With a hand wave from Beck and not another word, I stand up from my seat and walk out of his office.

This whole conversation could have been a phone call or a damn email, for that matter.

I head back to my office, closing the door behind me before taking out my phone to dial a number when the phone starts to ring.

It's an unknown number.

"Madden," I answer the phone not thinking twice about it, and heading straight to my desk.

"I need to call a meeting." Leonardo Morales's voice comes through the other side.

Speak of the devil himself.

"You need to call a meeting? Shouldn't that be my line?" I lean back in my chair, getting comfortable since I have no idea how long this conversation is going to last.

"I don't have time for your bullshit, Madden. I need to call a meeting, and I would like to do it sooner than later." The man growls through the phone.

I scoff a little. Does he not know who he's talking to?

"Fine. When?" I ask. Might as well let him lead this, as long as he gives me information that sticks.

"A week from now. In Austin." Of course, he is having this meeting in his territory.

"Fine. Send me the address and I will be there. Dress conspicuously." I say before hanging up the phone without letting him answer.

I don't know what this meeting is about. I should have asked, but it's too late now.

Hopefully this meeting gives me the information that I need to finally put the whole case to rest.

Waking up my computer, I start looking for flights to Austin and a hotel for next week.

I will be there for one day max, but that still doesn't help to divert my mind to something completely unrelated.

Cami is in Austin. Or at least close to it. I saw her boarding pass when I was checking for a gate number.

Maybe this trip could be an extension of these last few days.

Maybe I can call her and we can meet up.

I'm slightly taken aback by my thought process. Just met the girl two days ago and I already want to see her again, this time in her home state.

Isn't that a little stalkerish?

Possibly, but I feel like there was something there between us. It might be a good idea to see if it was just something that we experienced in New York or if it's actually something.

Or maybe it's just me looking to get laid again.

No, I do want to see her. I could care less about the sex.

Without thinking I book my ticket to Austin and my hotel and after all that is set and done, I pick up my phone.

I find her name in my contact list right away and soon

I'm shooting off a text to the twenty-year old I think I might have developed a connection with.

Fingers crossed this is a good trip all around.

Get to see Cami and get information to end Ronaldo Morales once and for all.

7

CAMILA

REFRESH. Refresh. Oh my god, refresh!

I've been hitting refresh on my email every five seconds for the past three hours, and nothing new has come in.

It's been over a week since my interview with the art department at NYU and according to the main decider, I'm supposed to get a response today. Now it's three hours past the specified time and I'm freaking out.

It's okay, Camila. It's okay.

They probably are just writing every single email out and that takes time. I will get an email soon.

God, I hope it's a good email.

Good email or not, this whole thing is stressing me out beyond belief.

It's a good thing that I'm going out tonight to distract myself from all this.

The thought of going to dinner brings a smile to my face like it never has before.

I'm going out to dinner with Nate!

When the message popped up on my screen last week, I thought for a second that my brain was playing tricks on me.

Because no way was I reading the message right.

No way did I read that the person, the older detective that I spent a lot of time in bed with while in New York, was going to be in Austin. And no way was I reading that he was inviting me to dinner.

Here was a guy fourteen years my senior and he was flying from another state to take me to dinner. Sure, he could be coming to Austin for other reasons, but he was asking me to dinner.

Surely that was all fake and just my imagination playing tricks on me

But it turns out that it wasn't fake, and he had really sent that message.

I might have screamed just a tiny bit from the excitement.

Of course, I accepted the invitation right away, even if it was just a "friendly" dinner. I'm going to take what I can.

Abandoning my laptop, I go to my newly organized closet and start pulling out outfit ideas.

I say newly organized because while I was away in New York, my sister's boyfriend, Santos, who is also like a brother to me, moved both of us out of her apartment and into his townhome.

He said that it had to do with space, but I know he wanted to have Isabella closer to him. Especially with everything that has been going on with her these last few weeks.

I found it sweet, and I wasn't going to complain about it.

It's like I have two roommates that bang each other's heads off every chance they get.

Okay, not a visual I needed.

Moving on.

Looking through my closet, I settle on a little black silk dress that is designed by the one and only Isabella Morales. One of the many perks of having a sister that is a fashion designer.

Once the dress is picked out and so are the shoes, I check the time and see that I have plenty of time to do my hair, makeup and to shave my legs.

I'm all ready to go with half an hour to spare before I have to head out to meet Nate.

Grabbing my small bag, I make my way downstairs where I hear my sister's and Santos's voice flowing.

"You look pretty, " Isabella says as soon as I step into the kitchen.

"Thank you. I have a dinner date." I say, spinning around giving her a better look at my outfit.

"Ooh fun. That dress is definitely the right choice," Isabella says as she continues to chop some vegetables.

"It's short," Santos grumbles next to her, which earns him a stomach slap.

"Isabella made it," I say, sticking my tongue out at him.

I swear he and Leo are going to be the death of me. They both are way overprotective.

"You need to make your dresses longer," he tells his girlfriend, who just shakes her head at him.

"You never complain when I wear them," she says with a shrug.

"Talk about double standards," I say on my way to the fridge to take out some water.

I swear I hear Santos let out a groan at my comment.

"Fine," he grumbles and when I turn, he is pinching the bridge of his nose. "Who are you going out with?"

I raise an eyebrow at him which just makes him more frustrated.

Isabella just looks at him in confusion, probably wondering where this is coming from.

"She's living under our roof." He waves at me, his voice going up a little. "I have a right to know who she goes out with. At least to prepare if I have to go after the bastard and kill him if he does something."

I look at my sister, who just looks at me and rolls her eyes.

"You don't know him and he won't do anything." At least not anything I don't want, I want to add but I don't. Santos already looks like he's going to pop a vein, don't need him to have a heart attack too.

"How do you know that?" he asks, raising his own eyebrow at me.

You know I would find this man scary if he wasn't so domesticated and wrapped around my sister's finger.

I shrug. "I just do."

Grabbing my water and my bag, I make sure I have my keys and my phone and start to head out the door.

"Don't wait up!" I yell as I walk away from them. "I probably won't be home until tomorrow morning!" I say before I step through the doorway and close the door behind me.

"Camila!" Santos growls out but I'm already out the door.

That last comment might have been an exaggeration but hey, it caused Santos to have a reaction. I see it as a win.

I jump into my car, the one that my brother bought me, and head to the address that Nate sent me to meet him.

He offered to pick me up, but given the reaction that Santos had with the dress and me going out, meeting up with him was the best idea. Nate could have been tied to a chair and tortured before we even went to dinner.

I make it to the restaurant a little bit early, which takes my attention away from dinner and back to checking my email.

Still nothing.

Damn, I was really hoping to share with Nate if I was going to NYU or not.

At the very least so I can know if this will be the last time I see the man or not.

I let out a sigh. Hopefully I get the email soon, because not knowing if I will be staying in Texas is driving me crazy.

My finger continues to meet the refresh button on my email until a message pops up at the top of the screen.

It's Nate.

He's here.

A big smile forms on my face as I put my phone away and step out of the car.

The smile on my face grows as I approach the restaurant and see the fine specimen of a man standing out front, waiting for me.

If I thought that this man looked delicious in the suit he was wearing last week, I was mistaken. No, he looks absolutely mouthwatering in the one he is currently sporting.

This man gets hotter every time that I see him.

He looks up from his phone as he hears my heels approaching, and the smile he gives me makes me want to squeeze my thighs tighter.

"Hello, beautiful," he says, as he walks over to me.

My smile grows even more when I hear the term of endearment and he leans in to place a sweet kiss on my lips.

Legit butterflies flying in my stomach.

"Hi there, Detective. Long time no see," I tease him a little, fluttering my eyelashes at him a bit.

He lets out a small chuckle. "Such a long week it has been."

It really has. Ever since his text came in last week, I've been counting down the minutes until I saw him again.

"If I'm being honest, I didn't expect to hear from you. But I'm glad I did," I tell him, throwing a bright smile in his direction.

He nods in understanding. "I guess you must have left an impression, because when this trip came up, the second thought after finding a flight, was you."

Butterflies continue to flutter.

"Well, I'm glad that I was a thought. Want to go in?" I say, pointing to the door and he places a hand on the small of my back, guiding me in.

We approach the hostess stand and wait for the girl to look up from what she is doing.

"Welcome. Do you have a reservation?" she asks, fluttering her eyelashes at Nate.

I guess she doesn't notice me standing next to him.

"Yes. It's under Nathaniel," he answers her.

She nods and does something on her computer before she gives him a bright smile.

"Your table is ready. I will take you back," she says, again only addressing him.

Nate must have noticed how all the attention was on him because he grabs my hands and positions me to walk behind the hostess with him behind me.

My hand never leaving his.

When we reach the table, the hostess looks me up and down, assessing me and giving me a fake smile.

"Here you are." She places the menus on the table and waves us to sit.

Nate goes around her and pulls out a chair for me to take. When I do, he leans down and places a kiss on my cheek before he takes the chair across from me.

"Are we celebrating anything special tonight?" the hostess asks. If I'm not mistaken, there is a small hint of disappointment in her voice but also irritation.

"Yeah, we are celebrating our anniversary," I tell her, a bright toothy smile thrown in her direction.

I hear Nate cough up a little, but I don't turn to look at him. I keep my eyes on the hostess.

"That's amazing," she says, her eye twitching slightly. "I will go get your waiter, enjoy your dinner."

With that she walks away, and we are left alone.

"Anniversary?" Nate asks, a smirk on his face and an eyebrow raised.

I shrug. "She was giving you 'fuck me' eyes, besides she doesn't know we only met a week ago."

Is a one-week anniversary a thing?

"You're something else, aren't you?" he says letting out a small laugh.

I just throw a wink at him.

Before long, the waiter comes and takes our food and drink orders. The latter stumps Nate a bit when he remembers that I can't legally drink just yet, and ends up ordering a club soda.

"You can drink, you know. Don't let my age put a damper on your night." I say, taking a drink of my water.

"It's fine, I have a meeting tomorrow morning anyway. Not drinking might actually be a good idea."

"Is that why you're in Austin?" He didn't really tell me why he was here for in the texts, I just assumed it might have something to do with work.

He nods. "Yeah, it's a work meeting pertaining to a case."

"Do your cases always take you to different states like this?" I know he told me he traveled a lot for work, but being that he's a detective, wouldn't he have like a home base or something?

Is that New York?

"All depends on the case. This one landed on my desk even though it should be handled by the Texas division and not New York. But I don't mind it."

He gives me a shrug.

Interesting.

"What kind of detective are you? I know you said you didn't work for the NYPD, but working around the country on cases has to be some big-time stuff, right?"

As I ask the question, I notice the tightness that forms around his eyes. Just like last week, I get the impression that he doesn't like to talk about work.

But he answers either way. "It's a federal agency. My home office is in New York, but I'm able to work cases outside of my jurisdiction."

I nod. "So do you carry a gun and a badge on you at all times?"

He nods. "I do. I actually had a gun on me when we met at the bar."

"Do you have one on you now?" I ask. I don't have an aversion to guns. Given my father and brother's career choice, I've been around them almost my whole life.

All the men that my father hired to protect my sister and me, carried guns.

Hell, I even got one for my eighteenth birthday. I know that both Leo and Santos are always carrying, and given that Nate is in law enforcement, it makes sense he carries one too.

He looks at me for what feels like an eternity before he gives me a very slight nod.

"My badge is also in my pocket."

I don't know why but I find that hot.

When I don't say anything for a few seconds he speaks again. "Does that scare you?"

I shake my head. "No. I know that sometimes, it's a necessary thing. Guns don't terrify me." It's the people that use them that are sometimes the issue.

He gives me a nod, and as the waiter comes by with our food, all gun talk is set aside.

For the rest of dinner, we just talk and get to know each other a little better.

He tells me that he is an only child, who grew up in Pennsylvania and that his mother lives down in Florida enjoying her retirement. He talks about how in high school he was the star quarterback and even got a few offers from well-known schools and ended up going to school in Kansas and playing. Apparently, there were even NFL scouts that were looking into him once he was about to finish school, but he decided to go into law enforcement instead.

When it comes to me, I try to give him all the details that don't include anything on the cartel. I tell him about Isabella and how she is a clothing designer. I tell him about my own high school experience and how I was the artsy student. I tell him how one day I hope to travel all over the world and just paint, something that I have never told anyone, not even my siblings.

By the time we are both finished with our dinner, we both have a better understanding as to what the other is like. When we are about to call for the check, the waiter comes by and places a small lava cake on the table, in celebration of our anniversary, he said.

I guess the hostess relayed my message to the kitchen.

Because I love chocolate so much, I have a smile on my face the whole time I eat the heavenly dessert. I even feed a few bites to Nate before I finish it all.

Once the bill is paid, Nate takes my hand and guides me out of the restaurant.

It's outside when he takes my face between his hands and places a kiss on my lips. His tongue sweeping my lower lips right away.

"I think the chocolate tastes better on you than from the spoon," he says pulling back slightly before planting another small kiss against my lips and taking my hand.

"Want to come back to my hotel?" he asks, and I'm nodding before he can even finish asking the question.

He lets out a small chuckle and starts to guide me to my car. No need to call for an Uber.

As we are walking to the car, a ding sounds through the air.

Instantly I recognize it as my email app.

I got an email.

Is it *the* email?

Pulling my hand out of Nate's, I reach into my small purse and take out my phone.

Right there looking back at me is a small notification that a new email has arrived.

"Holy shit."

"What is it?" Nate asks, concern filling his voice.

"I got an email." I open the app and right away I'm taken to the message. Sure enough, it's from NYU.

"What?" The concern is now covered in confusion.

"I got an email. *The* email. I've been waiting for this email all day."

"What email?"

"The one that tells me if I got into NYU." I say not looking up from my phone, keeping my eyes on the subject bar.

It doesn't say anything. I have to actually open the email to see if I got in or not.

"Well?" Nate comes closer to me, but I still don't look up.

I take a deep breath and press on the message, opening it.

Scanning through the words, I see what I have to see. I re-read the message one more time before looking up at my date.

"I got in." Tears start to well up in my eyes.

Holy. Shit. I got in.

"You got in? You're going to NYU?"

I nod. "I'm going to NYU."

I let out an excited squeal and soon I'm in Nate's arms getting spun around.

"I think this means that we need to go and celebrate," he says when he finally puts my feet back on solid ground.

That idea excites me so much that after I give him a nod, I throw myself at him and give him a big sloppy kiss.

"Take me to your hotel and have your way with me, Detective."

He lets out a small growl as he palms my ass.

"Gladly."

We get in the car and head to his hotel.

Once in the room we celebrate. Nate celebrates me getting into NYU and I celebrate that I'm going to be as far away from my father as possible.

8

NATHANIEL

THE FACT that I don't want to leave this bed or the beautiful woman that is sleeping in my arms, tells me that I'm becoming attached. That thought alone should scare me, but the reality of it is that it doesn't, and I have no idea why.

Last night after dinner and Cami finding out that she got into NYU, we came back to the hotel, with a stop at a liquor store to get a bottle of champagne of course.

The second that we walked through the room door, there were hands and mouths everywhere. It was like the week we had spent apart was too much and we needed each other right there and then.

And that's what happened.

Right there at the door, I lifted Cami in my arms and pressed her back against the door. No foreplay, no her coming on my tongue, no cock being wrapped around her mouth, nothing but animalistic need. One handed, I hiked up her dress, took myself out of my slacks, and after I coated myself with her wetness, I slammed into her.

It was fast, hungry, and everything we fucking needed at that moment.

There was also a lapse of judgement, because I had slammed into her without a condom, but after she came, she detangled herself from me, got on her knees and took everything that I had to give. Swallowing every last drop.

After that, we got rid of our clothes, and I opened the champagne bottle. Instead of drinking from glasses, I laid Cami down on the bed, and poured the liquid into her belly button, drinking every drop off her body.

After the champagne was done, we fucked until we both fell asleep. I had her count again, getting her to seven before she passed out fully.

Now, the sun is starting to peek through the curtains and my phone is telling me that it is almost time to head to the meeting with Leo Morales.

I pull myself out from under Cami's body, before heading to the restroom quickly to freshen up. When I return back to the room, she is still sound asleep.

Pulling on the same suit from list night, I situate myself before I climb back into bed, taking in her scent.

"I have to go, baby girl." I run my nose along her exposed neck.

She must feel the featherlike touch because she starts to wake up.

"Stay," she mumbles, rolling onto her stomach and cuddling further into my body.

I let out a small chuckle. "I wish I could, but I have that

meeting to get to." I place kisses on any inch of skin that I see, and she lets out a contented sigh. "You could stay."

I place a kiss against her pouting lips.

"If only. My sister-in-law is coming over for breakfast. Maybe after that." Her brown eyes open and even though they are filled with sleep, there is a small hint of lust in them.

If only I can stay and make the lust part more prominent.

"I'm heading back to New York in a few hours." I don't know what Morales is going to tell me, but whatever it is, I will have to work on it. And I have to do that from home where I have all my resources.

Cami's pout becomes more prominent.

"So, you're going to leave me high and dry?"

This girl.

Shifting on the bed, I position us so that I'm lying on top of her, with my hands on either side of her head.

"You got into NYU. We'll see each other again." I place a kiss on the tip of her nose.

"Promise?"

This time I place a kiss on her lips, prolonging as much as I can. "I promise you."

I grind against her to drive my point. My cock already getting hard at the thought of having her again.

If only I had the time to feel her tight, hot pussy wrapped around me right now.

Finally, when we pull a part, Cami gives me a nod. "Okay. I guess I will see you when I get to New York. If you still want to see me, of course."

"I think that I've proven that, Camila Diaz."

With one final grind against her body, I move off her, telling my dick to calm itself down.

Cam watches me as I grab another jacket, my wallet and phone and stuff them in my pockets, and my eyes find hers when I grab my gun and hide it in my waistband.

I'm going to a meeting with the second in command of a cartel, of course I'm going in strapped.

After I have everything, I head back to Cami and place a chaste kiss on her lips.

"See you later, Camila." I repeat the words that I said at the airport.

"See you later, Detective."

"Stay as long as you like, maybe this will end quickly and we can get one more round in before your breakfast." I wiggle my eyebrows at her which causes her to giggle.

With one final kiss, I walk out of the room and try to get in the right mindset for this so-called meeting.

———

I PULL up to the address that I was sent from an unknown number. It's a café in a secluded part of Austin but it still has a small amount of people around.

Never pegged Morales to frequent places like this, but I guess even the most dangerous man has to eat breakfast.

Walking into the café, I am able to find Leo easily. He's in the back eating and from the looks of it he brought someone with him.

It was a good idea to bring my gun with me.

I walk back to their table, and right away Leo makes eye contact with me.

"You're late," he grumbles, but I don't respond. I just take a seat next to his man, who happens to be Santiago Reyes, better known as Santos and grab a menu from the middle of the table.

The waitress comes by to take my order and once all that is all said and done, I give my attention to Leo and Santos.

"How are you, boys?" I say to them, trying to tick them off more than anything.

"Oh, you know, just waiting for your ass to show up," Leo throws my way, a hint of annoyance in his voice.

I sigh. "Yeah, sorry about that. Had something to take care of and it took a little longer than I thought I would."

A lie, but they don't have to know that I was preoccupied by a certain twenty-year-old with an amazing body.

The waitress comes back with my coffee and places it on the table and she walks away.

Taking a drink of the hot liquid, I turn back to the two men. "So, what brings you to this lovely breakfast? Not that you two aren't my favorite people, but I got shit to do."

Like possibly taking Cami a few more times before I head back to New York.

Leo looks at me before he nods to Santos. I watch as he reaches under the table and produces a backpack. He opens it and pulls out a file.

"This is all that information that you need to close a cold case from five years ago," he says when he places it on the table and slides it over to me.

Cold case?

I open the files and ask. "What cold case?"

"The murder of Cristiano Reyes," Santos says before my eyes can register anything in the file.

When I hear the name, I look up at Santos. I can see it in his eyes that he knows I recognize it.

Cristiano Reyes is, or was should I say, Santos's father. He held the position that Leo holds now. Cristiano was the second in command of the Muertos and was Ronaldo's right-hand man. That is until he was killed five years ago.

But the recognition of his name doesn't come from his death, no it comes from his actions. Cristiano Reyes is the man that killed my father.

At least, he executed the plan that ultimately killed him. He was the only member of the Muertos that was in the same country as my father when he died in a car accident.

Cristiano may have caused the accident, but it was Ronaldo that called the orders. It's for that reason that my vendetta is against Ronaldo and not Cristiano. Reyes was simply doing what he was told to do.

I found this all out when I went to the lead agent on my father's case when I was sixteen. I learned every detail from when my father's death occurred to who they suspected did it and why they didn't go after him.

"Who did it?" I look over the file trying to familiarize myself with the case, but it's your standard police report and pictures of a grey SUV.

"Emilio Castro."

Oh what the actual hell?

Castro is the son of another cartel leader. Last I heard of him, Leo had shot him in the leg after he kidnapped his wife.

I thought that he would be dead by now.

"He still alive?" I have to ask.

"Died three weeks ago," Leo answers me.

Three weeks ago?

How?

The man went after his wife, why in the hell did he let him live that long. If it were me, he would have died a long time ago.

"How?"

"Shot in the chest at his wedding." Leo gives me a shrug like that is the most casual thing in the world.

"He got killed at his wedding?" I ask the question in a low voice, hoping that none of the other restaurant goers hear me.

Leo nods, and that is all I need to know that the two of them were at the helm of it.

Santos reaches into the backpack again and places another file in front of me.

"He was shot with an automatic reloader, which is owned by Ronaldo Morales."

Holy shit.

I open the new file and look it over. It's an autopsy report which describes the type of gun he was shot with.

"I'm not even going to ask how in the hell you were able to prove that the gun belongs to Ronaldo."

That is something that I've been trying to do for years, but Ronaldo Morales is anything but stupid and when it comes to weaponry, he doesn't have any. At least not any legal ones under his name.

Santos reaches forward and shifts through the papers in the new file, pulling something out.

"He did all the work for us. The one and only weapon registered to Ronaldo Morales in the state of Texas."

I take the registration from him and look it over. This piece of paper is legit. I look at every piece of information, even the date to see when this registration is from.

The state of Texas has a law that no known members of any crime affiliations have the legal right to own a gun. Ronaldo is at the top of that list.

"This registration is from the late eighties," I muse.

Given the date, Ronaldo wouldn't have been on the FBI's radar until a few years later.

"When Ronaldo wasn't very well known as a cartel member." Leo finishes my thought process.

How Ronaldo missed this little detail is beyond me.

He must have bought the gun and registered it, but never used it.

"Fuck." I run a hand over my face. And here I thought that this meeting was going to be for nothing.

I now have something to bring Ronaldo down.

"Now you can add murder to his rap sheet," Leo says to me.

But I don't answer, I just continue to look at all the information that they provided me. It is all legitimate evidence.

Everything in these files is enough to tie Ronaldo to murder and put him away for a long time.

I can't help but wonder how it got to this point. What did Ronaldo do that drove Leo to the point of ratting him out? Of risking everything that his family has built?

But one other thing is more pressing than Leo's relationship with his father.

"I'm not one to ask if anyone has a moral compass, I've done my fair share of heinous things." A few bodies come to mind. "But I do have to ask this. What happens to the cartel once Ronaldo is taken down?"

Do the Muertos completely disappear, and my job becomes a lot easier?

"I can't very well tell you that the cartel is going to continue, can I? Whatever is decided, that's going to be between me and my brother-in-law here. Not you. But I can promise you this, you won't find another file on the Muertos on your desk after this."

I want to hate the guy, I do, but if I don't have to deal with him or this cartel after all is said and done, I will be good.

"I can get behind that." I give him a nod. The less I have to deal with him, the better.

With that, I grab all the paperwork that was handed over to me and stuff them in the inner pocket of my jacket.

Throwing a few bills on the table to cover the breakfast, I stand up and give both men a nod.

"I'll reach out if there's a development," I say.

Without a response from either of them, I leave the café.

By the time that I reach my rental, my mind is a bit blown.

I don't have anything that will put Ronaldo away for drug-related charges, but I do have enough to possibly put him away for murder. I don't know what made Leo and Santos do all this, but I don't really care.

As long as I get to put the bastard away, that is all that matters.

I start the car and head back to the hotel to grab my things. The ball needs to start rolling and I won't be able to do that until I get to New York.

It's time to put Ronaldo Morales behind bars once and for all.

9

CAMILA

I THOUGHT that I would have a mental breakdown.

I thought that I would cry all the tears that my body could produce over this.

I thought that it would be harder.

But it wasn't.

It wasn't hard at all to pack up all my things and move to a different state. A state that was almost two thousand miles away from my siblings. A state where the only person I know is fourteen years older than me.

In reality, this move should have terrified me to the very core, but it didn't. The move actually brought peace.

Peace that I wasn't in Texas.

Peace that I wasn't just a drive away, that my father would cross the Mexican border and take me back to his estate.

Sure, my father is capable of coming to New York and dragging me away, but he won't. Especially if my siblings have anything to say about it.

In the almost three months since my sister's failed wedding and since I left the family estate, I haven't heard a peep from the man that was once a role model to me.

No phone calls.

No text messages.

Nothing. Not a single form of communication when it comes to my father.

A part of me wants to go to San Pedro and talk to him, to make things right and show him that he could still be the father that I know that he is capable of being. I want to talk to him and have him tell me that I don't have to be fearful of him.

But even though it's been a few weeks since I've seen him, or spoken to him, I'm not ready to make the jump and actually do it.

Maybe with a little more time, I will be able to do it.

But for now, I'm going to concentrate on moving everything into my new place and getting settled.

"This place is tiny as shit," Leo grumbles as he brings in the box that carries about twenty percent of my art supplies.

"I like it," I tell him, grabbing the box from him and taking it over to the corner I'm deeming my art enclave.

I wanted to make the most out of this whole experience, so instead of taking the apartment that my brother offered, I decided to live in a small studio offered by student housing. I did agree to getting my own room though, there is too much family shit to living with a stranger.

Leo didn't like the idea, but I was able to get him to let

me live like this for at least a year. Anything after that, he can put me in any apartment that he thinks is worthy.

"It's a shoe box," he argues back. It is tiny, but I not going to tell him that.

"Leave her alone," Serena yells out from the bathroom.

Hey, at least that has a door and not a part of the open concept.

"I can't believe you agreed to this," Santos groans when he walks in behind my brother with yet another box of art supplies.

I was going to do this move by myself, possibly convince Isabella to come with me for a few days. But when I asked Isabella, Serena jumped at the opportunity to leave Austin and well since Leo and Santos are little puppies when it comes to their women and won't let them go anywhere without them, they came too.

All fine by me, I was able to leave all the heavy lifting to my brother and his friend.

"Trust me, I didn't want to," Leo grumbles back before crossing his arms across his chest and giving me a stern look. "She somehow convinced my wife to withhold sex until I agreed."

Did I do that?

Oops. Looks like I did.

"I feel sorry for the fucker that ends up married to her," Santos mumbles before leaving the studio.

"Hey! *¡Yo soy una angelita*! Whoever I marry will be happy to have me!" I yell after him and even with him out in the hallway I still hear a grumble.

Leo just shakes his head and follows my sister's boyfriend out.

"Ignore them. They'll get over it," Isabella says from where she is fixing my clothes up on a rack.

"I don't know how you two deal with them on a daily basis." The two of them are infuriating and together they are even worse.

"Trust me, there are times where I want to dump my coffee on your brother's head." Serena says coming out of the bathroom.

"Oh, if you do it, can I watch?" Seeing Leo suffer like that is what dreams are made of.

Serena just laughs and goes to my small kitchenette to grab a bottle of water.

After countless hours, the place is coming together. Everything is in its place and makes the shoe box look like home.

All that is left is to get my art supplies in order and I will be all set. Then all I will have to do is wait for the first day of class to arrive, which is in two days.

"Thank you guys for coming with me. I know you guys have jobs and all that, but I really appreciate it. It saved me a lot of headaches trying to do this all by myself."

I think that is why I'm so okay with the move, because I had people here to help me make this whole thing a lot easier.

I'm blessed to have three people that have loved me unconditionally all my life and a fourth that has only been in my life for a year, but I can already feel the love she has toward me.

The guys come back to the studio with the last of my boxes. I tell them where to put them, not wanting to touch them until I'm alone. Because I'm going to need something to preoccupy my mind just in case my mental breakdown comes later.

"I guess that's everything," I say. Why do I feel like I'm saying goodbye to them and never going to see them again?

"Yes," Leo says, nodding, "Do you have everything you need?" he asks, looking at me like a father and not a big brother.

I nod.

He's not asking about my everyday things.

"I have everything. Gun under the bathroom sink, and phone under my mattress."

The gun for protection and the phone to communicate with my family.

In this family, it's not normal to have just one phone, you have multiple.

I have two.

One with a number that I use as Camila Diaz and use on an everyday basis and another that only the four people standing in this room with me have the number to.

It's a precaution. Something to have just in case the FBI started looking deeper into the cartel and started tapping into our phones.

"Good." He gives me a curt nod.

I give him a nod back. I know what I need to do when it comes to the family business and that's not to talk about it.

"Well since we're all here, Leo and I have something to

tell you," Serena says coming over and wrapping an arm around my brother's waist.

The look on her face makes me go on high alert, and it gives me a bad feeling.

"What?" I ask cautiously.

Leo looks down at his wife and lets out a sigh. "Serena's pregnant."

I feel my jaw fall open.

By the way Serena was looking, I thought for sure my brother finally convinced her to get a divorce.

"You're pregnant?" I turn to my sister-in-law, a smile forming on my face.

She nods. "Three months along. We wanted everything with Emilio to die down before we said anything. It's still not a good time, but it's happening and we wanted to tell you guys."

The room is silent for a second, all of us trying to digest the news. The silence is over when both Isabella and I let out a shriek before heading over to our sister-in-law and hugging her tightly.

This is the best news since Isabella and Santos finally were able to be together.

"Oh my god, all the baby clothes that I can make," Isabella declares.

"Can I paint the nursery?" I ask excitedly.

My brother and Serena are having a baby! After getting married in Vegas and everything that they went through the first few months of their marriage, I wanted them to be able to be happy and live their lives. And now they are and I couldn't be happier for them.

"I would love that. Both the baby clothes making and the nursery being painted." Serena's eyes tear up as she speaks.

Serena comes from a family that isn't very close. She doesn't have any siblings and her parents aren't a huge part of her life. Her being pregnant must be a terrifying thing for her.

But she has us. She has Leo, who I know won't let anything happen to her. She has me and Isabella that will spoil that baby to death with so much love. And she has Santos, who will be the best uncle that that baby will ever need.

She has a family.

This baby has a family, and nothing is going to take that away.

Serena is going to be a great mom and my brother is going to be a great father. I know for a fact.

"Should we go out to dinner to celebrate?" Isabella offers, excited about the news.

I love that my sister has finally come to accept Serena and is excited about this baby just as much as me.

"I could go for some Italian food," Serena suggests.

"Anything for you, *princesa*," Leo tells her before he places a kiss on her head.

I wish that when the time comes, I'm able to find what my sister and brother have.

The five of us get all situated and soon we are making our way out of my studio and out to the streets of New York.

As we jump into the car, the rental Leo got to move all

my boxes from the plane to the studio, Isabella calls an Italian restaurant and makes a last-minute reservation.

While we make our way to the restaurant, my phone dings.

When I pull it out to see who it is, a smile forms on my face.

DETECTIVE: *Glad to hear that moving is going great! Let me know once your family has left and we will do something to celebrate the big move!*

I HAD TEXTED him when we got in last night that I was finally back in New York, and then this morning, when he asked how moving was going, I told him that my siblings and their significant others were helping me out.

We haven't seen each other since he had that business meeting in Austin when I got my acceptance email. We have talked somewhat, but it was mostly just conversation about the move and him telling me what restaurants I should try, nothing too serious.

Now that we are in the same city though, maybe that will change. Maybe we will move from friends that occasionally fuck to something more.

Do I want it to be more?

I don't know, but it would be nice and if it's with Nate, it would be even better.

I guess we'll see what happens.

I text him back.

. . .

ME : *I will!!*

"WHO'S DETECTIVE?" Isabella asks from next to me, making me jump a little.

I lock my screen and turn to my sister, a small blush crawling up my face.

"No one," I say a little too quickly.

Thank God, I didn't send Nate a boob pic, her seeing that would have been embarrassing.

"I don't believe you." She narrows her eyes at me, a smile playing at her lips.

I sigh. "Just someone that I met while I was here for the interview," I tell her.

It's not a lie.

"Is this person a *he*?" she asks. Instantly my eyes go to the front where I see my brother looking through the rearview mirror, waiting for an answer.

I dislike this family sometimes.

I let out another sigh. "Yes."

"Is he cute?" Serena asks, leaning around my sister, wiggling her eyebrows at me. I swear I hear a groan being let out in the front seat.

"Yes, okay? He's cute." More than cute, but I digress. No need for my brother to hear how mouthwatering this man is and what magical things he can do with his cock. "We're just friends, so can we drop this?"

Isabella shrugs. "Whatever you say."

I swear if anything ever comes out of whatever is going on between me and Nate, I'm not bringing him around my family.

My brother may actually cut off his dick.

And I may or may not be partial to it.

10

NATHANIEL

My phone dings with a notification, but I ignore it to keep my concentration on the task at hand.

For the past two months, ever since the breakfast with Leo and Santos, I have been working tirelessly to bring everything together to bring Ronaldo Morales down. Unfortunately, in the last two months, I haven't been able to move any further than I was before.

Don't get me wrong, the information that Leo handed over was helpful, but it's not what the DEA wants to be able to handle the case. They need something that has to do with the drugs that Ronaldo moves. And the only way to do that is getting some sort of photographic evidence of the man himself at one of his warehouses, or he steps foot on American soil.

Being a known drug lord isn't enough.

So I ended up handing the case files that Santos and Leo gave me over to the FBI. We're working to take down the same man after all. They'd have a better chance of taking him down for murder than I will.

Now, I'm trying to get any footage I can of Ronaldo. My attention right now is in Austin, Texas, since that is where one of his bases of operations is. I will comb through every single piece of footage and information I can, before I move on to looking for him in Mexico.

I know his home base is in San Pedro, but that isn't where he handles his arms and drug trade. No, that happened somewhere else in the country, but after years, I'm still not able to find it.

This fucker is smart. Nothing is tied to him. Not his properties, his warehouses, nothing. Before his wife was killed, everything was in her name, now everything has changed names so many times, I have no idea if they are still tied to him.

My mind stays on his wife though as I pick up the police report on her death. Or should I say murder?

Rosa Maria Morales was killed twenty years ago in a border town in Texas. She was walking out of a fabric store when she was gunned down.

Her killing didn't make national news like it would have if it had happened today, but it did pique the interest of the local news stations.

I was in Kansas at the time and anything that had to do with the Muertos Cartel grabbed my attention. I was a year away from becoming an agent to go after Ronaldo, of course I was interested.

Every news article and every news station that reported

on her death, I looked through it like a fine-tooth comb. Trying to find anything that would lead me to Ronaldo.

But nothing brought me closer to bringing the man down. If anything, it drove me further away.

There is something that I knew about this case that was never said by the news reports, though. That is that her husband had something to do with her death. I just don't know what.

Twenty years later, that thought still boggles me.

Makes me wonder if Leo was able to find a connection with Cristiano's death, how come he wasn't able to find one with his mother's?

Was that even something he considered?

I shake that thought out of my head. I really need something to take my mind off the Muertos and Ronaldo.

Picking up my phone, I check the notification that had come in earlier.

Cami.

A smile forms on my face just thinking about her. She's been back in New York all of a few hours and I feel the need to see her again.

To touch her.

Feel her body under mine.

Dangerous thoughts to have really, but with everything that I have going on with the Muertos case, they are welcomed ones.

I slide on the message, opening it and seeing that it's a message informing me that her family has finally gone back to their hotel.

We've been texting off and on for the past two months,

so I knew when she was officially making the move to my neck of the woods.

We've kept our conversations as clean as possible, not really diverting things to anything besides her move.

I have a feeling, though, now that she is here, that might change.

Do I want it to change?

I don't know.

Cami is young. She should be out and exploring the world and grabbing at every single chance she can get.

She shouldn't be spending all her free time with someone who is almost twice her age.

She's in her second year of college, for crying out loud.

But you're the only person that she knows in Manhattan.

True, but wouldn't her family find it weird if she said she was friends with a guy in his midthirties?

Are we friends though or are we in a friends with benefits type of situation? Kind of how I was with Ava, but the major difference being that I actually want to spend time with Cami outside of the fuck session.

Okay, maybe Cami and I need to talk about all of this, before my mind blows up.

I'm about to type out a reply to Cami when an unknown number pops up on the screen.

The last time an unknown number called it was Leo.

I sigh before I press the green answer button.

This should be fun.

"Madden." I answer, already feeling frustrated.

"You have any updates?" Four simple words and my hatred toward this man grows more.

I pinch the bridge of my nose, trying to center myself. I lean back in my chair finally answering him. "Straight to the fucking point, aren't you, Morales?"

"When it comes to my livelihood, fuck yeah I am. Now do you have anything for me or not?

"All the case files that you gave me?" I say, trying to probe his brain.

"What about them?"

"They're in the hands of the FBI. I was told by my boss that we can't do anything with them. So, I handed them over, and they should be able to do something with them."

"Did you tell them where you got the information?" he asks, his tone rising a little bit.

"This isn't my first rodeo, Morales. When asked I told them that I had a few connections with the coroner's office that handled Emilio's body. They won't ask questions. Especially with the fact that the gun is registered."

"What does that mean for me and my men?"

"It means that for right now, that you are in the clear. No one is going to come after you at the moment." I tell him but I hear a small growl come through the other end of the line.

"For the moment?" There is the growl that was brewing.

"Look, Morales. I'm trying my damn hardest to keep your name and your men out of this. But there are other people in this department that want to see all the Muertos behind bars. Or better yet, dead. I'm trying to do everything that I can to keep my promise to you, but I'm only one man. So, if I say for the moment, I mean for the fucking moment."

Fuck, man. Why is talking to him so damn aggravating?

"And if anyone's name besides Ronaldo's starts to flow around, am I going to know about it?" I guess given my title he has every single right to mistrust me.

Should he trust me?

We do have one thing in common, we both want to see Ronaldo pay for his actions.

"If I hear anything, your name, Reyes's name, I will let you know. In the meantime, though, I need to ask you something."

"What?"

"I need something, anything, that will give me a better chance at getting Ronaldo behind bars." I waited my whole damn life to see this man pay for his actions, no way in hell am I going to wait any longer.

"Like what?"

"A warehouse, one that he frequents. If not the location, at least some footage that puts him there."

Maybe it's asking a lot, but given some of the information that Leo has given me in the past, like the warehouse locations in Austin, this seems like a reasonable request.

Leo is silent for a while, so long that it makes me think that the line was cut off. That is until he speaks.

"Fine. I'm about to get on a plane, but as soon as I get back to Austin, I will get you the information that you need."

I let out a sigh of relief. "That is all I ask."

Without anything else from Leo, the call ends, and I feel like this big chunk of stress was just taken off my shoulders.

Soon I will have information to bring down Ronaldo. Soon all of this will be over.

I just hope that Leo is telling the truth about sending me that information, otherwise I'm back at square one. It will suck, but if I have to start all over again, I will do it. But it won't be for me, it will be for my father.

As I put down my phone after the phone call with Leo, I remember that I was about to text Cami back before the phone started to ring.

Earlier I was going to text her because I needed some sort of distraction from the case and maybe to figure out where we both want what is going on between us to go, but now it's different.

After a conversation with the kingpin's son. I just want to see her. To live her in hopefulness for a little while and get lost in what she has to offer.

Opening up the texting app, I press on her name and start typing out a message.

ME : *DO YOU MIND IF I COME OVER TO YOUR PLACE?*

11

CAMILA

Do I mind if he comes over to my place?

Do I mind?

I look around the studio apartment and try to figure out how it went from all organized when my family left to the chaos it currently is.

Yet the chaos didn't stop me from texting him back and saying, "sure come on over!"

I sent that message about half an hour ago while I was sitting on a paint-stained floor cover and painting when I should have been organizing. Now it is just a bigger mess than it was before.

There is no time to clean up. Something that I should have started when I got the message, but I was so into the painting I lost track of time.

Well fuck. I guess the big detective is going to be meeting the chaotic Camila tonight.

And when I hear the knock on the door, that is happening sooner rather than later.

Scrambling to my feet, I check in the mirror I have in my bedroom/living room if I at least look presentable.

I don't.

There's paint on my face and my messy bun is all over the place. I fix my hair, but the paint, I leave because no way will I be able to scrub it off before I open the door.

When my hand hits the doorknob, I take a deep breath and center myself before opening the door.

There is a smile on my face as I swing it open, when I realize that it isn't Nate on the other side, it dwindles.

"Um, hi," I say to the stranger standing in front of me.

"Hey," he says, cringing slightly before he holds out his hand to me. "Sorry, my name is Devon. I live across the hall here. I saw you move in, and I thought I would come and introduce myself."

I look down at his hand for a second before I shake off the stupor that I'm in and shake it.

"It's nice to meet you, Devon. I'm Cami." I give him a small smile, using my shortened name.

I'm all for meeting new people, but I would like at least some sort of warning next time.

"Given by the paint on your face, I would say that you are an art student at NYU." He smiles at me.

I nod. "Yeah, I start next week. Are you also an art student?"

I have no idea how housing works here. It could be that all the people on this floor are art majors or it could be all over the place.

"No, actually, I'm a journalism major. I'm about to start my final year."

"Oh, that's cool," I say.

"Yeah," he says, and it becomes even more awkward when someone clears their throat.

Turning, I find Nate standing a few feet away with a bag of food in his hand and an eyebrow raised in a questioning manner.

"Hey," I say to him. The smile that I had when I first opened the door, making an appearance again.

"Hey., he says, not moving to come closer to where Devon and I are standing.

If I thought it was awkward before, it's definitely awkward now.

"Um, it looks like I'm interrupting your night," Devon says, taking my attention away from Nate. "I'm going to head back to my place, but it was nice to meet you, Cami. If you need anything, I'm just across the hall." He points at the door behind him.

I give him a nod and a silent thank you. "It was nice meeting you too," I tell him.

And with one final smile in my direction, he turns around and heads into his apartment.

Okay then. That was a little strange.

I just shrug it off and turn back to my visitor, whose eyes aren't on me but on the door that Devon just went through.

"Do you want to come in?" I ask, holding my hand out for him to take.

It takes him a second, but he finally takes my hand and lets me lead him into my apartment.

"Sorry the place is a mess., I say, closing the door

behind us. "I was organizing my art stuff, when you texted and then I got lost on a project and I didn't have time to clean up."

Nate places the bag on my small table before he turns to face me again.

"It's fine." He comes over to me and places his hands on my hips. "I'm sure that it's just the way your artistic mind works."

I smile at his words.

No one has ever said that they got the chaotic side of being an artist. No one but my mom.

"It is. Sometimes I get so wrapped up in what I'm doing, I get lost in my mind. And the chaotic mess helps sometimes."

"I'm the same way, so I can appreciate the mess."

I'm liking this guy more and more.

I place my hands on his arms and slide them up until my body is a little closer to his.

"Hi, Detective," I say to him, giving him a bright smile.

The hold he has on my hips grows a little tighter. "Hi there, beautiful."

"We haven't seen each other in a very long time." I run my fingers through his hair, loving the silky feel of it.

"No, we haven't." He leans down so that his face is only a few inches away. "Maybe we should give each other an official hello."

His lips are only inches away from mine. All I have to do is lean forward just a little bit and they will be touching.

"I think we should." Instantly my mouth is on his.

My hands form iron grips around the strands of his hair, bringing me closer to him.

The second his tongue meets mine, I'm in fucking heaven and I continue to be in bliss when his hands go from my hips to my ass. I let out a moan, when I feel his fingers digging into my shirt.

"Do you always wear oversized t-shirts, with nothing under, when you open the door?" he says when he slides his hands under the fabric and feels my bare ass cheek.

"It's what I wear when I paint in my space," I say against his lips. "Besides, I thought that it was you."

I nip at his bottom lip, which earns me a slap on the ass.

Nate pulls back slightly. "We should eat before the food gets cold."

For a second it looked like he was going to say something else, and even though I want to ask what he was about to say, I drop it.

"Fine," I say, giving one last kiss before pulling away from him and making my way over to my small table.

Nate opens up the bag and places all the food on the table, instantly filling my nostrils and making my mouth water.

I've certainly doing a lot of that with this man around.

"It smells good," I say, grabbing some plates and a few bottles of water.

"Figured with all the moving you've been doing, that you needed something to get you through," he says with a shrug.

"I will never say no to food." I give another smile.

Nate continues to situate the food and soon we're eating the Thai food.

"How was it with your family leaving?" he asks as I slurp up my pad Thai

I give him a shrug. "It feels a little weird. I'm so used to having them at least a forty-five-minute flight away. And since I've been living with my sister these last three months, it's going to be a little hard for sure."

I'm happy to be in New York, I am, but I've always had Leo and Isabella around. Even when they were living their lives in Austin through my teens, I saw Leo almost on a weekly basis and talked to Isabella almost on a daily. Not having them close by, when I might need them at a drop of a hat, is going to take some getting used to.

"If you don't mind me asking, why were you living with your sister?"

Why indeed.

The question doesn't take me by surprise, I expected it, especially if I was going to be seeing a lot more of him now that I'm in New York. But nonetheless, the subject brings me down a bit.

I set down my fork, put my hands between my thighs and give the man sitting across from me a smile.

"My siblings and I don't have the best relationship with our father. In the last couple of years, it's been like a down-ward spiral and it kind of exploded a few months back. I didn't want to be in the house anymore, so when my sister offered for me to come live with her, I did."

It's the truth without telling him about the cartel and

how power hungry my father got. I also keep the face slaps that I received to myself.

Nate puts down his own fork and looks at me with so much care in his eyes, it throws me off a bit.

Never has a man, or should I say boy, ever looked at me like that. Like he actually cares what I've been through and hearing about my life.

"I'm sorry to hear about your relationship with your father," he says in the sincerest way possible.

I nod. "Yeah, me too." Shaking my head I turn the conversation to him, not wanting to talk about the drug lord any longer. "How is the relationship with your mom?"

Please let it be better than the one I have with Ronaldo.

"Good. She's down in Florida living her best life. I try to visit her whenever I can. But she doesn't miss me too much, what with my stepdad keeping her company and all."

I'm glad that at least one of us has a decent relationship with our last remaining parent.

Asking about his mom though, does spring an idea in my head. Now that I'm in New York, I can visit Amelia Reyes, since she's in Quebec.

A smile forms on my face.

"What has you smiling like that?" Nate asks, oblivious to why I may be smiling like a crazy person.

"Oh, I was just thinking about visiting my sister's boyfriend's mom up in Canada, since I'm in New York and all."

The more I think about it, the more excited I get about seeing the woman that was like a second mother to me.

She did raise me until she moved back to her home country when Cristiano died.

That was a tough few weeks. Not only did we lose Cristiano, but I was also losing my second mother. Yeah, she was still alive and I would be able to talk to her almost on a weekly basis, but it wasn't the same.

When she left, she told me that she hated leaving me, and that if she could take me with her, she would but we both knew it was never going to happen. Not with Ronaldo.

"I'm guessing you two were close?"

I nod. "After my mother died, she was the one that looked after me. She became a second mom to me and my siblings."

"Then you should definitely plan to go see her."

I smile even more. "I think I just might."

We finish our dinner and when I go put the food container in the garbage can under the sink, Nate wanders over to my chaotic mess.

"Your place is tiny," he voices, and I can't help but snort.

"My brother said the same thing," I say, walking over to him.

"Looks like your brother and I would see eye to eye on a few things," he says, looking around one last time before the canvas I was painting on catches his attention.

He walks over to it, and a feeling of uneasiness comes over me. It's the same feeling I felt at the bar all those months ago as he was looking over my portfolio.

"It's beautiful," he says, looking over every single inch of it.

"Thanks, it's not even close to being done, but it will get there."

"A New York view from a plane window," he muses and I nod.

"Yeah, it's been in my head since we landed, so I figured I would paint it out." I look over the painting and see all the things that still need to be done and once they are, it will be perfect.

"It still blows my mind just how talented you are. I actually have the one that you painted at my place hung up in my study," he says, not taking his eyes off the painting in front of him.

"What?" Did he say what I think he did?

Nate looks at me, realizing what he said and lets out a small chuckle. "You said you finished it. And I couldn't just throw it away or put it in a closet, so I hung it up."

"You hung up my painting? In your apartment?"

The only people that have ever done that are Leo and Isabella. Never has it been a person I barely know.

Nate nods. "I did."

Okay, the butterflies that I once said appeared when it came to this man, has now become a swarm and there is nothing that will stop them.

Going with my gut feeling, I walk over to him and reach up to take his face between my hands, bringing down his mouth to mine.

It takes him by surprise, but he is able to compose

himself and place his hands on my hips, bringing me closer to him.

After a few minutes of some tongue action, I pull away from him, placing my forehead against his.

"Thank you for hanging up my painting."

"I will proudly display anything that you paint." He places a sweet kiss on my lips, and I melt a little more into his hold.

We continue to kiss in the middle of my mess. Tongues everywhere, hands on anything that they can grasp. That is until I get an idea.

An idea that will make my chaos even more crazy.

I pull away from him and give him a bright smile. "Strip."

"What?" he asks, a little breathless, but he still returns the smile.

"Strip."

12

NATHANIEL

"Not that I don't mind ridding myself of the suit, but why am I taking off my clothes?" I ask as I place my suit jacket and my shirt on her bed.

Did I come here with the intention that it would come to me taking off my clothes? Maybe but in all honesty, I just really wanted to spend time with her. I didn't care if it led to this or not.

"You'll find out soon enough," she says, grabbing what looks like a big canvas cloth from one of her boxes and laying it on the floor.

I may have an idea of what she is planning on doing but I continue to rid myself of my clothing and not ask questions.

Once I'm down to my boxers, I take a seat on her bed and watch her as she sets everything up.

There is a look on her face of determination and maybe a hint of happiness swimming somewhere in between.

It's the same look that she was wearing when we went back to my apartment when we first met. I like seeing her like this.

I wasn't the only person that liked seeing her, though.

"Have all your neighbors come by?" I ask, feeling slightly stupid even asking the question.

"No." She shakes her head without looking up at me. "Just Devon." She continues to place paint all around the canvas.

"He seems like he was into you." At that statement, she finally looks up at me, giving me a questioning look.

"Okay?" she says the comment coming off more like a question, tilting her head slightly to the side.

Did she not notice how he was looking at her? Like he was hungry? How his eyes moved to her exposed legs when she turned to greet me?

"You didn't notice how he was looking at you?" Why am I getting angry at this? Wasn't I just thinking earlier today about how she is young and should be out enjoying life?

Besides we aren't anything at this point, so there is no reason for me to be pissed over it.

Cami abandons what she is doing, before she comes over to me.

"Are you jealous or something, Detective?" She settles between my legs, with her arms going around my shoulders.

"I have no right to be jealous." My hands settle on her hips.

"And why do you say that?" She comes closer and I feel her fingers against my scalp.

"Because you should be out there enjoying yourself and not in here with someone who is fourteen years older than you. You should be having dinner with David instead of me."

She should be doing what normal twenty-year-olds do. Going to college parties, enjoying every aspect that the city has to offer.

"One, his name is Devon." She gives me a smirk. "And two, if I wanted to be out enjoying myself and having dinner with my neighbor, I would be. I don't like doing things that I don't want to. Case in point, why I'm here with you and not with him."

"You should be hanging out with people your own age."

"School starts in a few days, so I will, but there is nothing bad about hanging out with you." She looks at me with the most sincere eyes that I have seen.

I let out a sigh, pulling her closer to me. "I was thinking about something earlier. About how you being here could change things. How it might be a good change, but then guilt started to creep in. It kept telling me that whatever change I wanted to happen, might not be the best thing for you. That even being friends might not be the best thing for you."

My words cause her to pull back slightly, but she doesn't step away from my hold. She looks down at me like she is trying to figure me out.

We stare at each other for a few minutes, all while she mulls through my words.

When I think she is going to say something, she surprises me by shifting slightly until she is straddling my lap.

"I choose what's best for me. I decide who I want to spend time with. I don't care if they're ten years older than me or thirty. That decision is on me. Yes, there is an age difference between us, but there is also an age difference between me and my siblings. Hell, you're only a few years older than my brother." She shifts slightly, somehow her body moving closer to mine, my hands moving from her hips to her ass. "I'm okay with hanging out with you and seeing whatever change that might happen play out. That is if you are."

Am I?

Am I okay with seeing what may play out?

"And if I say that I'm okay with it, what will that make us?"

Is a thirty-four-year-old man asking for a label? It sure as fuck sounds like it.

Cami grinds a little against me. "I wouldn't be opposed to dating and getting to know each other a little better. There is no real reason to jump into things right away, right? You must be busy with work, and I'm starting school. We can take it slow but still have fun along the way."

When she says the word fun, she grinds herself against me a little more. My cock instantly loving the attention.

"I can get behind that." I bring her a little closer to me, continuing the motion of her body grinding against mine.

"Yeah?" That sweet smirk she gives me, makes me want to kiss it off.

"Yeah." I give her a curt nod before surprising her with an ass slap.

Cami lets out a yelp and when I'm about to lean and press my lips against hers, she gets off me.

"No kissing. We are still doing this." she says waving over to the tarp on her floor.

"What are we doing exactly?" I stay seated, telling my dick to calm down.

"We're going to paint with our bodies," she says, an excited smile spreading across her face.

"With our bodies?" What does that mean exactly?

"Yup." She nods and waves for me to stand up. "Boxers need to come off."

So it's that kind of painting.

I listen to orders and pull down my briefs. When I'm standing back upright, that is when my jaw falls a little bit.

In front of me, Cami is taking off her shirt, leaving her in nothing but a small piece of material between her legs.

I've seen this woman naked before and every single time it gets better.

Without missing a beat, I go over to her, just as she is sliding her thong, if you can even call the flimsy material that, down her legs. When she stands back up, the piece of material is hanging from her finger.

"Not going to need that." She flings it somewhere behind her.

My hands make their way around her waist and bring our bodies together.

"So how is this going to work? Am I painting you and you me?"

"More like rolling around until we've had enough."

With another smile, she pulls back from my hold and starts to grab the paints that she had placed around the material.

With a smile at me, she starts to dump all the paint on the floor, covering the material in all the different colors.

I watch from the middle of the fabric as the colors are spread.

Once all the colors are dumped out, Cami comes back to me.

"Now what?" I say when her arms go around my neck.

"Now you kiss me." I don't let her finish her sentence before my lips meet hers.

Our kiss is full of passion and there is nothing sweet about it. It's like all the sexual tension that we've been holding in since the last time we saw each other finally has the opportunity to come out. Our tongues dance against each other and I swallow every sweet moan that leaves that luscious mouth of hers.

Soon, instead of falling to the bed, we fall to the floor, the coldness of the paint meeting our skins.

But we don't give a fuck about the coldness we are feeling, now all we care about at the moment is getting what we need from the other.

"Touch me," she moans against my lips, panting when my mouth moves down her neck.

I smirk against her skin and move my hand from her ass to her pussy.

Cami throws her head back, loving the motions that my fingers are doing against her clit.

"You like that, baby girl?" I suck on her skin, wishing with everything that it was her pussy against my mouth.

"Yes," she moans again, her legs thrashing a little, moving some of the paint around.

I move my body down hers, taking her right tit between my mouth biting down on her nipple.

"As much as I want to eat this sweet pussy of yours." I move a finger to her, her wetness letting it go in easily. "I think that would disrupt our painting here."

Cami doesn't say a word, she just arches her back and gives me better access to her chest.

"Maybe I should just fuck you, and then eat you out later tonight." I move my finger faster and when I slide it out of her, I slide two back inside her.

"Yes." Her legs start to tremble more, telling me that she is getting closer to where I want her.

"You want me to fuck you, make this painting of ours worth hanging?" I move my legs feeling the coldness of the paint covering them, but I don't care. All I care about in the moment is getting Cami to the edge.

"Fuck me, Nathaniel. Please fuck me," she begs, her pussy tightens around my fingers.

I fucking love it when she says my full name like that.

"Come first, Camila. Come and I will fuck you all over this canvas." I move my mouth from one tit to the other, giving it the same attention as its counterpart.

My fingers move in and out of her faster, bringing her closer to the brink.

"Nathaniel!" she yells out when I bite down on her nipple and have my thumb move against her clit.

"That's it, baby. Come on my fingers. Coat them." And with that, she does.

As she thrashes under me, I take my fingers out of her and pull away from her. But only for a second while I grab a condom from my wallet.

I sheath myself as I keep my gaze on Cami as she catches her breath. The part of her body that I can see is covered in paint. I can help but smirk at the thought at how covered it will be once we are done with our little project.

"Ready?" I ask her as I go back to her, situating myself between her knees.

"Yes." She bites her lip, and gives me a cute smile, opening her legs wider for me.

I grab my cock and slide into her hot wet core.

"Fuck." This woman is tight, and if we continue to do this, eventually she will be the death of me.

She lets out a moan, and I start to move in and out of her.

Without taking my eyes off her, I run my hands against the wet canvas and cover my hands in paint before placing them on her chest.

I slide the paint all over her chest, covering it with a mixture of colors.

Cam arches her back, filling my hands perfectly.

"Such a beautiful girl," I say, admiring the way her body looks covered in paint.

"Nate," she starts to pant out, her legs tightening around me.

"I know, Cam. I know." I continue to move, in and out of her. The sound of our bodies slapping against each other fills the room along with the paint moving around us.

"I'm right there." Her eyes slam shut, her body thrashing all over the canvas.

"Come, baby girl. Come," I say as I lean forward and press my lips against hers.

I pound into her, getting her closer to the edge.

Moving my mouth from hers, I take one of her nipples in my mouth again. That's what causes her to let go. For her to tighten around my cock and bring my own release to the brink.

"Fuck!" I growl out against her chest, my fingers digging deeper into her hips.

With one final thrust into her pussy, I slide out of her and fall onto the canvas.

I wrap an arm around Cami as I try to catch my breath.

We lie there, all wrap up around each other for a few minutes, just enjoying each other's bodies.

I shift a little bring her closer to me.

"Next time we do this, can we have a padded surface?"

Cami lets out a laugh, that is like music to my ears.

"Is your back not liking the concrete, old man?" she teases, sitting up slightly giving me a smirk.

"Did you call me old?" I pinch her ass.

She nods.

"Do you need another demonstration on how I can fuck better than any little boy has ever fucked you before?"

"Yes, Detective. I think I do." She throws me another smirk and soon we are adding more paint onto the canvas.

I lay on my back and have her lay herself on top of me, her pussy to my face and her mouth on my cock.

A loud groan fills the room when I feel her warm mouth wrap around me.

Her sweet mouth working me and sucking me dry.

We continue our little art project until every single inch of the canvas is covered.

In the end, I think that this may be my favorite piece from her.

Maybe I can hang this one above my fireplace.

13

CAMILA

"ISABELLA!" I yell at the screen as my sister shows me the big ass rock she is sporting on her finger.

"I know! Isn't it pretty?" Her eyes get this dreamy look in them that just tells me that she's happy. My sister is finally happy.

"Pretty? That thing is gorgeous! *Ahora, dime todo!*" I find the nearest bench to me and get comfortable.

Isabella starts going off and telling me every detail of how her proposal came about. Everything from her being at work at selling each and every one of her designs and how the girl that bought them gave her a card so that she can branch out to do her own thing. Then she goes on to tell me how when she got back home she and Santos celebrated, and thankfully she spared me of those details.

No way in hell was I going to be able to survive if I had to hear about my sister's sexual preferences with someone I see as a brother. Gross.

She then tells me how they were all cuddled up in bed

and she told him to propose. That she realized that she was happy and how she knew that no matter what they were going to go through, they had each other.

I find the whole thing romantic as hell.

"Oh my god, I can't believe that you told him to propose," I say to my screen, my sister's smile not going away anytime soon.

"It was either tell him to do it or have to wait for him to go through with his plan. This gets us to that stage sooner." She gives me a shrug and I absolutely love it.

"Ahh! I'm so happy for you two! You are finally going to be able to be together forever."

"That's the plan." She gives me another smile through the screen and I return it. And it's there until I think of something.

"Do you think..." I stop, trying to come up with the words. "Do you think that *Papá* will be okay with this?"

The man tried to marry her off to another man, and from what Isabella has told me, threatened Santos when it came to getting her out of that marriage.

Shit, I even saw my father go after him after the shooting at Isabella's wedding. Never have I seen my father so angry before.

I don't know how he will take this news.

"No," Isabella says, her voice getting harder. "I don't think he'll like this, but honestly, I don't care. I already let him control a lot of my life. I'm not going to let him take this away."

I give her a sad smile. I guess this isn't a good time to mention that I want to talk to him.

"Anyway," Isabella says changing the subject and getting away from the topic of our father. "How is school going? Everything going okay? How did this last month go?"

It's been a month since I have officially been in New York. In the one month, I have been trying to find my footing and for the most part, everything has been going okay. My classes have started out fine and I've even made a few friends in a few of them. I've even made friends with a few people in my building, including Devon.

I've also been spending more and more time with Nate.

Since our night together at my place, we've gone out and seen each other as much as our schedules will allow.

Matter of fact, everything is going good, and I tell my sister as such.

"Everything has been going good. Made a few friends and I like my classes. They are definitely better than what I was taking at the community college. I'm really liking New York."

I give my sister a bright smile and soon the face of anger she was wearing while speaking about my father has disappeared.

"*Qué bueno.* It makes me happy to hear that everything is going so well. It also makes me feel a little better that you're meeting people. I didn't know if being that far away was going to be a bad move, I'm glad to be proven wrong."

I nod at her. I get it. It's one thing having me live under my father's roof, it's another thing when I'm a three-hour plane ride away.

"I think I felt the same way, but I think I got comfort in

the fact that I at least knew Nate when I arrived so I had him to lean on if I needed to."

I'm so lost in the words that I'm saying, I don't notice my sister's expression. It has now gone from one of excitement to one of curiosity.

"What?" I ask her.

"Who's Nate?"

Crap. I mentioned his name, didn't I?

I let out a sigh. "Do you remember that guy I was texting in the car?"

"The detective?" Her smile turns to one of a smirk.

I nod. "Yeah, that's him."

"So, you guys kept in touch since you move there?"

"Yes?" My statement comes off as a question, and I might have cringed a little bit.

"Is there more to him than you just keeping in touch?" I sometimes hate having an older sister like Isabella, she's so observant.

I sigh again. "We are dating."

Well sort of, can't very much tell my sister that I let this man fuck me whenever he pleases.

The second the words leave my mouth, Isabella lets out a squeal.

"We're taking it slow. Dating and seeing where it goes."

"Oh my god, Camila. That is so exciting. I can't wait to meet him."

I should probably tell her, and not take her by surprise when that happens.

"If that does happen, you should know something," Again I cringe.

"What?"

Here goes nothing. "He's, um, thirty-four."

Silence.

For the first time in my life, I have rendered my sister silent. And by the way she is looking right now on my screen, she's a little shocked too.

I can see her play back my words in her head, and even opens her mouth a few times but doesn't say anything.

I let her digest the words though, but trust me I want to hang up on her, but that will just earn me a lecture later.

"He's thirty-four?" she finally asks.

I nod. "Soon to be thirty-five."

"And how did you meet?" She still has an expression of confusion on her face.

"At a bar. After my interview," Another statement that makes me cringe.

"Camila!" Isabella reprimands me.

"I didn't drink! I ordered a club soda with lime and chicken strips. It's not my fault that Nate happened to show up, and we hit it off."

She cannot be mad at me because I met someone that happens to be in his midthirties.

Isabella goes back to being silent, but this time she is shaking her head. At least this time around the silence isn't all that long.

"I can't believe that you're dating a thirty-four-year-old."

"Believe it, *hermana*. Believe it." Sometimes it's even a little mind blowing to me, especially in the last month.

"Is he hot?" I snort a little at her question.

"Um." I start trying to find the words, when something in the distance catches my eye.

Nate.

I texted him when I was out of class and since his work is close by, he said that he would meet up with me here.

"Yeah," I say, a smile growing on my face as he gets closer. "He's hot. He has a certain daddy vibe to him that I kind of find sexy."

"Oh my god, I can't believe you just said that." Isabella fake gags through the screen. I may have also said the words when Nate was only a few feet away from me, and by his raised eyebrows he heard them too.

"What? It's true!" I give both of them a shrug. "You'll see if you ever meet him." I throw a wink at her and she just laughs.

"Well at least you're not lonely."

"Oh definitely not. Or cold." That causes Nate to cough which he tries to shield as best he can, but does not succeed. Isabella is still able to hear him.

"He's right there with you, isn't he?"

I nod to my sister trying not to laugh.

"You're something else, Camila." I just shrug and she continues to laugh. "I gotta go, so I will let you enjoy your 'date'. See you in November?"

I nod. "I wouldn't miss it."

"*Te quiero.*"

"*Yo te quiero mas.*"

And with that I wave bye and our call is over.

"Daddy vibes?" Nate asks as soon as I set the phone down.

I shrug. "I think it's the whole being older thing and the gray hairs that are masked within the blond. Like I said, it's hot. I can start calling you daddy if you want?"

I throw him a wink which causes him to snort. "At this moment and time, I will have to decline that offer."

"Suit yourself."

He shakes his head, trying to hold in a laugh. "And I guess that was your sister on the phone?"

"Yes, sir."

"Well I guess," — he comes to sit on the bench next to me— "It's a good thing you called me a daddy to your sister and not your brother."

"I said you had daddy vibes, not that you were a daddy. And also, I would never have that type of conversation with my brother. He would probably jump on a plane just to come here and cut off your dick."

"Ouch, he says, crossing his legs, like it's something that will happen any minute. "Remind me that if I ever meet your brother, not to cross him."

I laugh, but in all honesty, I will have to do just that if that ever does happen.

Leo can be scary. Add Santos to the mix, and Nate will have to be armed just to handle those two.

I lean toward him, my lips only inches from his. "Deal."

I plant a kiss on his lips and when I pull back I give him a smile.

"How's work going?" I lean into his arm when he throws it against the back of the bench.

"Stressful. I feel like this case is never going to close.

I'm trying to work every lead that I get, but it still doesn't feel like enough."

I rub a reassuring hand against his thigh. These last couple of days, I have noticed that he looks a little over-worked. The times that I've been over at his apartment, he spends most of the time in his office, until I have to force him to come out.

"It will work out. Probably when you least expect it."

He sighs. "I sure hope so. It would be nice to have my life back."

"If it helps, you can tell me about it. I may not know a whole lot about crimes but I'm a good listener. Maybe I can help you find something that you haven't been able to see."

It's the least I can do, right? I'm sure that Leo's research skills have rubbed off on me in some way.

"Thank you, beautiful." He places a kiss against my temple. "But it's not something that I want to burden you with. The time will come where I can put this behind me."

I hope so.

"Maybe you need something to distract you." I lean my head on his shoulder.

"You help with that." He brings me closer to his body. "And maybe you can help me with something else?"

"And what is that?" I lean up slightly, not really pulling away from him.

"I have this work gala that I have to attend, be my date?"

I smile against his shoulder, a part of me absolutely loving that he asked me.

"As long as it's not the first or second of November, I will be happy to be your date."

"Then I guess we should find you a sexy dress to wear."

I can hear a smile on his face as he says the words.

Butterflies fly around in my stomach, and I hope they never go away.

14

NATHANIEL

THE CHAIR BENEATH ME SHAKES, *as if someone kicked it.*

It vibrates as if whatever hit the metal chair was made of metal itself. Whatever it was I was able to feel it all the way to my pounding head.

My eyes feel heavy, every inch of my body feels cold and I have no idea why.

Why am I cold?

Why does it feel like something is in my chest causing a fire?

"Nathaniel Madden." A voice says. A voice coming from the darkness. A voice that I don't have any idea who it might belong to.

I try to pry open my eyes, but I don't succeed. I'm just met with more darkness.

"No me puedes matar." The voice continues. It's speaking in Spanish, but what is it saying?

"No me puedes matar."

I grunt, trying to pull myself against the restraints that hold my hands down, but nothing gives.

A hand lands on my shoulder, and that's when my eyes finally open and I'm met with a pair of dark brown eyes.

Eyes that have no life to them. Eyes that I have seen before.

"You will never kill me."

It's my phone pinging that wakes me. My eyes pop open right away, and the darkness of the room tells me that it's the middle of the night.

Before grabbing my phone, I shake off the dream and I look over and see that Cam is still fast asleep with her back facing me.

Throwing the blankets off my body, I grab the phone and walk out of the bedroom and into my study. I turn on the desk lamp and get situated in my chair before I press the lock button.

On the screen a message shines bright, waiting to be opened. It's from an unknown number, but I know who sent it.

It's the same unknown number that has been calling my phone for over a year.

Leo Morales.

Swiping it open, the message opens and once it's on the message thread, I see what looks like coordinates.

Once I commit the coordinates to memory, I look at the message that came after them.

UNKNOWN : *You will find him at this location.*

.   .   .

I LOOK AT THE WORDS, and quickly type out a message in response.

ME : *Cameras?*

As I WAIT for a reply to come through, I star tup my computer. Once everything is up and running, I open up my database and type in the coordinates.

The system takes a few seconds to think before the screen shifts. It's pixelated for a few moments before it clears up and shows me a piece of land in the middle of what looks like a forest.

The more I look at the picture, the more I see that there are buildings all over, but are being covered by the trees, giving them protection. If someone looked at the picture quickly, they wouldn't be able to notice them.

Perfect for a drug operation.

I expand the picture, and I see that the location is in Mexico, in the state of Nuevo Leon.

I guess Ronaldo doesn't like to keep business far away from him, since San Pedro, the small town that he calls home, is located in the northern part of the state.

My phone dings, taking my attention away from the screen.

Looking down at the phone, I see that another message has come through. It's a link.

. . .

UNKNOWN : *The footage is erased every twelve hours.*

I GUESS I can't fault the Muertos for being overly cautious with their security footage.

I send the link over to my computer and open it. If the footage is erased every twelve hours, it could be days, maybe even weeks before I am able to get Ronaldo on camera.

"Fuck." I rub a hand over my face, just thinking about the amount of work this will be.

But I have to do it.

I have to do everything in my power to take down this man. To bring justice to every single person that he has killed, to bring justice for my father.

I will do everything to take down Ronaldo Morales, I don't give a shit if he ends up in a body bag or behind bars. One way or another, this fucker will pay.

I grab my phone again, and type out a message.

ME : *I will let you know if there are any developments.*

I PUT THE PHONE DOWN, but it's only for a second before it starts to ring.

Seriously?

I roll my eyes, but either way I answer.

"Madden."

"Don't you sleep?" Leo's voice comes through. I don't really feel up for his shit this late.

"I can say the same thing about you."

"Cartel business never sleeps." Neither does being a special agent.

"What can I help you with, Mr. Morales?" I let out a sigh, getting comfortable.

"I don't want developments," he states and instantly I'm on high alert.

"Then what do you want?" I try to keep my voice as low as I possibly can, not wanting to wake up Cami.

"I want action. I don't care how long it takes you to do it, just concentrate on the job and that's it. Take the man down."

His words take me by surprise. This is a different Leo Morales than what I'm used to.

"What the hell brought that on?"

Leo is silent for a few minutes before he lets out a sigh. "Things are changing with my family. I don't need this man to continue tainting my life or my siblings' lives any further."

He's being genuine. Never have a heard him speak like this. It makes me hate this man a little less.

"Okay. I will let you know when it's time or if I need anything else." He's giving up his father, it's the least I can do.

"Thank you." And with that the call ends.

I place the phone on the desk and lean back in my chair.

Never did I think I would be working with Ronaldo's son to take him down, yet here I am.

Eventually, I turn back to the screen and look through the security footage. I find that the twelve-hour intervals start at midnight and at noon. Meaning that the hours from yesterday are already erased and I can only go through the ones for after midnight. Given that it's three in the morning, there isn't much. Just a few men putting together some kilos. It's not live though, there is a delay of about fifteen minutes, if the timestamp in the corner is accurate.

I look through the footage and at the map with the coordinates until I hear the door to the study open.

Cami.

She probably turned in her sleep and noticed that I was gone.

I look up and right away I'm met with brown eyes filled with sleep.

"Come back to bed," she says, holding out a hand for me to take.

I look at the woman standing in front of me and for the first time, I feel grateful for her. Grateful that she came into my life when she did and that she is still here.

If she was"t here tonight, I probably would be driving myself crazy with the dream that I had, the footage and the coordinates until I had to go to work.

After closing the screens on the computer, I stand up and make my way over to her. When I'm close enough, I take her face between my hands and place a chaste kiss against her lips.

"Thank you for being here tonight," I say to her and she awards me with a sleepy smile.

"I will be here every single night you want me to be."

Why is it that I want to tell her that I want her every single night?

Because even without that label, I'm starting to fall for this woman.

I give her one more kiss and then finally take her hand in mine, guiding her back to the bedroom. Once we are back in bed and she is in my arms, all I can do is look up at the ceiling and think about the dream.

"Cam?" I say softly.

"Hmm?" she hums against me, telling me that she's close to going back to sleep.

"What does '*No me puedes matar*' mean?" I ask her in my broken Spanish.

Whatever the words mean, it must be bad if Cami sits up right away and even in the darkness I can see that she is looking at me with concern.

"You can't kill me." She answers.

You can't kill me.

That's what Ronaldo told me in my dream. That I can't kill him.

Even in a dream, he's challenging me.

Now way in hell and am I going to let him be right.

15

CAMILA

I INSPECT myself in the mirror absolutely loving how the dress that Isabella sent over is sitting on my body.

Everything about this dress is perfect for tonight. My sister is seriously a genius when it comes to this type of thing and I absolutely love it. I love it even more when I get to reap the benefits.

Moving my eyesight away from the dress, I next look at my hair. The grayish strands are in a half up, half down updo. Given my short length is perfect and still makes it look like it's ready for a fancy occasion. My dark roots are showing but I like it, it gives my hair dimension.

Maybe I will let it grow out from the gray and go to my natural hair color. Maybe.

Once I'm happy with how my hair is looking, I move to my makeup. Everything looks good and once I add my red lip, I am ready to go.

Perfect.

I open the bathroom door and head to the nightstand to pick up my earrings and then go look for Nate.

Tonight, is the night of his work gala, and since it was a small hassle for him to go to my place to pick me up, I got ready here. It wasn't a hardship, since I've been spending a few nights a week here already.

The good thing about it is that his place is close to mine, so I can leave in the morning and head over to my place to grab what I need for class.

"Cam! You ready to go?" Nate calls from the kitchen as I walk out of the bedroom while I put on my studs.

"Yes, Detective. I'm ready," I say, entering the living room, my heels helping to announce my presence.

Nate looks over from where he is standing by the floor to ceiling windows and his jaw pops open.

"Holy fuck," he says, his eyes going from my toes all the way up. He looks at every inch of me, so I give him a twirl to give him the whole view.

"Is it too much? Too little?" I ask, a little nervous that maybe I need to cover myself more. This is a work thing. Is it appropriate to wear a dress like this?

"It's absolutely perfect," he says, finally being able to find his voice.

"You like it?" I give him a shy smile.

Nate abandons his place by the window and comes over to me, instantly his hands going to my waist and bringing our bodies closer.

"I love it. You look absolutely breathtaking." He leans down and places a kiss behind my ear.

"Thank you." I start to melt into his hold.

"As much as I want to drag you back to the room and lift up this little dress to see which panties you are wearing, we have to go. The car should be here already." He pulls away from me and holds out a hand for me to take.

It takes everything in me to avoid that comment about my panties and just take his hand.

"You got a car. Fancy." In all the time that we have been exploring this between us, which is almost two months, we have always walked places with taking his car on rare occasions.

"Hey, my girl deserves a night of pampering, even if it is for a work thing." He gives me a wink before guiding me to the elevator.

His girl.

He called me his girl.

It could have been a slip up, Camila.

I know, but let me bask in it for a few seconds.

It is something we need to talk about, though. Things have shifted. Feelings have gotten stronger, and I might think that we are past the whole 'seeing where it goes' phase. I know where I want it to go, and now I just have to hope he does too.

Maybe tonight after we leave this thing, we can have that conversation. Because I really like being called his girl.

We make it down to the front of the building and sure enough, a car is already out there waiting for us. The driver opens the door and after we slide in, we are making our way to the Upper East Side.

The whole drive over to the hotel, Nate has a hand on my thigh rubbing methodical circles on the exposed skin.

Silence fills the space, but it's comfortable silence and it's one I'm okay with. If we were alone, I would be having him find out what exactly I'm wearing under this dress, but I don't think about it much. Since I don't care for voyeurism.

"Does your work always hold their galas at luxury hotels?" I ask when we arrive at the designated location and start to get out of the car.

Nate laughs before taking my hands and escorting me into the hotel.

"It's their way of showing off to some of the other agencies. Trust me, the hotel portion isn't the only over the top thing that they do."

The second we walk into the ballroom; I understand what he means.

"Holy crap." And I thought that my father was one to flaunt his money.

There are flowers everywhere, and chandeliers that make the room sparkle. The center pieces on the tables all look like they cost hundreds of dollars and at the very front of the room there is a light up sign that announces the New York Division Gala.

It looks more like a wedding than a gala for a bunch of cops.

"Told you," he says guiding me into the room and stopping to let me admire every inch of it.

"Everywhere I look, there is something new. Is that a cheese fountain?" I ask when I spot a bunch of yellow liquid flowing out of a machine in the corner.

"Looks like it." Nate chuckles, but then the hold he has on my hand, shifts to my waist.

The movement causes me to abandon my drooling over the cheese fountain and turn to face him.

He's not looking at me though. No, his eyes are in front of us, looking at something else.

I follow his line of sight and see that there is a woman approaching us. She looks to be around Nate's age if not a few years younger. She is wearing a beautiful gray dress and she looks absolutely stunning.

"She's pretty. Who is that?" I ask, just curious, given his reaction to her coming our way.

"A coworker," he says with a sigh.

Am I missing something?

I'm about to ask why he's acting so weird when the woman steps in front of us with a welcoming smile on her face. At least I think it's a welcoming smile. The way her eyes are assessing me tell me that she doesn't care for me much.

"Nathaniel, you made it!" She leans forward and places a kiss on his cheek.

Nate leans away from her quickly giving her a strain smile.

"Ava. Yeah, I am here," he tells her and while he says the words, he pulls me closer to him.

"Who's this?" she says, looking me up and down like I'm the enemy or something. Something about the way she asks the question is rubbing me the wrong way.

Look, I'm not normally a jealous person. I'm the type of woman that loves everything about women and hypes them up. But if you bring out the claws, you will get them back.

So, I put a bright smile on my face and extend my hand to her.

"It's nice to meet you, Ava. I'm Camila." I give her my full name and add some of that Latina to my voice.

"Oh, are you a cousin of Nate's?" Really? His cousin?

"No," Nate says, his grip on my hip getting a little tighter. "She's my girlfriend."

"Your girlfriend?" Ava asks her smile faltering a little.

I try to keep my composure, but did he just say that? Did this man really just call me his girlfriend?

Right now, I'm trying incredibly hard not to jump up and down and do a happy dance.

Nate nods. "Yes."

Ava looks at him and then looks back to me with a tinge of confusion on her face. "Isn't she a little young to be your girlfriend?"

"We're both consenting adults. There is no harm in what we're doing. Besides, the age difference between us is minimal compared to other couples," I tell her.

This has been something that I have been practicing with saying. I knew the day would come that people would question not only Nate's intentions with me, but also the whole relationship in general. I'm sure Ava, or anyone for that matter, wouldn't have a problem with this if I was in my thirties and Nate in his forties.

"I guess so," Ava says, her eyes still bouncing between the two of us, like she still doesn't believe it.

"It was good seeing you tonight, Ava. I will see you at

the office on Monday." Nate says, giving her a nod and turning us to walk around her.

"It was nice meeting you." I give her another smile, one that she doesn't return.

Something is going on between her and Nate, because no way in hell is that a normal reaction.

Nate guides us through the ballroom until we reach an empty table. Pulling a chair out for me, I take it and once I'm pushed in, he sits next to me, taking my hand and placing it on his thigh.

"You okay?" I ask him, feeling as if something is a little off.

"Yeah," he says, giving me a curt nod, and a smile that doesn't reach his eyes.

"You and Ava have history, don't you?" There is nothing malicious about my question. It's just genuine curiosity.

He lets out a sigh and nods. "We were coworkers with benefits if you want to get technical. When we needed a stress reliever we would get together, but it hasn't been a thing since the start of this year."

I give his thigh a reassuring squeeze.

"Well, she's really pretty, so I can see why you two got together."

He looks at me and gives me a raised eyebrow.

"You're not mad that I had a sexual relationship with a coworker that I still see on a daily basis?"

"Do you want me to be?"

He just continues to look at me. Maybe he thinks I'm from another planet or something.

I take my hand that is on his thigh and bring it up to

his face, cradling it. For a few seconds Nate closes his eyes and leans into my touch.

"We both have a past. There is no reason for me to be upset about that. Unless you have a wife somewhere, and you are just using me to get some booty on the side or whatever, then that would make me mad." That causes him to pop his eyes open and give me a 'not amused' look. I let out a laugh. "I'm kidding. But besides that, no, I'm not mad. That's not the type of person that I am. I was actually going to say that she looked hot in that dress before she started looking at me like I was a piece of gum under her shoe."

Nate lets out a small laugh before leaning in and giving me a small kiss on the lips, one that is appropriate for being out in public.

"Have I told you that you're something else?"

I give him a smile. "Maybe, but I like hearing it."

He gives me another kiss, and when he pulls back, I give him a bright smile.

"You told Ava I was your girlfriend."

"I did." His blue eyes get darker, a hint of mischief in them. "Are you okay with that?"

I want to scream yes, but again, we are in public. So I just give him a slight nod.

"Yes, I'm okay with that."

"Good."

I'm about to lean in for another kiss when the music starts to play, announcing that the event is about to begin.

Both Nate and I straighten up in our seats, and soon a man is coming up to the microphone and announcing the start of the twenty fifth annual gala dinner for the DEA New York division.

"The DEA?" I ask Nate.

"The agency that I work for."

"Like the FBI and CIA?" I ask.

He nods. "Yeah, just a different branch that deals with different types of crime."

A part of me wants to ask what type of crime. That same part wants to ask if they deal with things like the Mafia, or most importantly the cartel, but I don't.

If I was dating someone that worked with those types of cases, they would know who I was.

Wouldn't they?

If they were after my father, they would know if he had kids and what they look like on top of their names, certainly.

Maybe I should ask Nate after this dinner is done.

Or maybe I should just let things be, because no way does my new boyfriend have any knowledge of the Muertos Cartel and what they do.

If he did, he wouldn't be with me, that's for sure

Because he would know exactly what my family does and that alone would terrify him.

16

NATHANIEL

MY EYES FEEL like they are about to crawl out of my head after spending countless hours watching security footage.

Even after watching hours of video footage from the warehouse, I still have no footage of Ronaldo stepping foot on the premises. I've been at this for days and absolutely nothing has come my way.

The only saving grace that I have at the moment, is that I have figured out a way to record the footage and not have to worry about it deleting after twelve hours. Now if I need anything, I can just go back and find it.

I just need the fucker to show up and I can get a plan into motion.

What that plan is, I have no idea.

But for the moment, I need coffee.

Pushing my chair away from my desk, I leave my office and head to the break room where I know there is a fresh pot of coffee brewing. Given the number of hours us agents work, coffee is a staple in this building.

When I walk into the break room, it's empty, but as I'm pouring my cup, a set of footsteps sound behind me.

"Hey, Nate," Ava greets me. I turn to her and give her a small smile.

"Hey, Ava." I move away from the coffeemaker to give her some room.

"Thanks, "she says as she grabs the pot,. "So how is it going?"

I guess we're doing pleasantries. "All good. I have no complaints."

"That's good. How is your girlfriend doing? Cameron?" She turns and gives me a fake smile, one that I'm not used to seeing when it comes to her, but I choose to ignore it.

It's been two weeks since the gala, and this is the first time I've seen Ava since then. From what I know, she was working a case in California.

"Camila, and she's good." I check my watch and see the time. "She's actually heading home to visit her family for the weekend."

She had invited me to go with her to Texas, but with the security footage, I wanted to stay on top of it, so I told her to go and have fun spending time with her family.

Besides, we've only been together officially for two weeks, it didn't seem all that right to intrude in her family time.

"Oh, that sounds fun. I thought that I noticed a hint of a southern accent in her voice."

I find it interesting that Ava noticed an accent, since Camila doesn't have one.

The Spanish does come out often though and that's a

different story. When she's talking in Spanish an accent is a lot more prominent. There're times when she's talking, and she could say every other word in Spanish, and I won't understand a single thing. But I think it's hot.

"Yeah." I nod to Ava. "So, I'm just going to drown myself in my work until she gets back." Just like I was doing before she came into my life.

"If you need any company, I'm just down the hall," Ava says before she gives me another smile and leaves the room.

I shake my head and start to make my way out of the room too when Beck walks in looking as snarly as ever.

"Madden."

"Williams."

"Any leads on that footage?" he asks, keeping his voice low.

Given that Beck is a higher up, when he pulled me into his office to ask for an update, I told him I got my hands on some security footage. I didn't tell him where I got it and he didn't ask. He just watched everything that I showed him and told me good work.

I shake my head. "Not yet. I'm hoping soon. I do have a few men we can go after but not the one we want. I'm hoping that will change in the next couple of weeks."

It's a bullshit answer but it's all I got at the moment.

The DEA doesn't get breaks in their cases like the FBI do. There's a reason that the Muertos have been going for so long.

Beck nods, accepting my answer. "As soon as you get something. Let me know."

"Yes, sir." I give him a curt nod and he leaves the room.

Looks like my eyes are going to be crawling out of my head after I'm done looking at all this footage.

I head back to my office. Before I turn back to the computer, I grab my phone and see that Cami has texted me that she has arrived in Austin.

A smile forms on my face and I type out a response.

Once the message says delivered, I put my phone away and get back to the task at hand.

Looking through the footage and trying to find out when Ronaldo will slip up.

Hopefully it's not in another thirty years.

———

CAMILA

I'VE ONLY BEEN in New York for a few months, and it already feels weird being back in Texas. I seriously thought that as soon as I stepped off the plane in Austin, I wouldn't want to go back, but not the case at all.

It's home, but New York is home too and I might be missing it just a little.

Or maybe you're just missing Nate.

He's part of it, but I miss New York in general.

That doesn't mean I didn't miss my family though.

That's why I'm currently at Leo's and Serena's house, drawing out a nursery.

"You do realize we don't know what it's going to be yet, right?" Leo's voice takes my concentration from the paper in front of me. I turn and find that he is standing in the doorway.

"That's why I'm planning out two." I stick out my tongue at him.

"I can't believe I agreed to this," he grumbles.

"You didn't. This is my gift from me to the baby, and you have no say in what I paint on the walls. I will need your credit card though." I give him my sweetest smile and I'm a little surprised when he rolls his eyes and takes his wallet out, walks over to me and hands me a few hundred.

"If you need more, just let me know."

"You're such a softy."

He grumbles before he takes a seat next to me on the floor. "Don't tell anyone. It will ruin the whole 'most feared man' thing I have going on."

I laugh. But after a few seconds, I somber "How are you handling that, what with the baby coming?"

I don't really get involved in cartel business. I know what happens behind closed doors, I know what is smuggled into this country, and I know that the cartel is the reason why my family is as well off as it is.

But I have nothing to do with the business side of things, not like Leo does at least.

"I'm trying not to let it get in the way of what's supposed to be a happy time, but it's hard not to. It's hard not to think about what could happen if someone finds out that Serena is pregnant, or about the baby after they're born. And not only that, but there are also a bunch of what-ifs. What if I can't protect them? What if I become just like Ronaldo and traumatize the kid? What if I can't be a good father? Worse yet, what if I get one of them killed?"

I hear the pain in his voice, and it just breaks me that he's going through this. I hate that instead of enjoying the fact that he is going to be a father, that he is thinking of the worst possible outcome. One where he might lose everything, all because of the life that we were born in to.

And there is nothing that anyone could do about it. There is no way to leave this family, this business and live a normal life.

I wrap an arm around my brother and hold him as tight as I can.

"It will work out and that baby will have the best dad in the whole world."

"How do you know that?"

I give him a smile. "Because I have faith, and I know for a fact that you will do everything in your power to make sure that none of your fears come true. Because you have an army standing next to you and Serena who will do everything they can to help you keep everyone safe."

"I guess I do." He leans over and places a kiss on my hair, and we sit like that for a little bit.

There is something I need to ask, and I know If I go to Isabella, she will say no. Leo might be worse, but I have to do it.

"I have to ask you something," I say, finally pulling away from him.

"What?" I can see the wariness in his eyes. He knows what I'm about to ask is going to be bad.

"Is it okay if I go to the estate tomorrow?"

"Camila," Leo starts to say, his head is already shaking no, but I stop him.

"It won't be long. Just a few minutes, I just want to talk to him."

"Why?"

Why indeed.

My father has done a lot of wrong in his life, and that includes going after his son's wife and forcing his daughter to marry someone she wanted nothing to do with. He has even made me fearful of him from his actions all those months ago, but he's still my father.

He's still the man I looked up to until Cristiano Reyes showed me what a real father was like. He is still the man that I lived with when my siblings were living out their lives.

I know the man that still cares about his children is still there under the hard exterior, and I just want to see if he will come out.

"I know he's a bad man. I know that he has done unforgivable things to us, but a part of me thinks that the man he once was is still there."

"And if he isn't?"

"Then I guess not only will we have lost our mother but are father as well."

I know what Leo and Isabella think of him, how he's dead to them, but I'm not there yet.

Even if I have some hate and anger toward him.

Leo continues to look at me for a few more minutes, not saying a word. Finally, his eyes close and he gives me a nod.

"Okay, you can go to the estate, but you'll have a man waiting for you outside and you'll come straight here afterward."

I give him a nod. "I will."

Will anything come from this? Probably not.

But I have to at least try.

17

CAMILA

IN MY FAMILY, the *Día de los Muertos* celebration is a big deal. It all started when my mother was still alive. From what Leo tells me, she used to place flowers on every single grave, as if to honor them, no matter if they had family. He said that she would also honor every single person whose life was ended by the Muertos.

It was some sort of penance, in a way. She would honor those who died on her husband's hands.

When she died, Isabella made sure that we continued the tradition. Maybe not honoring the individuals that my father or his men killed, but honoring the people in the town that passed.

We would build an altar for our mother and surround it with flowers, food, and pictures and then we would go into the town square to honor those who we didn't know.

When I was about fifteen, I noticed that there were a lot of gravesites that didn't have the same amount of decorations as the others had. Some didn't have anything at all.

So I made it my mission to show those people some love and place flowers on their graves. Like my mother did in a way.

This year is slightly different. This year an altar for my mother was still built, but this time at Leo's compound outside of Austin instead of here in San Pedro. Another difference is that I'm out placing flowers on the gravesites as the daylight shines, instead of when the sky is covered with the night.

The last major difference, I'm here by myself, hoping to speak to my father.

When Isabella heard what I wanted to do, she said that she would go with me, but I just shook my head and told her no.

This was something that I wanted to do for myself.

She wanted to fight me on it. I know she did, but she conceded and let me come without her at my side.

It's strange being in San Pedro for the celebration without my siblings being within a walking distance but I can handle it.

I finish up with putting the bouquets of flowers on all the graves before I head over to Cristiano's and my mother's.

First is Cristiano's where I put a set of flowers that were sent by Santos with his mother in mind. I look down at the grave and smile.

"They're happy, Cristiano. *Están feliz.* They're getting married."

I know he would have been happy for Santos and Isabella. Those two don't know it, but Cristiano told me once that he had hope that they would get married one day. That they would get over all the problems that they caused for themselves and be happy together.

Unfortunately, he was killed before he could see that happen.

I press my fingers against my lips and press them against the stone before walking away.

As I walk over to my mother's grave, my phone starts to vibrate in my dress pocket.

Yes, I had Isabella sew pockets into my traditional style dress, it's more conventional that way.

I smile when I see the name on the screen.

"Well, if it isn't my favorite detective," I say instead of a regular greeting.

"I better be the only one on that list," he says with a chuckle.

"There is a high possibility that you are," I tell him, the smile I'm wearing growing a little bit more.

"How is everything going over there?" I told Nate that I was planning on going to speak to my dad. That I had reservations about it but I still wanted to do it. He said that he thought it was a good idea, and if that's what I wanted to do, then I should.

I love his support.

"It's okay so far. The hard part hasn't happened. I'm just visiting my mom's grave right now."

"Sounds like there's music in the background."

"Yeah, that would be the day of the dead celebration. There's music and food and vendors doing face painting."

"It sounds like a nice time," Nate says and I'm finding myself nodding.

"It is. It's one of my favorite traditions. Most years I even dress up and go all out with my face paint." Face painting is always my favorite thing to do and I'm a little disappointed that I didn't do it this year.

"Most years? You didn't do it this year?"

I sigh. "I think if I wasn't meeting up with my dad later, I would have." My father has never really cared for my painting. He's told me countless times that I should find something more useful to do with my life.

"Maybe next year you will be able to go all out. I would love to see it," Nate says nonchalantly, but I'm trying really hard to keep myself intact over what he is saying.

Next year.

He wanted to be here with me next year? He's thought that far out into the future?

"You would?" I ask, my voice shaking a little bit. I clear my throat just in time to hear him let out a small chuckle.

"Yeah. You can show me why this is your favorite tradition."

He has no idea just how much hearing him say that means to me.

I try to swallow down the lump of emotions that is forming in my throat.

I smile even though he can't see it. "I would like that."

"Then we will make it happen." I can hear a smile in his voice and I love it.

"Madden, I need you in my office," someone says from his side.

"Okay, I'll be right there." Nate pulls away from the voice piece. "Sorry, baby girl. I have to go."

"It's okay. Go work, I'll see you in a few days."

"Alright. Bye, beautiful."

"Bye." I hang up the phone and put in my pocket as I walk the last remaining feet to my mother's grave.

Not caring about the dirt under me or, getting the dress dirty, I kneel before the grave and start spreading around the flowers.

"I'm in New York, *Mami.*" I place all the flowers that I can as I speak. "*Estoy estudiando,*" I smile as I tell her I'm going to school. "I'm getting my art degree at NYU and I really like it. I think you would have loved visiting me there. Everything feels so big and it's so pretty, you would have loved everything about it. You would have also loved to meet the guy I'm with. He's kind and cares about me very much. I think this thing between us is going somewhere very important and I love everything about it."

I finish putting the flowers around her grave and just sit there for a few minutes, looking at the engraved words.

"There is so much I want to tell you. About Leo and Isabella, but I think I will let you hear it from them when they come visit you. You will love everything they have to share."

I close my eyes and I let the November air flow around me, letting me feel as if my mother's spirit is right here with me.

After a few minutes, I open my eyes, letting out a sigh, and push myself off the ground.

"*Te quiero muchísimo, Mamí y te extraño con todo lo que soy.*"

Like I did with Cristiano's grave, I do the same with hers.

Soon, I'm leaving the cemetery and making my way over to my father's estate.

This is a walk that I have done on countless occasions but for some reason, today it feels heavier, like I don't know what is waiting for me at the estate. At the place that I once called home.

I walk onto the grounds, and I'm surprised that I'm not surrounded by my father's men right away.

My palms are sweating a little as I approach the main door, and they feel like a they are under water when I walk up the steps and a security guard approaches me.

"*Buenas tardes, Señorita Camila,*" he says, giving me a nod and opening the door for me.

"*¿Si está mi Papá?*" I ask him and I get a curt nod.

"*Si, señorita. Está en su oficina.*" He opens the door for me to walk through and give a nod.

"*Muchas gracias.*" I give him my thanks and walk over the threshold of the estate. The last time I walked through it, I was walking next to Isabella as she was taking me away from this house.

My heart beats faster the closer I get to my father's office. By the time that I'm standing in front of the door, it feels as if it's going to pop out of my chest.

Here goes nothing.

I lift my hand and knock on wooden door.

I stand there for a few seconds, and I finally hear something from the other side.

"*Pasen*," he announces and I try to control my breathing as much as I can before pushing the door open.

I step into the office and right away see my father sitting at his desk, looking down at some paperwork. His glasses are on and his dark hair with sprinkles of gray looks like he has been running his fingers through it. He doesn't notice that I walked in, so I clear my throat.

Right away, he looks up. A hint of surprise comes across his face, but it's quickly masked with one of indifference.

"Camila."

"*Hola, Papá.*"

He takes off his glasses and looks at me straight on. "What are you doing here? I'm surprised that your brother and sister let you come here alone."

"It wasn't without a fight," I say. but he just continues to look at me.

"What can I do for you, Camila? Did you come to ask me to move back into my home? Or maybe it's to ask for your inheritance?"

Inheritance?

I didn't even know that existed.

"I wanted to talk to you."

He nods. "*Entonces, habla.*"

I just stand there looking at the man that as a little girl I looked up to, that I thought would move hell and earth for his kids, but I guess I was wrong.

"Was the cartel really so much more important than your children?" It's a fair question.

"You don't know what you're asking, Camila." He waves me off, like the question that I just asked isn't important either.

"Don't I? You made both Isabella and Leo hate you because you decided that taking over another cartel was more important. You cared more about money and all the power you were set to get that you didn't care that your son's wife was taken or that your daughter was marrying a killer. All you cared about was yourself and you threw your kids to the wolves as payment."

I can see that he is starting to get angry, I can see it flowing in his eyes. Without saying a word to me, he stands up from his chair and walks over to me.

For a split second, I think he is going to strike me again, but he doesn't. He just continues to look down at me. No emotion on his face.

Finally he speaks. "I gave you three everything, a house, food, money. Everything that you could have ever asked for, I gave you. And this is how I get repaid? By having you go against my word, not doing anything that I say? *Esas son pendejadas.*"

"We never asked for any of that. All we wanted and needed was our father, a father that cared, but I guess that was too hard for you." I look at my father and then turn away, realizing that this was a bad idea.

"I cared.," he says to my back. I stop in my tracks and turn back to him.

"If you cared, you would have dismantled this cartel

the second that our mother died. And you wouldn't have gone after Cristiano."

At the mention of Cristiano's name, his nostrils flare in anger. Coming here was a big mistake, I know that now, but I came and there isn't a thing I can do about it.

With one final look at my father, I walk out of his office.

A part of me wished that he would run after me, to stop me, but he doesn't. The door closes behind me and it stays that way as I make my way out of my childhood home.

I hope that my father comes to his senses, I hope he sees that his children are the most important thing in the world.

I hope that does happen, because I don't want that to be the last time I speak to my father.

Because even with all the evil that he has done, I still love him. He's still my father.

18

NATHANIEL

"WHEN DO I get to meet her?" My mother's voice sounds through my ear as if she were speaking through a megaphone and not a phone.

I pull it back to keep my eardrums from exploding.

"Ma—" I start to say but she cuts me off.

"Nathaniel, you have been with this girl for months, and I have yet to meet her."

I sigh as I make my way into the living room and join Cami on the couch, where she's wrapped up in a blanket. With a smirk on her face, I know she's hearing everything my mother is saying.

"You will meet her," I say into the phone, pinching the bridge of my nose.

"Answer me this, Nathaniel. How long have you been with this woman?"

I sigh and lean my head against the back of the couch. "Officially, two months."

"And unofficially?"

"Six months," I say and I jump a little when both Cami and my mom yell out six months at the same time.

I look over at Cami and she is looking at me funny. I mouth 'what' at her but my mother's voice keeps her from responding.

"You've been together for six months?" Why I answered my mother's call, I have no idea.

"No, I said officially two months. The six months is when we met and I'm counting it. You're the one that asked."

"Don't talk back to me, young man, I can still fly up there and kick your ass."

Jesus.

Of course, that's what Cami hears and starts laughing at my expense.

I narrow my eyes at her, and she instantly stops.

"Sorry," she voices.

"Wait, is she there with you?" Of course, my mother heard her.

I let out a groan. I don't have time for this.

"Ma, I have to go. The office is calling. Talk to you later. Love you, bye."

I hear my mother scream at me as I hang up the phone and as soon as I press the red button, Cami starts laughing uncontrollably.

"Why are you laughing?"

"Because I have never seen a big bad detective afraid of his mom before." She continues to laugh and when she throws her head back, I pounce on her.

She lets out a yelp when she lands on her back with me on top of her.

Right away, the laughter stops and she gives me a sweet smirk that I'm about to kiss off.

"You count us being together from the very beginning?" She pushes my hair back and her eyes start to fill with a bit of lust.

I lean forward and place a kiss on the tip of her nose. "I do."

"Why?" she asks me when I pull back.

How do I answer that without sounding like a total pussy-whipped bastard?

I shrug. "It might have to do with how since day one, things between us have seemed like they were on the right path. Like even from our time at the bar, we were supposed to be here, where we are right now. There is this sense that this all feels right."

It's all true. There is something about being with Cami, that I have never felt with a woman before. In the one or two serious relationships that I had in my life, they didn't feel like this.

They didn't look hopeful and had me wondering what we would be doing in a month, a year or several years from now.

"I feel the same way," she tells me as she continues to run her fingers through my hair. "And it might scare me a little bit."

I shift slightly, making sure that not all my weight is on her. I move a few strands of hair out of her eyes and just look at her.

"What scares you?"

Cami looks me in my eyes and stays silent for a few seconds.

Finally, she speaks. "That we're moving too quickly. That maybe our age difference is a bigger deal than we make it out to be and we're just blind to the disasters we might bring to each other."

I know where she is coming from. In the last two months, I've had the same thought process.

The doubt creeps in occasionally, but I hear her laugh or see her smile and all that doubt melts away.

"I think with any relationship those types of fears are normal. I've had the same fears."

"What if it doesn't work out?"

I shrug. "Then it doesn't work out, but that doesn't mean that we didn't try."

And fucking try I will because I have a feeling that Camila Diaz is worth every single second if it.

"Have I told you something else completely?" The words and the smile on her face make me chuckle.

"You haven't, but I will take the compliment whenever you want to give it."

"How about this one? You are a very special man, Nathaniel Madden."

I smile a little bit, this time I lean in and place a kiss on her lips. "As long as I'm the only special man in your life, then I will be happy."

"Would you settle for being at the top of the list?" she says as my lips move to her neck. A growl escapes my throat at the thought of there being some asshole on her list.

"There are other men?" I lean back up, my face mere inches from hers, my eyes locked on her.

"Calm down, caveman. It's my brother and brother-in-law. You hold the number one spot, well that is until my nephew is born, then you might be at number two."

I guess if I have to be dethroned from the number one on the list, a baby would be the only acceptable replacement.

Two weeks ago, after her last final of the semester, Cami went home to spend the Christmas holiday with her family.

She came back yesterday, and she told me all about her trip home. The wedding planning for her sister's wedding and how her brother and sister-in-law finally told them that they were having a boy.

I told her that she looked excited and she said that she was happy because for the first time in her life she was seeing her brother over the moon about something.

She then spent hours buying the kid clothes and trying to get her hands on some baby size Doc Martens.

Who was I to stop an excited aunt?

Wait, no. I was corrected when I said the word aunt, it's *tia*.

"I can accept a baby coming before me."

"Good." She places her hand behind my head and brings me down to her.

As her lips meet mine, her legs wraps around my waist bringing her body closer to mine.

My tongue sweeps over her bottom lip and as soon as she opens up and our tongues meet, she lets out a sweet moan that I swallow down.

Even with us partaking in a few rounds of sex last night, there is still an animalistic pull toward this woman that I can't avoid.

Any chance I get, I want her wrapped around me and have the feeling of her body against my palms.

My hands start to slide down her body, with the intention of getting her undressed as quickly as possible, but she stops me.

I pull back slightly, and I'm awarded with a smirk.

"What are you up to?" She continues to wear her smirk as she moves her hands from my hair to my chest, where she starts to push me off her.

I abide by the motion and pull away from her. When I'm fully off her and sitting on the couch cushion, Cami, who now has lust filled eyes, gets off the couch and settles on her knees in front of me.

My mind instantly clicking where she is going with all of this.

With her eyes not diverting from mine, her hands move up and down my thighs and with a small gleam, she stops at the waistband of my sweatpants.

I lean back and place my arms on the back of the couch, letting myself enjoy every minute of this experience.

Cami takes me out and the smirk turns into a grin, licking her lips in the process.

"Like what you see, baby girl?"

She nods, taking her lip between her teeth not saying a word.

Kissing her and feeling her under my body got me going but seeing her on her knees in front of me with her licking her lips at the sight of my cock might take me over the edge.

"Take me in your hands, baby. Stroke me."

Keeping her lip between her teeth, she does as I say and takes me in her small palm.

I keep my eyes on her hand movements and watch as she methodically strokes me up and down.

"Now be the good girl that I know you are and take me in that pretty mouth of yours."

"And if I don't, are you going to put me in handcuffs, Detective?"

My cock twitches at the thought of her all tied up for me to play.

"I think I will do that whether you listen to me or not."

Cami shifts bringing her face closer to my cock, opening her mouth but she doesn't place it against the shaft.

No, she hovers her mouth over it, not inching to even touch it.

"If you handcuff me, what will you handcuff me to? Your headboard is made out of cloth."

She's testing me. She is trying to see how far she can take me before I break.

"I'll buy a new one. Better yet, I'll find one of those beds that already come equipped to tie you up," I growl out, about to place my hand on the back of her head and have her take me, but I don't.

"And what will you do to me while I'm handcuffed? Will you lick my pussy until I come? Or fuck me until I scream out?" Another methodical stroke.

Fuck. This girl is really going to be the death of me.

"I'm about to take your hand away and order you to take me in your mouth," I growl again, my hands itching to move to her hair, but I keep them in place.

"Tsk, tsk, Detective. That's not very Boy Scout of you."

"Never said I was a Boy Scout, pretty girl, and I will never be. So be a good girl and take me in your mouth."

With mischievous eyes, she does as she is told and takes me in her mouth.

"Fuck." I throw my head back, loving the way her mouth wraps around me, and when she sucks on the tip, I'm almost done.

That's what this woman has done to me, a few swipes of her tongue and a few sucks and I'm almost done for. I try my hardest to control myself.

"Do you like what I do with my mouth?" She takes my cock out of her mouth with a pop before moving down to my balls.

"Baby girl, I love everything you do. But what you do with your mouth is a close second from the things you do with your pussy." This time, I don't hold myself back and reach forward and place my hand in her hair.

She gives me a smirk and before I even have to ask she takes me in her mouth and works me as if to prove a point.

I hold her hair tighter, as she sucks and licks every single inch of my cock.

"Pretty girl, I'm close," I warn, pulling at her hair for her to come up to breathe.

She doesn't budge. She keeps at it, sucking on me harder and moving up and down faster. She does this until I can't take it anymore.

"Cami," I say but she just shakes her head.

Seconds later my legs start to spasm out and I'm filling her mouth with my release.

Once she is done taking down every drop, she pulls back from me, wiping at the corners of her lips.

It's the look that she is giving me, that makes me grab her by her upper arms and bring her up to sit on my lap.

Cami settles on me sideways and right away her mouth meets mine.

We stay like that for a few minutes, until we both pull away. Her head ends up on my shoulder and my arms go around her waist.

"Round two?"

I laugh at her comment. "Give me a few more minutes and I will give you as many rounds as you want."

"Such an old man." she teases but cuddles deeper into me.

"You and I both know that I'm better at giving you what you need than any boy would." I pinch at her side and she just lets out a laugh.

"That you do."

We continue to sit like that for a while, just both of us feeling the warmth of each other's bodies.

"This view is absolutely beautiful when it's snowing," she voices.

"It is," I say not even turning to the window, just enjoying her in my arms.

"If only I could experience it every single day," she says, sighing into me.

"You can." I say without thinking.

Cami pulls away from me and turns to look at me with confusion written all over her face.

"What?" she asks, her eyebrows bunching up.

Did I say what I think I said?

Yes, I did.

Is Cami interpreting it in the same way I'm meant for it to come out?

Also yes.

"You can. You can experience that view every single day, for as long as you want." I look into her chocolate eyes, trying to convey as much sincerity as possible.

"What are you saying, Nathaniel?" The way she says my full name has me shifting a bit.

"I'm saying." I tighten my hold on her. "Move in, and you can experience the view every single day."

Her eyes go wide at my words, and I might be a little surprised myself, but I'm not taking them back.

"But we've only been together for two months, you literally told your mom that."

"And I also told her that we've known each other for six." I shift her from sitting sideways to straddling me so I can take her face between my hands. "This is a big step I'm bringing to the table, but here's the thing Cam, I want to be with you. It's only been a short time, but I know deep in me that I want to be with you, and continue exploring a future with you."

"I want to be with you too," she says, slightly shaking her head. "Is that crazy? Especially after knowing each other for such a little amount of time?"

"People have fallen this deep in much less."

She nods agreeing, but still seems a little shell shocked by everything.

"We don't have to take that big of a step just yet, if you're not comfortable with it or if it's not something that you want." That's what our relationship has been based on, right? It being Cami's decision. It has and will always be her decision.

She spends most of her time here and most nights as well, so this would just be that added step to a process that we have already started.

Making it official.

"I do want to, but I'm not sure if I'm fully ready to live together." She places her hands over mine, and for a second, I think she's trying to tell me that she doesn't want to hurt my feelings with her response.

She's not.

I nod. "Then we can do this slowly, not move in fully just yet. You keep your studio and you can be there as much as you want, but you can spend as many nights and days here that you want. And when you fully believe you are ready for that step, that we are fully ready for that together, we can take it."

"Really?" She strokes her fingers along mine.

"Yes, really. I want you here, but you have to fully want to be here too."

She looks at me. Really looks at me, like she is trying to find the catch or where I don't mean a single word I say. Soon a smile is taking over her beautiful face.

"Okay. We do this slowly."

I give her a smile that mirrors hers. "We do this slowly."

A noise from the outside takes us away from each other for a moment, lights filling the room with different colors. For a few seconds it looks like one of her paintings.

Cami turns back to me and gives me a smile that I have come to know and love.

"Happy New Year, Detective."

"Happy New Year, beautiful girl."

We start the new year with a kiss and a new adventure of living together.

Well, somewhat. For now.

19

CAMILA

"A REMINDER that abstracts are due in two weeks. I can't wait to see what you all can come up with. Have a good weekend," the professor announces and soon every single person in the room is cleaning up their art supplies.

Whereas everyone is doing it slowly, I'm doing it at lightning speed so that I can make it to Nate's work in time to catch my flight.

I got a text from Leo about an hour ago that Serena was in the hospital ready to have the baby.

I had hoped that she was going to go into labor two weeks ago during Isabella's and Santo's wedding, but I had no such luck.

After a beautiful wedding and finally seeing my sister get her happily ever after, I left Austin with a new brother-in-law, but not a new nephew. I was sad.

That sadness might have caused me to go crazy and text my brother and Serena a few times a day for the last two week just asking if it was time.

Every single time they told me no. I think I might have annoyed them a bit. I might have also annoyed Nate with my constant moping that the baby wasn't here yet.

Of course, on the one morning, that I have class and forget to text my brother, I get the message that Serena's in labor.

Leo better hope I make it to Austin in time, or I'm going to kick his ass for me missing my nephew's birth all because he didn't message me sooner.

I stuff all my art supplies without caution into my bag and run out of the room.

My first order of business, head over to Nate's office and tell him that it's baby time.

Next would be to head to the airport. It's a good thing that I didn't bring all of my clothes to New York.

As soon as I'm out of the art building, I leave campus and head to where I know Nate works. I've been there a few times with him when he has forgotten a file or two. I always stay in the car though, so actually finding his office will be a mission.

I make it to his building after twenty minutes of speed walking and walk in probably looking like I just ran a marathon or something.

As soon as I make it inside of the building, I beeline it to the security desk that's in the lobby.

"Hi, I was wondering if you can point me to the office of Nathanial Madden." I give the security guard a big smile.

"Your name?" he asks, not even looking up at me.

"Camila M—" I stop myself from saying Morales. "Diaz. Camila Diaz."

"Do you have an ID?" I pull it out and hand it over to him.

He takes it and does something on his computer before he hops on the phone. My guess is that it's Nate on the other line.

After about two minutes of me tapping my foot impatiently, the security guard finally hangs up and hands me a badge.

"You can head up. It's on the twentieth floor. Someone should meet you up there."

I take the visitor badge from him and head directly to the elevators. "Thank you!" I yell over to him.

Once I'm in the elevator, I press the button to floor twenty more times that I can count before the doors close and the metal box moves. Within seconds I'm on the floor that I need to be.

I step out of the elevator and head to the receptionist desk about to tell her I'm here to see Nate when I see him approaching.

"Cam," he calls out, concern not only coating his face but also his voice.

The fact that I came here is probably freaking him out, given that I've never been here before like this.

"Hey," I say, a little out of breath.

"Is everything okay?" he says moving me out of the walkway and closer to the wall.

I nod. "Oh yeah. I should have probably called or

texted, but I just got excited and decided to come and tell you in person."

"Tell me what?" His eyebrows come together and try to rein in the excitement.

"My sister-in-law is finally in labor. My brother texted me this morning. So, I'm heading to the airport right now so that I don't miss it. I'll be gone for a few days, but I will be back before classes on Tuesday. That is, if he is born by then. Can you imagine being in labor for that long? If I ever get pregnant I want that thing out fast because no way am I going to suffer like that."

Strong hands land on my shoulders and Nate bends down slightly to come into my line of vision.

"Cam. Calm down, breathe."

"Right."

Nate gives me a smile. "So you're going to Austin?"

I nod. "I booked a ticket as soon as I saw my brother's name on the screen."

Given that Leo doesn't text me just because, I knew it was something big.

"If I wasn't so swamped here, I would be joining you."

I smile at the thought. When it came to Isabella's wedding, he was originally supposed to come home with me, but something came up with a case that he was working on, so he decided to stay behind. I really wanted him to meet my family after all this time, but I understood. I understand this time too, especially with how sponta-neous this is.

"It's okay, this is definitely last minute. I just wanted to come and see you before I left and let you know I wasn't going to be home for a few days."

Home.

Ever since New Year's, I've been slowly moving my things over to his place. I still have my studio apartment, and I use it on occasion, but when I think of home in New York, it's at Nate's.

I paint in the spare bedroom and in the living room in front of the windows. I cuddle with him on the couch, and he has even added more of my work to the walls.

Moving to this step might have been quick but I don't regret a single thing.

"Well, I'm glad you came by." He's about to say something more, but someone interrupts him.

"Nate, I was looking for you," a female's voice calls out.

I lean to look around Nate and see Ava is approaching us.

Her eyes meet mine for a split second before she shifts them back to Nate. A smile that she wasn't wearing, suddenly appears.

Nate turns his head only enough to see who it is, but he keeps his body facing me.

He doesn't say anything as Ava closes the distance between us. I plaster a smile on my face.

"Hey, I was wondering if you wanted to get coffee," she says to only him and at the last second, she finally turns to me. "Oh, Camile. I didn't see you there. Did Nate bring you to work with him today?"

You literally saw me.

And it's Camila, *pendeja.*

Also, did she try to make an age joke with that last comment?

My smile stays in its place.

"Hi Ava, it's nice to see you again. And no, I just stopped by to tell Nathaniel that I have a last-minute trip to Texas and wasn't going to see him when he got home."

I try to put emphasis on the word home, but who knows if she caught it.

"How nice of you. Don't worry, I'll keep him company until you come back."

She's egging you, Camila. Don't fall for it.

"Oh, he's a big boy. He can handle himself." I pat Nate, who is hasn't said a word and is just leaning against the wall with his hands in his pockets, on the stomach. "I should get going though, I don't want to miss my flight."

"I'll walk you down." Nate finally speaks, pushing himself off the wall. "I'll be back in about fifteen minutes, Ava." He says without looking at her.

"It was nice seeing you again, Ava." I wave at her as Nate guides me back to the elevators.

"Safe travels," she says with a smile on her face and a slight roll of her eyes.

I guess she doesn't like me much.

The feeling might be mutual at this point.

Fortunately enough, the elevator doors open right away and Nate and I walk right in. As the elevator doors close I see Ava walk away.

"I'm not going to call you Nate again," I say. The way that Ava says his name makes me bring the claws out a bit.

He chuckles next to me. "I'm okay with that."

A hand lands on my waist and I'm being dragged closer to him.

"There're cameras," I say when his lips land on my neck. Even as I say the words, I lean my head back to give him more access.

"I've fucked you in front of the whole city to see back at our place, what's in front of a camera? Maybe we can have a quickie, before the elevator door opens." I feel his teeth graze my skin before he bites down.

A ding rings through the steel box.

I laugh. "Too late."

Nate lets out a groan when the doors open which just makes me laugh even more as I grab his hand and walk out of the elevator.

We walk out of the building hand in hand and when we get outside, Nate waves over a cab and when one approaches, he opens the door for me.

"Call me when you land?" His hands cradle my face, and I can't help but lean into his touch.

"I will but also be prepared for a bunch of baby pictures getting sent your way."

He laughs. "Send as many as you want." He leans in to place a kiss on my lips. "See you in a few days."

I place another kiss on his lips and repeat his words. "See you in a few days."

I want to say something else, but I keep it in.

We've moved quickly with everything else, we can go slowly with this.

Pulling away from Nate, I give him a smile and slide

into the back seat of the cab and once Nate hands the driver money to cover the cost, I'm on my way.

Fingers crossed I make it to Texas in time.

———————

I LOOK at the tiny face in my arms and my heart can't help but swell ten times over just looking at it.

I know that even without knowing this little being for very long, I will love it until my very last breath.

"I'm going to love you forever." I run my knuckle along the small cheek of my baby nephew.

There's a smile on my face that hasn't left since I found out that he was born.

My flight made it to Austin just in time, and thankfully Leo had Arturo on standby because he got me to the hospital with only a few minutes to spare.

Apparently, Serena was already pushing and had Leo and her friend Aria in the room with her. All the while Isabella and Santos were pacing the waiting room. I started pacing right next to them until Leo came out and told us that the baby had arrived.

Noah Morales has arrived into the world and is a healthy baby boy.

Of course, Isabella and I asked right away if we could see him and all we got was a roll of the eyes from our brother and were told to wait.

After an hour, he finally went to get us and we got to meet our nephew.

Now it's a few days later and I'm set to go home, and I don't want to leave.

"Can I take him with me?" I ask my brother and Serena who are sitting on the couch, both looking exhausted.

"Sure, but you have to wake up every hour and a half to feed him," Serena says before yawning and leaning her head against Leo's shoulder.

"I love you." I tell Noah, placing a kiss on his little cheek. "But I love to sleep too much, and *tia* shares her bed."

Leo lets out a small growl at the last comment, and I just laugh, not caring.

I told my family that I was seeing someone months ago, and that it has progressed to moving in together. I've told them about Nate without telling them everything. I want to keep some things for myself of course.

One thing I do want to happen, though, is that I want them to meet. At this point it feels like I'm two separate people and it might be time to join them.

Maybe I will bring it up to Nate when I get back to New York and see if he could take some days off and we can come back to Texas together.

"How is that going by the way?" Serena asks, her eyes almost completely closed.

"It's going good. We've been able to manage it with his work and me with school. I can see it going places," I say, a bigger smile forming on my face as I talk about Nate.

"Like you might marry this guy?" Leo says through his gritted teeth, not liking the idea, I guess.

I shrug. "Maybe. I wouldn't say no if he proposed when I got home." A smirk replaces my smile.

"How about you finish school first and then you can maybe, and that's a big maybe, think about marriage with this guy. Years from now."

God, Leo is so lucky that he had a son. God knows how he would be with a daughter to look after.

"Don't worry. I will." Leo worries too much, that's for sure.

The front door opens, and in walks Isabella and Santos.

"Are you ready to go?" Isabella asks as soon as she steps foot in the massive living room.

I sigh. "No, but I guess I have to."

I hold Noah to my chest and covering his little head with a bunch of kisses before handing him over to his mom.

"Can I FaceTime with him every night?" Is this what being a *tia* feels like? Loving the children that your sibling has like they are your own?

Serena laughs at my question. "He won't say much but he will try."

I guess I can take that.

Grabbing my purse, I start making my rounds of good-byes. First are Serena and the baby, and then it's my brother.

"Stay safe, okay? If anything happens, I'm just a phone call away and can be there in a few hours."

I nod, a small knot forming in my throat. "I will."

"I love you, Camila." Leo wraps his arms around me and holds me tightly.

"I love you too."

I hug him just as tight that he is me, but something feels off.

Like he's trying to say something else without actually saying the words.

"You stay safe too."

"I'm always safe, Camila." Leo gives me a wink when he pulls away.

I don't know if I believe him.

20

NATHANIEL

Do you ever do something so often that it becomes like second nature? Whether it's getting dressed a certain way or making your coffee at the same time every morning, doing something repeatedly, sticks with you.

That's what is happening to me right now.

For almost six months, I've been looking at this security footage, looking for any sign to take down Ronaldo Morales. Anything.

I got close once.

A few weeks ago while Camila was in Texas for her sister's wedding, the DEA got word from local law enforcements that there was a possible sighting of the kingpin in Austin.

Given that Camila was down there, I wanted to jump on the first plane out. Not because Ronaldo was on American soil but because I didn't want him within a hundred miles of her.

Ronaldo knows who I am, he knows that I'm after him,

and I wouldn't put it past him to be keeping tabs on me. So in my head, if he was keeping tabs on me, there was a possible chance that he knew I had a woman in my life that I cared for. One that would destroy me if anything happened to her.

I wanted to jump on a plane to Austin to make sure that he didn't go anywhere near her.

The only thing that was holding me back from heading to Austin and following this lead, was Beck.

He was the one that was notified that Ronaldo had possibly crossed the border.

The only reason that New York has this case and not Texas was because of me.

Because I begged New York to handle it when I was barely a rookie so I could be the one that took down Ronaldo.

When Beck got the call, he told me that he would have Texas follow through with the lead and if anything came of it, we would move.

Turns out, Ronaldo had crossed into Texas and was in Austin with some of his men. For what? We have no idea, since he didn't go to any of the warehouses that the DEA has eyes on. Camera footage proves that he was in Austin, but all we had to go off was that footage. By the time that the Texas division got to the location, there was no sign of him.

For days after, we kept a close watch on everything from Austin to San Pedro, but no other sighting of him came to be.

At that point I was ready to throw it all away.

I was ready to fly to San Pedro and just but a bullet in his head, no matter how long it took for me to find him.

But I didn't. I just continued to look at the security footage for the warehouse that Leo gave me access to, hoping that he'd show up eventually.

Because of the sighting, I'm no longer looking at the footage alone. Beck gathered a few agents to watch some of the footage with me and even deployed some agents to the Texas division to keep a close eye on things and to be on alert if needed.

But right now, it's just a waiting game.

A fucking long ass one at that.

At this point, I want to throw the computer that I have in front of me out the window.

"Nate?" Cam's voice sounds through the apartment, telling me that she's finally home from work.

A few weeks ago, sometime before going to Texas for the wedding of her sister and the birth of her nephew, she got a job at the art store I took her the day that we met.

Cami comes from money, at least from what I know and see, so when she told me she was looking for work, I asked why. I never asked her for money when it came to the expenses here at the apartment or everyday things, those things were handled. I think my words to her were that she didn't need to get a job. She stopped me though and she said that yes, she didn't need a job, but that she wanted one to pass the time when she wasn't concentrating on school or I was at work.

This woman was independent and after that conversation, my respect for her grew even more.

I gave her my support. If she wants to work, who am I to tell her no?

"In the study," I call out, closing out of the footage screen, giving myself a break from looking for Ronaldo a few hours.

Within seconds, Cam walks in, drops her bag on the floor and comes over to me.

I scoot back enough for her to get settled sideways on my lap and have her arms go directly around my neck.

With no words spoken, our lips meet and we kiss as if we haven't seen each other in weeks and not the hours since she left this morning.

I take her bottom lip between my teeth which cause for a giggle to escape from her pouty lips and fill the room.

Never will I get enough of hearing her giggle and the feel of her body in my hands.

Finally, we break apart and I give her a lazy smile. "How was work?"

"It was fine, nothing too special. Just helped a few people pick out some paints for a project. That's as exciting as it got."

I rub circles along the exposed skin of her back. "Sounds a lot more exciting than my day."

"Yeah, but you get to carry a gun and be a badass, I'm dealing with customers all day."

I snort a little. "I don't even remember the last time that I shot my gun on the job."

That's a lie. Actually, I do remember the last time that I shot a gun but I technically wasn't acting as a federal agent.

No, I was helping Leo Morales save his wife from Emilio Castro and had a shootout with Castro's men.

"Maybe we should go to a shooting range or something, put some excitement back in your life." She wiggles on my lap, my dick stirring at the friction.

"Because my excitement comes from a shooting range and not the twenty-year-old currently sitting on my dick." I throw out sarcastically.

Grabbing her hips, I move her body slightly over my lap, moving her body enough for me to feel her heat through her leggings and my slacks.

"Such a one track mind." She gives me a slight eye roll but she continues to rub herself against me.

"Only when it comes to you." I place a kiss on her jaw.

"Seriously though, we should go to a shooting range or something, change up your day from doing whatever it is that you're doing." She looks over at the mess on my desk. The same mess that has been growing for the past week or so.

"You want to go to a shooting range?" I feel my eyebrows raise at the question.

"Sure, why not? It could be a fun date or something and we can grab some pizza afterward."

I think that my cock is getting slightly harder at the thought.

Seeing Cami handling a revolver might be a sexy sight.

Why am I even questioning it?

"I know of a place close by if you're really up for it."

She smacks a kiss on my lips before she gets off me. "Let's go."

I smack her ass as she stands up. "Let me finish something real quick and we can head out."

Cami nods, already starting to make her way out of the room. "I'm going to change."

"I'll only be a few minutes." She gives me one final nod before leaving the room and closing the door behind her.

As soon as the door is closed, I pop open the security footage screen once again, even if I promised myself that I would give it a few hours.

At this point it, has become an obsession. If I don't get a hit, I will be thinking about it the whole time we're out.

It takes a few seconds for the screen to load and when it does, it goes back to the screen that I was on. Looking at the time stamp, a few minutes were added to the footage.

I slide the progression bar to the side just to reassure myself that nothing has happened or changed.

The screen is currently centered on the drive up to the warehouse. The first couple of seconds, there is no difference in sight.

Until a few seconds later, that is.

A car approached the property, and it's not one of the usual cars driven by the workers. Given how long I've been looking at this footage, I know those by heart.

No, this one is a dark SUV and looks something like a kingpin would be driven in.

I start the footage over at the point that the SUV makes an appearance and I just follow it with my eyes.

It drives up the long dirt path before it's surrounded by the trees of the forest. Only for a few seconds, then it reappears at the entryway of the hidden warehouse.

I switch to the camera facing the entryway. The SVU stops, and for a few seconds there isn't any movement, nothing from the warehouse and nothing from the SUV.

Then one of the back doors open, a man slides out, and a few seconds after him, is Ronaldo Morales himself.

The king has finally shown up.

I stop the footage and take a snapshot of the screen.

Looking at the time stamp on the footage, this was only a few minutes ago and given the lag on the footage, there is a chance that he is still there.

Maybe enough time to deploy a team.

This could be it. This could be our shot to get Ronaldo Morales and bring him down once and for all.

I send the footage to my phone, and after all of that is set, I pocket my phone, wallet, and keys and run out of the study.

"Camila! I have to go." I yell as I run into the bedroom where she's changing.

She looks up at me with confusion and concern in her eyes. She's currently just in a bra and her panties, a pair of dark jeans in her hands.

"Go where?" The pair of jeans get placed on the bed and she gives me her full attention.

"To the office, something came up. I have to go. I'll make it up to you, I promise." I walk in and give her a quick kiss before running out of the room.

"Nate!" she yells out, but I just continue my way out of the apartment and run to my car.

It takes me fifteen minutes to drive to the office, but I'm able to make it. As soon as the car is parked, I make my way into the building and head straight to Beck's office.

The man is so obsessed with his job that he is here almost every single day.

I get a few weird looks along the way, but I don't give a fuck.

The breakthrough that I've been waiting for has finally come through, I'm going to act accordingly.

There's no knocking when I arrive at Beck's office, just me storming in and him looking up like I might have lost it.

Maybe I did.

"Morales showed up at the compound less than half an hour ago."

He doesn't say a word for a few seconds, eventually he nods, standing up from his desk.

"Let's go into the viewing room."

Half hour later, both Beck and I, with a few other agents, are in the viewing room, looking over the footage of the warehouse.

Ronaldo entered the warehouse and from the footage we have from the inside, was inspecting his merchandise.

As soon as Beck got confirmation that it was him, I was able to deploy the team that we have stationed ten miles away, working with local police. Because of the lag on the footage, we have a short window for this to work.

"How long has it been?" I ask one of the junior agents that has been going back and forth and checking the times.

"There is a fifteen-minute backtrack on the video

footage. Given the time you said that you first saw him and the current footage we have now, it's been about an hour."

An hour.

We deployed our men twenty minutes ago, and as of fifteen, Ronaldo was still there.

"Any way we can get past the backtrack and get live footage?" I ask, already knowing the answer.

"Not from here."

Great.

We continue to watch the video, continue to watch Ronaldo from the inside of the warehouse. Waiting for something to happen.

Feeling frustrated, I take out my phone, hoping that it would ring with an agent on the other side telling me they're approaching, but all I see is a call from Cami and a few texts.

I should call her back. No, I need to call her back but for right now, I have to ignore her call and concentrate on this.

The phone starts flashing with a Mexican number and right away, I take the call.

"Madden." I put the call on speaker.

"We are approaching the compound now, sir," the agent on the other line says.

I inadvertently look at the screen in front of me, hoping to see our men approach, but nothing.

Of course, there is nothing.

"Okay, keep me on." I place the phone on a small table, trying to get every ounce of information I can from listening in.

"Going through the tree overhang now and approaching the front of the warehouse."

"You're about to encounter armed men. Be prepared," I say, knowing exactly where the men are stationed, I relay the locations.

Ronaldo's men likely have eyes on the agents, who they view as intruders, and are getting ready to shoot.

"We have eyes on the black SUV," the agent states.

He could still be there. If Ronaldo wasn't tipped off, he could still be there.

This could finally come to an end.

"Warehouse is in sight. There are about six armed men waiting."

Beck looks at over at me, giving me a nod, telling me that it's my decision.

I've wanted to be the one to take this bastard down. I wanted to be the one that got the pleasure of cuffing him or shooting him dead.

But I'm more than two thousand miles away.

"Engage. Ronaldo Morales is your target. Engage."

"Orders are clear."

There is shuffling coming through the speaker as our men get ready to head into the warehouse. Then there is silence.

A long beat of silence that has every single person in this room holding their breath.

One beat.

Two.

Then shots start to ring out. Men are yelling out in

Spanish. If only I could see it in person just to get a visual of what the fuck is going on.

The yells and the shots continue for about fifteen minutes, but the one thing that doesn't come through the phone is the confirmation that Ronaldo is there.

I need fucking confirmation.

Five minutes later, the lead agent comes back to the phone.

"Building secure. A total of seventeen men. No visual confirmation of Ronaldo Morales in the building."

"Fuck!" I yell out, grabbing the nearest item and throwing it against the wall.

"Good job, men. Finish the job, I will be in contact in a few," Beck says to the phone.

"Yes, Sir." With that, the call is over, and we don't have Ronaldo Morales.

"There had to be a way out of that warehouse that we didn't know about," another agent voices.

No fucking shit.

Did anyone really believe that the head of the Muertos Cartel was going to build a warehouse in the middle of fucking nowhere, with only one way out? Fuck no, he's going to build it with as many escape routes as possible for exactly this very reason.

"We'll get him, Madden. All in due time."

Due time, my fucking ass.

It's time that this fucker is finally brought down and I'm not stopping at anything.

I just give him a nod, before grabbing my phone and leave the viewing room.

I need to do something. I need to come up with a plan, something that I haven't thought of in fourteen years. I need to come up with anything to take this man down. To finally put this vendetta to rest.

To get the fucking revenge my father deserves.

Storming into my office, the only thing that I can think of is going after Ronaldo in the one place that we always overlook.

His family home.

I found the Morales compound years ago. It's well hidden and well protected but not a hard place to find.

The only reason that we have not infiltrated the compound is because we had no hard evidence that was the place that Ronaldo called home. The people of the town of San Pedro don't speak on the matter.

Leo has also told me to not go after him there, and I'm all for keeping promises, but things change.

With my mind made up, I pull out my phone and start to dial. I have never called him. The communication has always come from him, but I need to put an end to this.

The phone rings four times before it goes silent as if someone answered.

"I'm guessing if you're calling, you and your men are about to move." Leo's voice sounds through.

"I need your permission to storm the San Pedro compound," I say, ignoring his comment.

"Why?" Leo growls out after a few beats of silence.

"Because we just infiltrated the warehouse. We were so close to getting him, but our men were too late. My guess is that your father left through an underground tunnel before we could even arrive. If you really want to bring him down, then I need your permission to storm the San Pedro compound."

I can't wait any more for Ronaldo to be caught on his own terms. I need to take matters into my own hands.

Leo is silent for a few seconds but eventually he lets out a sigh.

"Okay. Just tell me when, and I will clear out my men."

"No. You have to be there. If we take him down, there will be questions as to why you aren't with him." No one will believe that the kingpin was without his second in command.

"Are you shitting me? My men could get killed. *I* could get killed."

"It won't come to that, but if it does, the only member of the Muertos that will be seeing a bullet is Ronaldo. Do I have your permission or not?" I growl out. The anger in me boiling over.

"You have my permission, but you better do this right, Madden."

"I will."

I hang up the phone.

The time has finally come for Ronaldo to pay for his sins.

I will finally be able to bring down my father's killer.

I will put an end to Ronaldo Morales, whether he lets me or not.

21

CAMILA

"HOW LONG WILL YOU BE GONE?" I ask Nate as I sit on the bed and watch him move through the room, packing a bag.

"It should be less than a week, but no longer than two." he says before heading to the bathroom to grab a few things.

"Two weeks?" When we first got together, Nate told me that he traveled a lot for work, that was why he didn't go looking for relationships. In the time that we've been together, he's been gone maybe a weekend, a day here and there, never this long.

"Yeah, but that's only if things go to shit." He comes back into the room with his toiletries in hand.

"And what can cause it to go to shit?" I'm trying to prepare myself for the worst here. I don't even know what type of case he's working on.

Is it meetings? Or a swat raid type of thing?

I know he takes down bad guys, but what kind of bad guys are we talking about here?

"Getting shot," he says nonchalantly as he shoves his more shirts in his bag.

"What?" He looks up when hearing the panic in my voice. He looks at me for a quick second before he forgets about packing his bag and climbs on the bed to come over to me. He sits and grabs me by the hips and sits me on his lap. I shift to straddle him.

"Things can happen, things can go wrong and I can get hurt or one of the other agents could. It's part of the job. But believe me when I say this, I will try my hardest to come back to you without a scratch on me. I will be home once this is all done, and we will be able to live our lives without the dark cloud of this case over our heads."

"What's so important about this case?" He's been working on it for as long as I've known him and from what I've put together, he's been on it for years. Whatever is taking him away from me for two weeks it's big.

"Once it's over, I will tell you. But for right now, let me do what I need to do to put a stop to this and to keep you safe."

The look in his eyes tells me that he is really worried that whoever he is after might come after us, might come after me.

"Okay. Just come home to me, please."

"I will be here as soon as I can." He takes my face in his hands and leans his forehead against mine. "Because I love you, Camila Diaz."

Those words.

Those are the words that I wanted to say so many times and stopped myself because I thought it was too soon.

Now he is saying them to me.

"I love you too, Nathaniel Madden."

I was just supposed to place a simple kiss on his lips, and I was going to pull away, but the second that my mouth meets his, it's like I need more. As if I need everything that he could give me so I could survive two weeks without him.

Nate's hands move from my face down my body, finally settling on my ass cheeks. He holds me so tightly that I'm sure that his nails are penetrating the fabric and he will leave marks on my skin.

I will take every single mark that he wants to place on me.

We continue to kiss, our tongues dancing with each other, trying to find more.

Without taking my mouth off his, I start to move, start to grind my body against his, wanting to get everything that I can.

Nate must feel the same way because he shifts so that his back is to the mattress and I'm on top of him, cowgirl style.

"Nate." I pant out when his hands travel under my shirt and snap at my bra strap.

"What do you need, baby girl? Tell me what you want me to do to you." He says against my skin when he moves his lips down my neck.

"Fuck me, Nate. Please fuck me." I plead, the friction that is happening at my core currently, isn't enough.

"Whatever you want, baby girl. Whatever you want."

He shifts us enough to rid me of my leggings and

panties and to pull down his slacks just enough for his cock to pop out.

I drool at the sight of his hard, girthy cock, just asking for attention.

"This is going to be fast and hard, baby. I'll give you nice and slow when I come back."

I just nod as I take his cock in my hand and give it a few strokes, before coating it with my wetness.

We had the protection talk around the time that I moved in. We aren't ready to bring a baby into this world, not even with how much I love Noah. So I shifted my birth control from the pill to an IUD and we've been going condom free ever since.

Once his cock is coated with my wetness, I shift onto my knees and place his tip at my entrance. Slowly, I sink down and let out a groan when I feel his bare cock fill me up in the best way possible.

My head goes back at just how amazing he feels inside of me.

Nate's hands land back on my ass, holding me in place until I'm ready to move.

Once I'm settled and want more, I open my eyes and look down at Nate, moving my hips methodically.

"Ride me, baby. Ride me, take control. Make my cock weep."

I follow orders.

I move, fucking myself with his cock, all the while his hands stay on my ass, moving me along.

Bouncing up and down this man's cock should be an Olympic sport. It gets me where I need to be, with sweat running down my whole body.

"Nathaniel." I moan, when he hits just the right spot, almost losing it with one simple motion.

"Take what you need, pretty girl. Take everything."

So I do. I ride him until we are both panting. I ride him until there is sweat penetrating my shirt. I ride him until I can't take it anymore.

Soon, I explode around him and when that happens, he takes charge. He plows into me, making me feel every last inch of him. Not long after me, he lets out a grunt that fills the room and I feel his body shake under mine as he releases his seed into me.

"I love you." I lean down and place my mouth on his.

It causes him to dig his fingers deeper into my skin and let out a primal growl. "I love you too."

We stay like that for a few minutes, not saying a word, our bodies connected as we kiss, just basking in the closeness between the two of us.

Eventually we pull apart and before Nate goes back to getting all his stuff together, he heads to the bathroom bringing back a washcloth to help me clean up. After everything is taken care of, it's time for him to head out.

Grabbing his bag, I follow him out of the room and to the front door.

"I'll call you when I can, okay?" he says bringing my body closer to him and pressing his face to my hair.

I nod against him. "Please do."

We kiss and when we pull apart, I feel like I'm going to cry, and I have no idea why.

"I love you, beautiful girl."

"I love you too, Detective."

With one last kiss to the lips, he pulls away and he's out the door.

I know he's only leaving for work. I know he will be back in a few days, but something in me is telling me that I need to worry.

Something is telling me that I have to look up at the sky and ask my mother and Cristiano to keep a close eye on him to keep him safe.

Dios cuidalo y protegelo.

22

NATHANIEL

I SLIDE my bulletproof vest on to my chest and pull at all the straps tightly. Once my vest is in place, I strap on my weapon to my shoulder and my rounds to my legs.

The day that I've been waiting for, practically my whole life, has finally arrived. It is finally time to take down Ronaldo Morales and make him pay for all the evil that he has brought into this world.

And no, I'm not talking about drugs and trafficking. I'm talking about all the deaths, all the lives that are gone because of him.

My father.

His loyal men.

Innocent people.

His wife.

Today, in a few short hours I will see Ronaldo pay, dead or alive. It hasn't been decided.

As I continue to get ready to go into a war zone, my

212 | JOCELYNE SOTO

mind wanders to only a few days ago, when this plan was put in place.

"You have one job and one job only. Do you understand me, Madden?"

I just continue to sit there as Beck gives me a stern look, not saying a word.

"You go in, get the target and you get out. I don't want this to be a bloodbath. The Admin is already on my ass for going about it this way. I don't need bodies too."

Again I don't say anything, I just continue to sit there. Not making any promises.

"Madden, I'm serious. Do not make it a fucking bloodbath. Just go into the compound and get Morales. Work together with the FBI and bring this bastard down the right way."

Beck is getting angrier the more he speaks. If I was in his position, I would feel the same way. I would feel the need to tell my men to follow the rules and close this case as clean as possible.

I want to do that, but I'm not sure I can.

Not after Ronaldo robbed me of a life where my father was still alive and breathing.

"Do it clean."

I just nod and stand up from my seat before heading out the door.

Not agreeing to anything.

And again, not making any promises.

I got a text this morning too telling me to do everything clean. To not let my head get in the way of things.

To not let the need for revenge take over.

But I ignored it.

I'm going to play this by ear. I don't want to shoot my gun, but if I have to, I will.

"Everything is set, sir," one of the agents, Acosta, says to me followed by a curt nod.

I look at him and then at the men behind him, all of them ready for what we are about to do.

I give them all a nod back. "Now we wait for confirmation that the target is inside and we move."

We are currently at the border between Texas and San Pedro, Mexico. It's safer for my men to start on United States soil, especially since it looks like San Pedro is a safe haven for Ronaldo and the Muertos.

With everyone ready to go, all that I need to move is a text from Leo.

This is why I needed Leo at the compound. I needed eyes inside, I needed confirmation that Ronaldo was there and that he wasn't going anywhere.

After our phone call, Leo said that he would get back to me as to when we would be able to go through with the plan.

Finally after a week, I got a message with a date and time and everything was ready to roll out.

Now, I'm just waiting for a text to come through that tells me that I can move my men.

I hear my phone beep, and I step away from my men to see if it's the message that I've been waiting for.

Pulling out my phone, I see that it isn't Leo, but Cami.

Since I left New York two days ago, my contact with her has been a bit sporadic. Mostly because I've been trying to get everything in place for tonight and by the time I'm done, I knock out without giving her a call.

I know she's worried about what I'm doing, especially with how quickly I left and not telling her exactly what was going on.

Wanting to hear her voice before I go into the unknown, I press on her name and step further away from the men standing close to me.

The phone rings once before she answers.

"Nate," she says, as if she is relieved that I called.

"Hi, beautiful girl." I feel a smile forming on my face just by hearing her voice.

"Is everything going okay?" she asks. She's probably nibbling on her lower lip right now. Better yet, the spare bedroom at the apartment is probably covered in canvases to get all the worry out.

"For now, it is." There is no need to tell her what I'm about to do.

"That's good. I've been freaking out a bit

I let out a chuckle. "Do I have a new painting to hang up?"

In the months that we've been together, I've made it a habit to keep every single thing that she has painted. There are a few hung up in the living room and some in my office. She tells me that I don't have to but I want a piece of her everywhere I look.

"I think so. This one could replace the one you have in your office. Oh and when you get back, I have a surprise for you."

"One," I say, my smile growing a little more. "The one

in my office is staying. It was the one that you painted when we first met. And two, what kind of surprise?"

"Just something that will top everything else hanging around the apartment," she says, a hint of teasing coming out in her voice.

"Well, I can't wait to see it," I tell her and I'm about to tell her something else when my phone beeps.

Pulling it away from my ear, I see it's the message that I've been waiting for.

"Baby, I'm sorry, but I have to go. I will call you as soon as I can, okay?"

"Okay, stay safe."

"I will. I love you."

"I love you too, Detective." I don't know if I will ever get tired of hearing those words come out of her mouth.

Hanging up the phone, I open the message right away.

UNKNOWN : *You have the all clear.*

As soon as the message is read, I pocket my phone and turn back to my men.

"Let's go," I order and straight away, we all start to file into a few indistinct black SUVs. The same that the Muertos use.

Within minutes, we are making our way to the Morales compound.

The twenty-minute car ride from the border to the

compound is completely silent. Not one person saying a word.

When we are five minutes out, I order for all men to mask up and to get ready because as soon as we arrive, we're moving in.

The second the wheels of our vehicles cross the entry point of the compound, I tighten the grip on my AR-15.

Our vehicles are able to enter the compound without notice, my guess that was Leo's doing. The main gates are even open for us.

We drive a little more before I tell my drivers to stop about fifty feet away from the entrance to the house.

"On my call, arms drawn," I say into my mic.

"Copy that."

"Remember, apprehend men, not kill," I once again order.

The last part wasn't a part of the original plan that I came up with Leo.

But it's the only way to make this whole thing clean.

I have to arrest every single person present before I can let them go.

If you can let them go.

Shaking that thought out of my head, I give my order.

"File out."

Car doors fly open, and men begin to storm into the house. I enter the house last, hearing shot after shot ring throughout the high ceilings.

There are men yelling, profanities shouted out left and right. Man after man are being apprehended or shot with non-deadly injuries.

I don't shoot though, no I have my target and I won't use it unless absolutely necessary.

Leaving my men, I continue to walk through the compound until I reach the location of the house that was given to me by Leo.

Ronaldo's office.

I wasn't going to come in here blind. I needed to know the layout of the whole property. After I got the permission from Leo to storm the compound, he sent me the plans.

There are footsteps around me, telling me that my men have my back.

Approaching the office, I see that there are men guarding the doors, guns drawn.

"Weapons down!" I order, but of course the cartel men don't listen, they just start shooting.

We take cover and start shooting back, but we are outnumbered when more men start to show up.

"On my count," I say into my mic and I get nods from the men that are with me.

Holding out a hand, I count down to zero. That's when we move away from the cover and start shooting.

Men start to fall, gunpowder is filling the space, the aftermath of the smoke floating into the air, making it hard to see.

As I get close to the doors, two figures appear in front of me, my gun is drawn but I know who they are.

Leonardo and Santiago. Both also with guns drawn

"Move," I order but the two men don't stand down.

They are trying to make it seem as if they won't stand down without a fight.

"We don't take orders from you, Special Agent." I watch as Leo pulls the trigger of his pistol, for a short second thinking that our deal is out the window but aims it over my shoulder.

Looking over slightly, I see that he hit one of his father's men.

My confirmation on whose side they are on.

The theatrics for this thing between the three of us has to be turned up a bit, because no way in hell will they let me through, that will just raise too many questions. The fact that they were informants for their own family is a killing offense.

Without warning, I charge at them, taking them by surprise and causing them to drop their weapons.

The three of us end up on the floor. Somehow Leo is able to land a punch to the part of my face that isn't covered by my helmet.

"Motherfucker," I groan, the sting of the punch radiating down to my jaw

"Have I ever mentioned how much I hate you?" He smirks, getting pleasure out of getting a hit in.

"The feeling is fucking mutual," I growl out, throwing a few punches for myself.

The scuffle continues until I draw my weapon back and the butt of the rifle meets Leo's forehead, causing him to fall back. Blood seeping from his scalp from the impact, ultimately bringing him down.

I'm soon able to get to my feet before I'm being charged by Santos.

This fucker tackles me to the ground, landing punch

after punch on my face and my rib cage. I take every single hit, until I grow tired of it and draw my weapon.

This time I don't turn it over to head butt him. No, this time I fire a single shot. I watch as the fired shot travels from the barrel and grazes Santos on the shoulder, before ultimately hitting the ceiling above him.

Santos fakes pain and falls to the side.

That gives me enough time to get back on my feet and get as situated as I can before I make my way to my intended target.

I kick open the office doors, the smoke from the rest of the house making its way in.

My eyes roam the room until I see a figure standing at the edge, their backs turned to me as they face the window.

I grip my gun a little tighter, the barrel pointing right at my target.

The noise from outside of the room filters in, but I zone everything out. I zone everything out and concentrate on the man in front of me.

"Nathaniel Madden. I was wondering when you were finally going to come knocking on my door." Ronaldo's voice drowns out all the outside noise.

"You're a hard man to find," I say, looking through my scope, keeping a tight grip on my gun.

"Your father was able to find me. Not only was he able to find me, but he was able to come into my home and become a member of this family. I guess the smartness that that man embodied didn't get passed down to you."

Ronaldo turns to face me, his face dead of any emotion. I don't let my gun drop.

"He was a member of this family, and you still killed him," I growl out, feeling the anger that I've been harboring for decades finally coming to the surface.

"He betrayed me. He made me trust him and he turned that trust against me, of course I had him killed. And for that very reason, I killed one of my other loyal men. Because they went behind my back and talked. They became disloyal to me, so they had to pay."

The anger in his eyes is something that I can see even through all the smoke.

I had suspected that Ronaldo was the one that called the hit on Cristiano Reyes. There was no reason for someone like Emilio Castro to go after him without merit. No, he had to be told to go after him. And in anything that has to do with the Muertos, Ronaldo calls the shots.

He holds anger toward the men he had killed, even if it has been years or decades, that anger is still there.

"You robbed two individuals of their father."

"Maybe those two individuals were better off without the bastards they had as a father."

"And your children? Were they better off without their mother?" A low blow, but it's enough to cause a reaction out of him.

"Do not bring my wife into this!" he growls, smashing his hand on the top of his desk.

"Why? It was your actions that got her killed."

"You don't know what you are talking about, *pendejo.*

Just because you are an agent doesn't mean you know everything. Not like I know about you."

The last six words that he spews out has the hair at the back of my neck to stand up.

"How's your mother enjoying Florida? What about your stepfather? Are they enjoying retirement?" Ronaldo finally moves from his spot, coming closer to me. I grip my gun as tight as I can, keeping it pointed at him.

"Don't come closer," I say through my clenched teeth, but the man just chuckles.

"How about Camila? Is she enjoying New York? Never thought that a man like you would go after a sweet, innocent girl like her. I honestly don't know what she sees in you."

"Don't you dare talk about her! You have no right!" I place my finger on the trigger.

My suspicions were right. He knew I had a woman in my life.

"Like hell I don't!" he yells and pulls out a gun from the holster that is hidden with his suit jacket. "You came into my house, infiltrated my family, and crossed the line with my own blood! You are threatening everything that I've built! I have every fucking right!"

Triggers are pulled.

Four shots fired, more smoke and the smell of gunpowder filling the room.

Both of us fall to the ground, but only one has blood spewing from his mouth.

Only one of us has anger swimming in his eyes at the failure of his gun.

Only one is succumbing to his injuries.

It's as if everything is happening in slow motion. That each second that ticks by is as long as an hour, a day.

I watch as the blood seeps through the shirt, as it becomes too much for him to hold himself up and eventually fall to the ground completely.

It's when he's on the ground, face down in a pool of his own blood, that I ignore the pain radiating from my chest and go to him.

I check his pulse.

That's my confirmation.

Ronaldo Morales is dead.

The kingpin to the Muertos Cartel is dead, and I was the one that discharged the fatal shot.

23

CAMILA

Camila

I DRAG *the brush along the canvas, watching each and every stroke come together and become something spectacular.*

There is no rhyme or reason behind my strokes, just the need to get whatever is clouding my head out.

The only reason I'm painting is to simply paint.

To get lost in the motions.

No sound is coming in from the outside world. No sound filling the room besides the brush meeting the canvas.

"Camila."

The sound of my name makes me turn, looking around the room for its source but there's no one else here.

For a split second, it sounded as if it were my mother calling me.

Could it be her?

"Camila."

That time around was definitely my mother's voice saying my name. I look around the room, but I don't see her.

How is she here?

My mind must be playing tricks on me.

I turn back to the painting in front of me and it takes my attention away from the thought of my dead mother calling out my name.

It's dark, the painting. Nothing like what I usually do.

There are reds and blacks everywhere and in a way it looks like...

"Muerte." This time the voice is as clear as day. It may be almost sixteen years since I heard that voice, but I could pick it up anywhere.

It's my mother's.

I turn to my right and there she is in all her glory. Dark chocolate brown hair swaying down her back. Eyes that are like my brother's, so dark that you can feel them sucking you into the abyss. She looks exactly the same as when I last saw her. Young and beautiful. Just as beautiful as when she was still alive.

The only thing about her that is slightly different, is that her face is painted the same way I paint mine every single year for the Día de los Muertos celebration.

I want to say something to her.

Ask her questions as to why she's here, but I don't. Instead, I turn back to the painting in front of me and see that she's right about it

It's death.

"La muerte no es algo qué se debe pintar."

Death is never something that should be painted.

Painting death in this kind of light is a bad omen, one that no painter or artist should ever aggravate.

This is far different from what I usually do.

So why is it that I painted it?

Good question.

"Tal vez algo va a pasar."

The words leave her mouth in the most nonchalant way, and it makes me wonder if I should worry, but I don't. I just keep looking at the painting in front of me.

Something is going to happen.

But what?

"Te quiero muchísimo, mi niña preciosa."

I turn back to my mother and give a bright smile, one that both my siblings have said looks like hers. I want to stand up, I want to wrap my arms around her and hold her tightly. Just like she did the first five years of my life.

I just continue to stay rooted in place as she starts to melt away.

"Te quiero también, Mamí."

"La muerte está cerca."

Then she disappears.

My eyes snap open right away. The darkness of the room looks like it's the middle of the night and when I look out the window, that I should really cover with blinds, I get my confirmation. It's indeed the middle of the night.

Groaning, I turn over and start to feel the bed next to me, hoping that maybe Nate came home and I will feel his body lying here next to me. That way he could take me in his arms and help me go back to sleep.

But when I feel the coldness of the sheets next to me

and the smoothness of the half made bed, that hope disappears. I guess he didn't come home to me in the middle of the night like I wanted him to.

If I could dream of my dead mother, I could make my boyfriend suddenly appear, right?

I guess not.

Only a few more days.

That's what I've been telling myself since he left, and that was only three days ago. I have no idea how I'm going to survive a full week, let alone two.

I don't know how long distance people do it man. I'm only a few days in and I already want to jump on a plane and go find the man.

Don't be a stalker, Camila. The man has to work.

I know, but still.

And yes, I've been away from Nate before, so I don't know why this time has been affecting me a lot harder. Maybe because unlike other times, I'm not with my family, and there's a cloud of unknown hanging over this whole trip.

I don't know why, but something doesn't sit right, what with the dream I just had, and my mind coming up with every single scenario known to man.

But only a few more days and I will be back in Nate's arms, feeling safe, and will be able to put all these bad feelings and this bad dream about my mother and death behind me.

Because Nate's the calm to my disaster. The light to this dark life that I was born into.

Finally accepting that Nate isn't coming home tonight, I roll over, grab his pillow and bring it to my face, taking in his scent and I try my hardest to go back to sleep.

But the second my eyes are closed, they fly back open when a phone starts to ring.

It takes me a second to realize that it's not the phone that I have sitting on the nightstand, but the phone that I have hidden in my dresser. The second phone that I have and only use to communicate when it pertains to cartel business. The phone that only four people in my life have the number to.

When I first moved to New York, I stashed that phone under the mattress in my studio. When I moved in with Nate though, or partially moved in with Nate, I put the phone in a bottom drawer where he wouldn't find it. As for my gun, I kept that at the studio since I knew there were already guns here.

Sitting up, I look at the time on the alarm clock that Nate has on the bedside table. I see that it's three in the morning.

It's late. Very late.

The only reason that phone is ringing is because something is wrong. No way would anyone call me on that phone if shit wasn't seriously wrong.

Tal vez algo va a pasar.

Was she right?

I never dream about my mother in that capacity, but what if she was trying to tell me something? What if there's a reason why I dreamed of my mother and painting death?

Throwing the blankets off my body, I try to walk over to the dresser at a slow pace, so that I don't have a panic attack over the phone ringing so late.

A big part of me wishes that Nate was home right about now.

Crouching down, I open the bottom drawer of my dresser as slowly as possible, as if a bomb were about to be detonated.

Once it's open, I just look at the clothes, not making the effort to move them out of the way. I take a few deep breaths before shifting the clothes and reaching for the small rectangular device. As soon as I have the phone in hand, the ringing stops.

I flip the phone over and I see that it was an unknown number calling.

I don't do anything but wait, just staring at the screen, for it to start ringing again. Because if something is really wrong, that unknown caller will call again. I know it will.

And I'm right because within seconds, the ringing starts up once more.

It's as if my brain knows that whoever is on the other side of this call has something bad to say. My hand moves without me telling it to and presses the answer button as slow as possible.

I take a deep breath and try to center myself as best as I possibly can before bringing the phone up to my ear.

"Hello?" I breathe into the receiver, trying to keep calm.

You can do this, Camila. You can do this.

"Camila." My sister's voice comes through right away.

It's shaky and something about the way she says my name that has me on high alert.

It actually takes me back to the time I told her about Cristiano Reyes's death.

Is this what is happening?

Someone died?

"Wh-why are you calling me so late? On this phone? Did something happen?"

Is it Leo?

Or what if it's Santos?

Worse yet, what if it's Noah? He's just a baby, but what if something happened to him? What if he was taken? What if Leo wasn't able to protect him like he feared?

"There was a raid at the estate. In San Pedro. Leo and Santos were there, and..." My sister starts but then stops.

A raid? Like the FBI stormed the property and went after the cartel? After my brother? My father?

"And what, Isabella?" I need an answer. I need to know what the fuck happened.

"Men were killed." Her voice hitches, telling me that what she has to say is a lot worse than what she wants to let on.

Which just causes me to freak out even more, to the point that I want to puke.

La muerte está cerca.

That's why I was dreaming about my mother. It was a warning that this was going to happen.

A lump forms in my throat and I feel wetness in the corner of my eyes. I try to push it down, but I can't. My next question almost breaks me.

"Leo? Santos?"

Please let her tell me that they are alive. *Please.*

"They are both alive." I let out a sigh of relief, one that lets the tears escape. Her words are able to reassure me but it's not enough. There's more to this phone call, I know there is.

"Then who, Isabella? Who was killed? Whose death is so important that you had to call me in the middle of the night to tell me?" I feel like screaming, but I keep it in.

Ya sabes quien.

La muerte está cerca.

My mother's voice rings through my mind.

I may know who it is, but I need my sister to confirm it.

"Camila." Her voice breaks again, and I know what she's going to say.

"Who, Isabella? Who?" I beg. I just want to hear her say the words so I can finally figure out how I feel about all this.

She is silent for a long minute.

I stand up and head to the bed, sitting on the corner of the mattress, just sitting there waiting for her to speak. As the silence continues, I start counting the tears that are running down my cheeks.

Say it. *Please* just say it.

"*Apá.* Our father, he's dead. They killed him."

A sob escapes my throat when the words come through the earpiece.

Even if my relationship with my father has been nonexistent for months, even if I hate him for the things that he has done, he's still my father.

The last living parent that I had.

And now he's gone. I never thought that if this day would come, that it would hurt this much.

I try to rein in my emotions as best as I can before I say something to Isabella.

"Ho-how do you know? Were you there?"

There are so many questions floating through my head, I just ask them in rapid fire.

"No, both me and Serena are in Austin with the baby. The three of us are safe. It happened about three hours ago. I guess Leo and Santiago were arrested, and were given the privilege of one phone call. It wasn't long, but they were able to tell us what happened. Leo said that he saw it happen. He's gone, Camila."

She lets out a strangled sob, and I lose it right with her.

He was our father, bad or good, he was a man that we once loved with everything that we had.

We sob through the phone for what feels like forever, but eventually we are able to calm ourselves down.

"Listen to me, Camila. I need you to be strong, okay? A lot of things are going to happen in the next day or so, and I need you to do everything as I say, okay?"

I nod, even though she can't see me. This is something that has always been a topic of discussion growing up. What to do when the cartel gets taken down, what are the proper steps, who to contact. Everything was discussed, but never did I think that I actually had to do it.

Now, I'm really wishing that Nate was home. He's in law enforcement, he would be able to help me with this.

But if I went to him, then I would have to tell him

about the cartel and who I really am. I'm not sure I'm ready for that.

I shake that thought away and put my attention back on Isabella. "Okay, what do I do?"

"Leo and Santiago were arrested, and according to them, they will be taken to a federal prison in New York City. Because of their charges, they won't be released on bail, at least not yet. Serena and I will be heading that way on the first flight out. In the meantime, I need you to try to see if you can talk to them once they arrive in New York. We need to figure out a way to get them out of there." Isabella is pushing through, and all the signs of sorrow over our father's death, gone.

Talk to them?

They are going to a federal prison, are people that are heading to a federal prison even allowed to have visitors.

"How do I do that?"

Isabella tells me exactly how. She goes into detail as to who I need to contact and what I need to say at the prison.

At the end, she tells me that she loves me and that she will see me in a few hours. That everything will be okay.

When the call ends, I just sit there in the darkness and try to digest everything.

There was a raid at my childhood home.

My brother and brother-in-law are in jail.

And my father is dead.

My father is dead.

It shouldn't hurt, but it does.

It hurts like there are a million pieces breaking inside of me.

So, that's what I do, I break.

I break until I have to built myself back up and do what I need to do to save the remaining family that I have left.

24

NATHANIEL

I LOOK at my face in the bathroom mirror, seeing that the dry blood is the only thing that I can concentrate on.

The swelling has gone down slightly, but even hours later after receiving a pounding to my face, the swelling is still visible and the bruises are starting to get nastier.

I'm sure as hell going to have a hard time explaining this to Cami when I get home.

Home. All I want to do right now is head home, grab a bite to eat, shower and then fall into bed with my girl in my arms and not wake up until it's absolutely necessary.

But I can't do those things. Why? Because I have to not only interrogate two pivotal members of the Muertos Cartel, before I have to get interrogated myself for killing the cartel kingpin.

I'm set for a long ass fucking day.

After the raid at the Morales compound, the one that ended with Ronaldo dead, and the FBI coming in to start their investigation, it was time to fly back to New York.

Because of the severity of the case and because we arrested two high profiled drug traffickers, I was advised by the head of the DEA to extradite the men that were arrested to New York. A process that usually could take weeks. But because New York is closer to DC than Austin is, we put our captures on a cargo plane and flew out.

Of course not before I was asked by the cartel's second-in-command if he could call his wife. He got his wish once every other agent was out of view.

In the eyes of the United States government, Leo Morales and his right-hand man will be spending a lot of time behind bars, but I have one more thing up my sleeve. Something that even Leo and Santos don't know about.

Something that the news outlets will have a field day with when the story hits in a few hours.

We arrived in New York about an hour ago. Now, it's close to eight in the morning, meaning that it's been eight hours since we stormed into the compound, and I pulled the trigger.

After decades of hunting the man down, the mission is finally over. I thought that when this moment arrived, I would be elated, yet I'm not.

I don't know what it is, but nothing about this whole situation feels right.

Shaking the feeling off, I splash water on my face and leave the restroom, not even bothering to clean up my face.

We are currently at the federal holding facilities in New York City, where Santos and Leo are being held and where I will soon be interviewed about my actions.

Beck wanted clean. That shit didn't happen.

In total, six men were killed. For this type of operation, that's a lot of bodies, so whether I killed Ronaldo or not, I'm still getting my ass chewed.

I approach the conference room that I know Beck is taking over for this and right away make eye contact with the boss.

Beck just looks at me, shoulders squared, jaw locked. Dude looks like a scary motherfucker that you shouldn't mess with.

"Ronaldo Morales was officially pronounced dead at one twelve in the morning by Webb County coroner's office. His body will be transported to Houston, where a full autopsy will be conducted. Then the body will be released to the family."

I nod.

The man really is dead.

"I said I didn't want a bloodbath, Madden," Beck growls out and I feel my jaw tensing up.

"It wasn't like I could fucking stop it. We were getting shot at," I say through my clenched teeth. "At the very least, not one of our men was killed."

If we had gone in blind, if I hadn't gotten the layout from Leo beforehand, half of the men that entered that compound with me would be right next to Ronaldo.

Death was fucking unavoidable. Beck should know that.

Beck looks at me in anger, but eventually the anger subsides.

"We will drop the subject for now, but trust me when I say this isn't fucking over."

"Fine with me."

"Now," he says, opening a file and pulling out two mug shots. "What are you going to do about these two?"

He slides Leo's and Santos's mug shots over to me, as if I'm going to pick them up and inspect them.

"Let me talk to them, alone. Let me see what else I can get out of them." It's an unprecedented request, but I'm banking on Beck's trust in me to let me do this.

"Nate," he starts, already shaking his head.

"We have nothing to lose. They already have a rap sheet a mile long. Me talking to them isn't going to change a damn thing." That he knows of.

I can see Beck bubbling with anger again, but eventually he gives me a nod. Of course it's not without his jaw locking in place.

"Fine, do it. But I'm only giving you thirty minutes. That's it. Then you are going to sit all nice and pretty and get interviewed by the FBI, am I clear?" He stabs the table with his finger.

I nod. "You're clear."

I leave the office and head over to the holding cells where Leo and Santos are.

"I need Morales and Reyes to be moved into an interrogation room," I tell the sitting agent keeping watch.

"Sorry, sir. I don't think that I can do that," he says a little sheepishly, like he's scared of listening to me.

"I didn't ask for your opinion, agent. I'm telling you that I need those two in an interrogation room. That means you do as you're told and make it happen."

"Yes, sir." He nods in my direction before he goes on his merry way and does what I say.

Within a minute, both Leo and Santos are being escorted to the interrogation room at the end of the hall.

Once in the room, they are both seated in their separate chairs, looking a little beaten up.

I nod at the agents that brought them in, dismissing them, but they don't make a move to leave the room.

"You are dismissed," I say in a hard tone. Both agents jump slightly before they scurry out.

As soon as they are gone, I lock the door and close the blinds before turning off all cameras and microphones that are in the room.

"Now I know why you're called a cold-hearted bastard. You scare all the rookie agents away," Santos mutters when I sit in front of them.

"Don't make me shoot you again, Reyes."

He scoffs. "Yeah, thanks for that. The wife will be very happy with the new fucking scar on my body."

"I barely grazed you."

"Yeah, and what about my face?" Leo calls out which causes me to turn to him. His face is bloody, worse than mine.

"You were punching me," I throw back.

"And that got me a gun handle to the face? My kid is probably going to cry when he sees me."

These two are fucking frustrating.

"Do you two want to talk about how we are going to get charges against you dropped or not? Because I can gladly walk out of here and let the government take care of you."

They both scoff, but they shut up and give me their full attention.

"Are they able to hold us?" Leo asks, placing his hand-cuffed hands on the table.

I sigh. "For being at the compound last night, there are also no open warrants for either of you, but that doesn't mean that they won't try to figure out a way to charge you for something."

"Everything that we run is clean," Santos voices, copying Leo's stance.

I nod.

There's a reason why I didn't go after any of the warehouses in Austin. Because in the eyes of the government, those warehouses are legitimate businesses and there is nothing tying them to the Muertos. Unless they are tied to money laundering or racketeering, there is nothing that the FBI can do to stop them from operating.

"I know that, and they do too, but that still won't stop them from finding something. You're known cartel made men. They will do anything in their power to take all of you down."

They both go silent and turn to face each other as if they are having a silent conversation.

After a few minutes, they turn back to me.

"Do you have a plan on how to stop them from doing that?"

"For right now, just trying to convince my boss that we can't hold you two. Being at the estate isn't enough. I will tell him to concentrate on tying up all the loose ends that come with Ronaldo being dead."

Leo nods, not saying a word. I killed his father, yes he was a bad man, but still it was his father.

"I apologize, by the way. For doing what I did."

Leo nods again, but this time he does speak. "If it wouldn't have gotten me killed, I would have done the same thing."

There is something in his eyes as he speaks, it looks a bit like gratitude.

It's a sadistic life to see a child be grateful for their parents' death.

I clear my throat and stand up from my seat.

"Sit tight. I promise I will have you out of here in no time. Let me work a few angles."

They both nod and I start to walk away when Leo stops me.

"Madden." I turn back to face him. "Thank you. Thank you for doing this."

His words are genuine, that much I know.

"You promised to keep the Muertos off my desk, I'm just keeping my side of the bargain. I'll be back with some food and something to drink."

We give each other nods and I make my way out of the room.

Walking to the elevator, I check my watch once I'm inside.

There may be a very short window of time for me to head home and check in with Cami.

Even though the raid is done and over with and Ronaldo is in a body bag, the work isn't done yet. There is still the whole Leo and Santos thing, so my guess is I won't be going home anytime soon.

Seeing her for a few minutes might actually keep me sane.

The elevator arrives on the first floor of the building and when my foot steps onto solid ground, I swear I hear a voice that sounds a lot like my girlfriend's.

Did I miss her that much that I'm hearing her voice?

Walking to the security desk of the building, I get confirmation that my mind isn't playing tricks on me. Cami is actually here.

"I'm telling you, he's here. If you can just send me up so I can see him, I would be out of your hair," she yells at the security guard. Her little body looking like it's going to fly over the divider and hit him in the head.

What is she doing here?

Is she here looking for me? If she is, how did she know that I was here? Or even back in New York?

"Cam," I call out, approaching the security desk.

Right away she looks up at the mention of her name, her eyes going wide with surprise when she sees that it's me.

"Nate? What are you doing here?"

Okay, so she's not here for me.

"I can ask you the same question." I approached her, grabbing her elbow and guiding her away from the security guards.

"My brother was brought here." Tears start to fill her eyes as she looks up at me. "Have you been in New York this whole time?"

I shake my head. "I got in about two hours ago. I was actually about to head home real quick," I say, but then her last statement makes me back track. "What do you mean your brother is here?"

Tears start to fall from her eyes, but she quickly wipes them away.

"He was arrested. Both him and my brother-in-law. My sister called me around three in the morning that there was some raid at my father's estate. Which ended with him getting killed." A sob escapes her and her body starts to shake. I don't even think. I take her in my arms and console her. "And my brother and sister's husband were being brought here."

Camila lets out a blood curdling sob as she wraps her arms around me tightly. As if she were gasping for air.

As I hold her crying form in my arms, realization strikes.

There was a raid at her father's estate.

Her father was killed.

Her brother was brought here.

Fucking hell.

That's why the picture at the back of her portfolio looked familiar the first day we met, because I had seen that woman before. It was her mother.

Rosa Maria Morales.

An individual whose picture I studied just as much as I studied her husband's.

And her name.

I knew all of Ronaldo's children's names, all three of them are engraved in my brain.

Leonardo. Isabella. *Camila.*

How the actual fuck did I not put this together sooner?

"Leonardo Morales is your brother." My hold on her tightening even more as I voice the realization out loud.

She nods against me. "Yes."

The confirmation makes my head spin just a bit.

"You're the daughter of Ronaldo Morales."

Cami pulls away from me, going to stand a few feet away, wiping at her eyes, giving me a head jerk confirming the parental lineage.

As tears continue to coat her face, I come to the biggest realization of them all.

Not only did I kill Ronaldo Morales, I killed the father of the woman I love.

She will never forgive me for this.

25

CAMILA

It's the surprised expression on Nate's face that has me wishing that I didn't just spill my darkest secret.

But the second I heard his voice call out my name, I thought it was God's way of telling me that everything was going to be okay.

That didn't stop me from asking what he was doing here when he should be gone for work. When he should be away for almost two weeks, but it's only been a few days.

It didn't matter though. As soon as I felt his hand touch my skin, I didn't care as to why he was here. All that mattered was that he was standing in front of me and, soon after, I was in his arms. Only that mattered.

Then he started putting two and two together as to who I was, and I couldn't hide it anymore. I had to tell him who I was, who my family is.

Of course he knew who my brother was. Of course he knew my father's name. He works for the special agency. I don't know why I put it past him.

"I'm sorry that I didn't tell you sooner. Who my family was, I mean." I wipe my remaining tears from my face.

Nate looks at me for a quick second before he gives me a head shake. "The fact that you just told me who your father is, isn't what is surprising me at the moment."

"Okay?" What else do I say? Obviously, the man is in shock.

"This may be a silly question to ask, but do you know if my brother is here?"

If Nate knows his name, then surely, he knows if he's in the building or not. Leo is a kingpin's son after all.

I gulp.

With my father dead, does that make Leo the one in charge now?

Nate nods, still the expression of shock on his face. "Yeah, he's here."

He doesn't move an inch, he just continues to stand there a little dumbfounded.

"Do you think that I can see him? Is that something that's allowed?" Can people who have been arrested have visitors this early in the game?

Nate just stands there, looking down at me, as if he were in a different world.

I step forward and place a hand on his forearm. "Nate?"

At me saying his name, he finally snaps out of whatever stupor he was in and responds to me.

"They aren't allowed."

Fresh tears spring out at those words. Nate must see them because he comes closer to me and takes my face between his hands. "But let me see what I can do."

I nod, taking it, because that answer is better than nothing.

Nate places a kiss against my forehead and for a second, we just stand there in the middle of the lobby and I feel like everything will be okay.

"C'mon. I'll take you up." He takes my hand and guides me over to the elevators, yelling over to the security guard. "She's cleared."

The security guard gives him a nod and lets us continue on.

Nate presses the button for the thirty-second floor and we watch as the doors close. The ride up is completely silent, the only sound surrounding us is the gears of the elevator pulling us up.

Silence like this is not normal with us, but given everything that was revealed down in the lobby, I get it.

The ding announces the arrival at the correct floor, and as soon as the doors open, Nate escorts me through the floor until we reach a conference room.

"Wait here," he says, leading me into the room and giving me a small smile. "I'll be right back."

I nod and he leaves.

As soon as I hear the door click, I crouch down to my ankles and let out a sob into my hands.

How did we get here? How did a dream about my dead mother lead me to this? Only twelve hours ago, I was just a girl living the best life she could in New York with her boyfriend and now she's lost a parent once again and her brother is in jail.

It feels like everything is going to shit way too quickly.

When I hear footsteps approaching the door, I stand back up and try to compose myself as best as I can before the door is pushed open.

The second the door is open; I'm met with a set of dark eyes. The same color that I dreamed of last night.

As soon as he is fully in the room, I throw myself at my brother, holding him for dear life.

"Camila," he groans out and when I pull away, I see that his hands are handcuffed behind him.

"Sorry, are you hurt?" I look him up and down trying to see any signs of injury but all I see is his face. "Oh my god what happened to your face? Are you okay?"

I reach out to touch his injury, but he cringes when my fingers barely graze the gash on his forehead.

"I'm fine. We're both fine."

The door closes and I look past my brother to our brother-in-law. He doesn't look as bad as Leo does.

Either way, I run to him and hug him just like I did Leo.

"I'm guessing your sister is on the way," Santos says when I pull away from him.

I nod. "Her and Serena should be here in an hour or two."

He nods, knowing that my sister has a mind of her own and wouldn't have stayed in Austin even if he bribed her to.

A clearing of a throat sounds through the conference room. I look over Santos's shoulder and make eye contact with Nate's gaze.

"I will give you three sometime," he says, reaching for the door.

"No, stay. Please. It's been a tough couple of hours and I want you here with me." I reach for his hand, giving him a small smile, but he pulls away from my touch.

Something that he has never done.

"Nate?" I ask him, but he's not looking at me, he's looking over my shoulder.

"You two know each other?" Leo growls from behind me. I turn and I meet my brother's deadly stare, but it's not aimed at me. It's aimed at my boyfriend.

"Yes," I say, my voice shaking slightly.

"How do you know him, Camila?" Leo's face is filled with anger, and it scares me a bit. Never have I seen him this angry at me.

"He's my boyfriend," I tell him, and I barely get the last word out before Leo charges.

"If I wasn't fucking handcuffed right now, I would be strangling you, Madden!"

I get pushed into Nate's body and then suddenly, I'm grabbed and pulled out of the way.

"When my hands are free, you're dead, Madden. You're dead for fucking touching my sister!"

"Stop it!" I yell, stepping in between Leo and Nate, and trying to put as much distance between them as I can.

Leo steps back but he doesn't take his eyes off the man standing behind me.

Once my brother is standing a few feet away, I move from Nate.

"How do *you* know each other?" I ask them. It's obvious by Leo's reaction to my statement that they know each other, that the three of them have history.

What history that is, I have no idea.

Nobody is saying anything.

"*How* do you know each other?!" I yell out, needing an answer.

"Cam," Nate says, reaching for my hand and turning me to face him. "There's something that I need to tell you."

"What?"

His face is composed, but there is something in his eyes that says I'm not going to like what comes out of his mouth.

Nate sighs, squaring his shoulders. "That case I was working on, the one that caused me to leave a few days ago, is a case that I've been working on for a while." He looks at me and takes a deep breath before he continues. "That case was to bring down the Muertos Cartel. Not only the Muertos but also to bring down Ronaldo Morales."

I hear the words that he's saying, but it's taking me a second to comprehend them.

The case he was working on was one to take down my family's business? To take down my father?

"What are you saying, Nathaniel?" I back up from him, fearful of what he's about to say.

"I was the one that was behind the raid at your father's compound. I was the one that put that gash on your brother's forehead. And..." He pauses, looking at me with so much sadness in his eyes, knowing that his next words are going to break me. "And I'm the one that killed your father."

The words ring through the room and I want to make

them disappear. I want him to take them back, to not make it real.

"No." I shake my head. "No, you didn't do that."

"Cami, I did. I was the one that pulled the trigger. I did it. I killed your father."

He approaches me, and when he gets close enough, I shove him back.

"No! Don't touch me!" I feel like everything has been ripped from me, like there is nothing holding me together anymore.

I start to breathe harder, and I feel a little lightheaded.

"I need to get out of here," I say to the room heading to the door.

"Camila," Santos starts but I hold up a hand stopping him.

"This is too much. Serena, Isabella and I will figure out a way to get you out of here, but I can't handle this right now. I'll tell them you're okay."

I walk out of the room without anyone stopping me.

Instead of heading to the elevator, I head straight to the stairs, needing to get out of this building faster.

When I reach the outside of the building, I lean against the brick wall and slide down until my ass is hitting the ground.

Nate did it.

Nate went after the cartel and is the reason my last living parent is dead.

The man I love killed my father.

I'm in love with my father's killer.

26

NATHANIEL

I SHOULD HAVE FOLLOWED her out. I should have stopped her and explained everything, but like the idiot that I am, I didn't.

Why?

Because I took something from her. I killed her father. I saw the pain in her eyes and heard it in her voice when she talked about his death. It's affecting her, and she is trying to hold herself together and the reason she is doing that is because of me.

"Out of all the women in this city, you had to go after the one that you shouldn't have." Leo's voice comes from the other side of the holding cell that he's currently in.

After Cami stormed out of the conference room, both Santos and Leo started yelling at me for going after Camila. I let them yell, I let them yell until I grew tired of it, and I escorted the two of them back to their cell.

They were right, I shouldn't have gone after Camila. I

shouldn't have gotten involved with her, but I don't regret any of my actions when it comes to her.

"I didn't know who she was, okay? Do you think that if I did, I would go after her? That I would start a relationship with her?"

At least I think I wouldn't.

There is something about Camila Diaz, fuck, I mean Camila Morales, that captivates me, and I want to be exposed to everything that she has to offer.

That doesn't mean that I shouldn't have done my homework. I should have investigated her. I should've found out everything about her. Her family, her friends, what her routine was back in San Antonio. Everything. Maybe then I wouldn't have been so blindsided by whose daughter she is.

"I swear, Madden, once I have my hands free, I'm going to punch your fucking face in for even thinking about my twenty-year-old sister."

After all the hurt I caused her, I'll let him, but I don't tell him that.

I do roll my eyes and start to make my way out of the holding cells.

"As soon as you are free to go, I will let you know."

I walk out and head straight to where Beck is holding the fort for the day.

Beck is already up and pacing the room, not stopping when I walk in.

"We can't hold them," I say, closing the door behind me.

He sighs and nods in my direction, not stopping his movements. "I know. We need more evidence to put them behind bars for good and what we have right now is not sufficient."

"I say we let Reyes and Morales go, and keep a close eye on them. They are bound to mess up somewhere. The time will come when we'll see them pay for their crimes," I offer.

Even after months of having the time to come up with a plan, this is the best that I can come up with. Let them go as if they didn't do anything wrong.

Beck finally stops pacing and nods. "Hold them for the remainder of the twenty-four hours. We'll have them back in our hands soon."

"Yes, sir."

We talk a few more logistics and how we are going to handle the press conference that we will be holding tomorrow with the FBI about the takedown of the head of the Muertos.

Eventually, I excuse myself and head out. I have one place in my mind, and that is going home.

I need to see if Cami is there.

We need to talk, and I need to explain everything to her.

Hopefully she can forgive me, even if it's a small amount.

———

I OPEN the door to the apartment.

For a moment, I just stand there listening for any noises. Anything that tells me that she's here.

One second.

Two.

After five seconds, I finally hear some rummaging coming from the master bedroom.

She's here.

"Cam?" I announce my presence, not wanting to scare her, especially when I don't know how she's feeling at the moment.

Walking to the bedroom, I see articles of clothing everywhere. Hers. Mine.

"Camila," I say when I enter the room and I find her on the floor stuffing clothes into one of her bags.

She doesn't look up when I call her name or when she hears me approach, she just continues doing what she's doing.

"Camila, what are you doing?" I walk deeper into the room, crouching down next to her.

"I'm packing my things," she says, still not looking at me.

From what I can see of her face, I can see tears running down her cheeks. The slight tan of her skin tone looking a bit pale.

"Where are you going to go?"

"To the studio. Away from here." She pushes herself off the floor and heads to the bathroom.

"Cam," I call out after her.

She storms back into the room.

"Tell me this, Nathaniel. Did you know who I was? When we met, did you recognize me and thought to yourself, here's my ticket to taking down the head of the Muertos? Is that what happened?"

Her face, her eyes, everything in her expression is covered in betrayal.

"I didn't know," I tell her, trying to keep my voice even.

"I don't believe you. You probably saw an innocent girl who was born into a shit life and you decided to take your shot." She storms past me, heading out of the bedroom and into the living room.

"I didn't fucking know who you were! I didn't know until an hour ago!" I yell after her.

I need to rein in my emotions, because I'm starting to lose it.

"How?" She stops when she reaches the kitchen. "How did you not know who I was? You went after my father, right? That means that you at least had to know that I existed, so how is it that you saw me at that bar and didn't recognize me right away?"

"Because," I start but have a hard time finding the right explanation.

"Because, isn't an answer, Nathaniel."

What I wouldn't give for her to call me detective right about now.

"Because the last known picture that the DEA or FBI has of you was from when you were around four. Yes, I knew you existed, but because you were just a child and you weren't involved with the cartel, I didn't keep tabs on you. It didn't feel right."

More tears start to escape from her eyes. Her bottom lip starts to tremble, and I want to go to her and wrap my arms around her. I want to apologize for each one of my actions.

"How long have you been working on this case?" Cami asks after a few minutes of silent cries.

I let my chin fall to my chest. "My whole career. From day one."

I don't tell her that I've wanted to take down Ronaldo since I found out he was the one that ordered the hit on my father. Since I was sixteen. Almost twenty years.

"I guess taking down my father was a big accomplishment for you. You should be proud." She grabs her sketchbook from the counter and heads back to the bedroom.

"That's not how I wanted it to play out. I never planned on pulling the trigger." I follow her down the hall.

I should tell her that it was a life-or-death situation. I should tell her that we both had our guns drawn. I should tell her that I had all intentions of placing cuffs around his wrist and taking him in.

But I keep every single one of those thoughts to myself. I don't want to her anger her more, to make her believe I'm spewing lies to get her to see that I'm speaking the truth.

"But you did." She stops at the threshold, turning back to face me, coming closer, stabbing a finger into my chest. "You did pull the trigger. You pulled the trigger and now my last living parent is dead."

"You said that your relationship with your father wasn't

great." It's a low blow. I know it is as soon as the words are out of my mouth.

"Just because my relationship with him was shit, it doesn't mean that it doesn't hurt any less knowing that he's dead. I still loved him. He was still my blood."

Tell her, Madden. Tell her why you pulled the trigger.

This time I don't hesitate, I do reach out to her, but like in the conference room, she steps away from me.

If it's in fear, hurt, anger, I don't know.

She shakes her head at me and heads back into the room. I watch as she finishes stuffing her things in her bags until she's finally done.

"Cam, you don't have to go."

"But I do." She slings a bag over her shoulder. "I can't do this right now. I need time to process all of this. I need time away from…"

From me.

She needs time away from me.

I nod, not needing her to finish her sentence.

"Okay."

She grabs the remaining of her stuff and walks out of the room. Before she is fully out of the door, she turns back to me.

"I don't know if I can forgive you for pulling that trigger." She squares her shoulders back and holds her head up high as she leaves.

I continue to stand in place not moving to go after her, not even when I hear the front door close behind her.

Fuck.

Never thought that I would regret pulling a trigger as much as I do right at this moment.

Never thought that finally putting an end to Ronaldo Morales would cause my life to go down in shambles.

But it has.

Fuck Ronaldo Morales.

27

CAMILA

I LOOK out the window of my sister's hotel room and it's nothing compared to the one back at mine and Nate's place.

Or should I say his place? Since I packed up most of my things and stormed out.

As I continue to look out the window, I try to figure out what hurts more. The fact that my father is dead or knowing that it was Nate that killed him.

Or maybe it's the fact that Nate even went after my father knowing full well that it could end in death for one of them.

At this point in time, I think it might be the second one, but my head is going in so many directions. I can't keep up.

"Camila?" my sister calls out for me. When I look up, I see that she's standing at the doorway. "Are you okay?"

I shake my head, fresh tears springing to my eyes and a sob forming in my throat.

Isabella looks at me with sadness before coming over to me and wrapping her arms around me.

"It will be okay, Camila. It will be okay," she reassures me over and over again, but I don't believe her.

How can it be? How can it be when Leo and Santos are in jail, our father is dead and the reason all of this has happened is because of my boyfriend?

I cry into my sister's arms, getting lost in the tears for a quick minute.

"We have to plan a funeral," I voice once the tears have stopped.

A small part of me is saying that instead of my father's it could have been Nate's. That thought gets grabbed and thrown away.

"I know."

"What if Leo and Santos never get out?" It's possible. Given what this family does, it's possible that they could spend the rest of their lives behind bars.

"They will," Isabella insists.

I pull away from her and look her right in the eye. "But what if they don't? We both know it could happen."

Isabella looks like she wants to fight me on this, like she will do everything in her power for that not to happen, but she knows just as well as I do, that's not possible.

Eventually, she lets out a sigh. "Then we continue with life. We continue it and fight for them to be free one day. That's all we can do."

I don't like that answer, but she's right. That will be the only thing we can do about it.

So, I give her a nod.

"C'mon, let's get you something to eat," she offers, and when she gets up to leave the room, I follow.

In the small living room of the suite my sister was somehow able to get in a few short hours, sits a cart full of food.

Serena is sitting on the couch feeding baby Noah and when I walk in, she gives me a small smile.

"How are you feeling?" she asks.

After I stormed out of the apartment, I was going to go to my apartment, but I got a call from Isabella as soon as I got into an Uber telling me that they had arrived and heading to the hotel.

So, I diverted the Uber and came here.

As soon as I walked into the room and I saw my sister, I completely lost it.

She held me tight as I cried in her arms and she consoled me about our father's death.

I told her that that wasn't why I was crying. I told her what I had just found out. I told her that Nate, the man I was madly in love with, killed our father. I told her every-thing I could while the sobs tried to escaped.

It still feels like the sobs are on the brink of escaping but I push them down.

"Like I got my heart ripped out of my chest over and over again." I go to my sister-in-law, ignoring the food and holding my hands out for the baby.

Serena finishes feeding him and then hands him over. I position the kid for him to burp.

"It's an understandable way to feel." Serena gives me a small smile, that is, until she shakes her head. "I can't believe that the agent that killed Ronaldo and your boyfriend are the same person."

Neither can I.

"Did you not know what he did for a living?" Isabella asks as she comes and sits next to me.

"I knew to some extent. He told me he was a detective the first time we met. Told me that he went after bad people, but he never talked about his cases in full detail. Hell, I even went to his office and went to a work function with him. I knew he worked for the DEA, but up until today, I didn't know what DEA stood for."

Drug Enforcement Agency.

I looked it up as soon as I left the prison. Apparently, this agency goes after all things that have to do with drugs in the United States. Including drug trafficking.

The very thing that my family does.

My whole life I was taught to fear the FBI, never the DEA.

"I met him once," Serena lets out.

Right away, my eyes go to her. "You did?"

How is that possible?

I didn't so much as show my family a picture of him. How did she meet him?

She nods. "It was when Emilio took me and Aria. He had stopped me before I had gone into the building. Had asked me to talk about what I knew about the cartel. He told me that my husband was a bad man."

"What did you tell him?"

"That I didn't know anything. That Leo and I weren't

together, and I had nothing to do with what he did. He actually gave me a card just in case I changed my mind."

I look at Serena a little dumbfounded. I guess Nate had a bigger connection to this family than just working on the case to bring my father down.

"He actually helped save me and Aria," Serena voices and again I'm in shock.

"What?"

She gives me a sad smile. "I don't know how it happened, but one second I looked up and he was there. He helped take Aria to the hospital. I even got flowers a few days after. At that moment, he wasn't working to take down the cartel, he was working with them."

How did I not know he did that? How is it that I'm just finding out that Nate took part in saving Serena from Emilio?

"Let me ask you this." Isabella places a hand on my thigh, taking my attention away from Serena. The movement tells me that what she's about to ask, I'm not going to like. "Did you tell him anything about the Muertos?"

"*¿Me crees pendeja?* I was told from a young age that I should never talk about what the family does. So I don't, not even when I start a relationship with someone I see a future with."

There were times that I wanted to come clean to Nate about who I really was. Why I was scared of bringing someone that worked in law enforcement anywhere near my family.

But I held it in.

I held it in because I'm not defined by my father's

choice of business. I'm my own person, and I have nothing to do with the Muertos, only in blood.

"Not even involuntarily?"

"No, Isabella. Not even involuntarily." Does my family really think I'm that stupid?

Isabella holds up her hands. "I'm just asking. There are just a lot of questions running through my head right now, and I had to know."

"What other questions are running through that pretty head of yours, *hermana*?" My voice sounds annoyed, and frankly, I am.

I can't believe that she thinks that I would talk. I wouldn't.

Isabella sighs, giving my thigh a reassuring squeeze, not taking her eyes off the baby in my arms.

"Do you really believe that he didn't know who you were? He was able to find Serena."

He was and at the time that Emilio took Serena, she and Leo were only married for about three months.

That's a short amount of time to know someone exists and ask them to talk.

But do I believe Nate is telling the truth?

Did he really not know who I was?

He was shocked when we were in the lobby earlier when I said I was Ronaldo Morales's daughter. It was like he was in disbelief.

And then the way he said the words back in the apartment, it was like he was angry at me for not believing him. Not only was he angry, he was hurt.

"I believe him," I state for the first time out loud. "I'm

not involved in the cartel like you are. There is no reason as to why the FBI or DEA would need to look at me. Like Nate said, I was a child. And as of at least three years ago I still was."

A part of me wishes that I had come to this realization a lot earlier in the day than right now.

But just because I believe him, that doesn't mean that I don't harbor anger toward him for what he did.

The room goes silent for a bit. The only noise is coming from Noah groaning about his position. Eventually, we drop the subject of Nate and we eat the food that was ordered for dinner.

After dinner, we turn on the TV to check the news, waiting to see if the news of the Muertos kingpin's death has hit TVs across America. It hasn't.

I even check reports in Mexico, but nothing is reporting that my father is dead.

But the news will hit soon. A man like my father can't die without it going unnoticed. The United States government is probably waiting for the right time to announce it.

And when they do, there will be no hiding from the limelight.

That, on top of the funeral, will not be a fun experience.

For the rest of the night, we keep the news on, even when my sister, Serena, and Noah fall asleep.

I stay awake though, not wanting the darkness to overtake me. There's this fear running through me, like if I close my eyes, I will dream of my mother again and something will happen. Maybe it will be worse than the last.

So, I stay awake for most of the night, only dozing off here and there.

At sunrise, I get up from the bed and I go down to get some breakfast. When I come back, both Isabella and Serena are awake watching the TV intently.

"What happened?"

"They finally announced the raid and Ronaldo's death. They are going to have a press conference later today," Serena answers me, not taking her eyes off the television.

My eyes focus on the footage scrolling on the screen.

There are pictures of individuals dressed in all black, carrying guns, getting ready for battle.

They also show photos of the aftermath of the raid, pictures that show damage to a house that I once called my safe haven. The pictures show the blood, the broken furniture, everything.

"It doesn't look the same," I voice, my heart hurting at just seeing everything destroyed.

"It's not the beautiful house that *Mamá* once loved." No, it's a whole different house.

We continue to watch the news and listen to the reporter talk about the men that were killed and the ones that were arrested.

"Do we have names of the men that were arrested at the compound?" the anchor asks the correspondent on the split screen.

"We do have confirmation of two individuals. Leonardo Morales and Santiago Reyes, two known members of the Muertos Cartel. As of right now though, we have no indication of what their charges are."

A phone rings through the room and right away our attention is off the screen and on the ringing phone.

We each pull out our phones and Serena comes out the victor.

"It's a New York area code," she says before answering the phone and putting it on speaker. "Hello?" "*Hola, princesa.*" Leo's voice comes through and instantly tears form in Serena's eyes.

"Hi. Please tell me that they are releasing you," Serena says, getting straight to the point.

He answers right away. "We are getting released."

We all let out a sigh of relief.

"Do we pick you up?"

"No, we will come to you. We've been told that there's a lot of press outside. We are getting escorted to wherever you are."

If there is press already outside of the prison, what is the scene like back in San Pedro?

"Okay," Serena sighs. I'm sure she's anxious about having her husband within arm's reach. "Okay, we'll wait for you here."

There is noise in the background, taking Leo away for a few seconds before he comes back. "Serena, I have to go, but I will be there soon, okay? Give our boy a kiss for me."

"I will."

With that, the call is over and the three of us just continue to stand there, looking at the screen.

They are getting released.

But just because they are free, it doesn't mean that any of this is over.

28

NATHANIEL

"You must be excited about finally putting this case to rest."

Ava's voice comes from behind me as I get ready in the changing room here at the office. The press conference on Ronaldo's death and the raid that led to it is happening in fifteen minutes and I'm currently making myself presentable. Suit, tie, the works.

If I could do this job without the involvement of the press or paperwork, I'd be a happy man.

"Just because a man is dead, doesn't mean that the case will be closed," I answer as I throw on my suit jacket.

"Well..." I watch as she comes deeper into the changing room through the mirror and comes to stand behind me. "At the very least you can rest for a little before you jump back in." She places a hand on my shoulder, as she smiles at me through the mirror.

"Yup," I say, stepping out of her touch and reaching for my tie.

"Here, let me help you with that," she says when I place the tie under my collar.

I know how to tie my own fucking tie.

Ava steps forward before I can even tell her that it's okay. She takes the ends of the tie and starts to form the knot.

I think I might be a little too shocked by her forwardness to stop her. So I just stand there and watch it happen.

It's just a gesture, but it feels way too intimate to be happening.

She smooths her hands over the lapels of my jacket. "There, you are all ready for your conference. You should send a picture to Camile."

I sigh, stepping out of her reach. "It's Camila. And sending her a picture of how I look right now is not necessary."

Without another word to or from Ava, I leave the changing room and head to where the press conference will be held.

Ava is making her stance known on how she feels about me having someone in my life and if it continues, I will have to put a stop to her advances.

Shaking it off, I try to get my mind in the right place for this stupid press conference.

I want nothing to do with it, especially since I found out just how connected I am to the person that died. But since I'm the head agent on this case, I have to speak. I have to be there to answer all the pressing questions that all the news outlets have.

Even if I cringe with every single one.

"Are you ready to face the vultures?" Beck comes up behind me, dressed in a suit as well.

"No, but you won't do it alone." I button my jacket and make sure that my badge is on display.

"Gotta have someone in the room to point the reporters to when they ask the big questions."

I grunt at his response.

Soon we are getting called by our public relations rep to head into the room. The second that we step over the threshold, we are bombarded with camera clicks, flashes and questions.

The questions don't quiet down until our public relations representative, Marie, stands at the front of the podium, silencing everyone in the room.

Once she has the room's attention, she goes through the press release that was sent out a few hours ago. The one that stated that the agency had successfully taken down the known drug lord.

I've been avoiding looking at my phone or even looking at a TV screen. I lived it, there is no need to relive it over again.

Once Marie is done speaking, Beck steps up and goes through what the plan was for this operation and how it was all conducted.

As soon as Beck is done with all the technicalities of this whole thing, the time comes for me to shine.

The second I step up to the podium, the questions start to fly.

I resist the urge to roll my eyes at every single one.

I keep myself composed and point to a reporter in the front.

"Agent Madden, is the war against the Muertos Cartel over now that Morales is dead?"

I guess I don't have easy questions tonight, do I?

"That's not an easy question to answer. Yes, the leader of the Muertos Cartel is no longer here, but that doesn't mean that the Muertos is dismantled. There is no clear way of knowing that it's over."

I point to the next reporter, this time a female that looks like she is trying to get her feet wet with the big shot reporters.

"It was reported that Leonardo Morales, the son of Mr. Ronaldo Morales, and Santiago Reyes were both arrested at the scene. What charges are being brought against them and where will they be held before their court hearing?"

Again, with the hard as fuck questions. This is why I hate reporters.

I clear my throat and give them the answer that they aren't going to like.

"Yes, Leonardo Morales and Santiago Reyes were arrested at the scene. At this moment in time, the DEA has not charged the men with anything pertaining to this case. As of a few hours ago, they are free with a few stipulations, those stipulations put forth by the DEA."

Right away, questions come out rapidly.

"You let them go."

"They are known to be connected to the cartel."

So many questions, I can hardly think straight.

"The DEA is keeping a close eye on both Mr. Morales and Mr. Reyes, and that is all I will say on that matter."

The room silences once again, all the reporters looking stunned by the news that we let Leo and Santos walk.

Another reporter holds up his hand, and I point for them to ask a question.

"Will the agents involved in the raid and in the shooting of Mr. Morales be revealed?"

The biggest question of them all.

Who is the face that pulled the trigger?

Who gets the glory of getting known for killing the biggest and baddest kingpin of all?

No matter what I learned yesterday morning, I wouldn't announce it to the world that I was the one that did it. But I did learn something and that warrants my response even more.

"No. Not a single agent will be revealed."

"Why is that, Agent Madden?"

Can you tell that this person has never dealt with something so high profile like the cartel, because I can.

"Because it's not only protection for the agents involved from retaliation, but also the man had a family. He had kids. Yes, he was the head of the Muertos Cartel. Yes, he has been rumored to have done some bad things in his lifetime, but he was still a person. Let those kids mourn their father in peace. Let them go about their lives without having to see their father's killer every day for the rest of their lives."

I look at the reporter, and then move to look at every other face in the room.

Not one ounce of remorse on their faces.

Not like the remorse I feel swimming through my body every time I think about what I did not more than thirty-six hours ago.

How much I hurt Camila for taking her father away.

"If there are no further questions, we are done here."

I need a drink.

A drink to get me through the dark times that are about to come.

29

CAMILA

I ENTER the bar and a sense of melancholy comes over me.

It might have to do with what happened the last time I walked into this establishment that is making me feel that way, but either way, I'm here.

Much like last time, I was walking down a New York street, coming from NYU. The only difference today is that I attend NYU and, well, my mood is nowhere near what it was that day all those months ago. So just like the time before, I walk in, notice the number of patrons that are occupying the place and head to grab a seat at the bar.

"Can I get you something to drink?" the bartender asks. This time it's a guy instead of the girl that was flaunting her boobs in front of my chicken strips.

I nod. "Can I get a Pacifico and a shot of whatever tequila you think is best?"

"Can I see an ID?" Right away, I pull it out of my purse without any hesitation.

He takes it, checks it, and hands it back to me. "Happy birthday. I'll get you that Pacifico."

"Thanks." I watch him walk away and retrieve my beer before coming back to me and pouring the shot in front of me.

"Enjoy," he says before walking away.

I take the shot glass between my fingers and hold it up as if to toast myself.

"Happy birthday to me."

I drink it down without thinking.

This is so not how I thought I would be spending my twenty-first birthday.

I had it all planned out. Even though it was my birthday, I was going to surprise Nate with a weekend getaway. I wanted to spend some time on the beach drinking all the alcohol with my man next to me and, well, he needed a vacation, so it was going to be perfect.

But a lot of things have happened in the time since I had that thought.

Like everything going down with the raid.

My brother's arrest.

My father's death but most importantly his funeral.

It's been six weeks since the death of my father and I think that I'm barely coming to terms with it. I've accepted his death, but just because it's accepted that he's dead doesn't mean that the pain is fully gone.

I think the pain is still there because I had hope that after our last conversation, he would change. I thought that he would see me walk out of his office and he would change for the better, that he would want to rebuild whatever relationship we had left. That he would stop being so damn power hungry and he would stop all this madness happening to our family.

But I guess I was just an ignorant little girl for wanting to believe that.

I did come to one realization when it came to mourning my father.

I'm not mourning the man that he was the day that he died. No, I'm mourning the man that he once was more than a decade ago.

The funeral was hard. After about three weeks and an autopsy ruling the cause of death, we were given the permission to bury his body.

My brother wanted nothing to do with it. He just said to tell him when to show up and he would. My sister wanted to act like burying our father wasn't affecting her, but it was. I saw it in her eyes every single day leading up to the funeral. She was hurting, but she was going to stay strong and get through as best she could.

As for me, I was composed around people, but when it came to being in private, I lost it every single time.

I cried for my father.

I cried for myself.

And I cried for Nate.

I cried even more when he showed up to the funeral. He didn't approach me or my family. He stayed in the shadows, but he was there.

Maybe it was for me, maybe it was some sort of penance, but he was there.

I wanted to hate him for being there at that moment,

but I couldn't. There was more gratitude than hatred for him being there.

The day of the funeral was when I saw Nate last.

He has called me though.

He has called, he has texted, and he has left voice mails, but I have yet to answer a call, reply to a text or listen to a voice mail.

When I walked out of his apartment the day of my father's death, I thought time would be only a few days, not weeks.

But I don't know if I'm fully ready to forgive him yet for pulling the trigger.

Especially when I don't know the whole story about why he went after my father and the cartel in the first place.

Was it because it was just for work?

Or was it because there is something deeper behind the case? Like there was more to the story?

But the biggest question of them all, why did he pull the trigger at all?

I have no idea, but for right now, I am planning on using my legal card and getting as drunk as I possibly can.

Grabbing my beer bottle, I put the opening to my lips and drink as much as I can in one gulp.

Once I'm done with it, I slam it down on the counter and wave over the bartender for another one.

He places the fresh beer in front of me and goes on his merry way.

I chug this one down too but when I slam my beer on the bar, I hear the stool beside me get pulled out.

I close my eyes and marvel at the possibility.

Could it be him?

Could he be here at this bar that we first met at and is taking the seat next to me?

The probability is low, but what are the chances?

Slowly, I turn to my stool neighbor and the disappointment rushes in.

I guess I haven't learned to stop getting my hopes up, so things don't get sucked up by a black hole.

Stool neighbor doesn't say anything, just sits there, orders his beer and then after a few drinks he gets up and leaves.

He didn't see that I was the life of the party, I guess.

I go back to my beer, which is almost empty, but I don't ask for another one. I just sit there peeling back the label, you know, making the best of my twenty-first birthday.

The stool next to me gets pulled out again. This time I don't look to see who it is. What's the point of being disappointed yet again?

"I didn't peg you as the type of person to come to this type of bar," a female voice says from next to me.

I recognize it, and I may be slightly regretting coming here today.

Plastering a smile on my face, I turn to my stool neighbor.

"Hi, Ava." *Be nice, Camila.* "Yeah, this bar has some sentiment to it. I didn't know you came here."

She nods and gives me a smile that I can tell right away is fake. "I've come here a few times with Nate actually, this was our go-to lunch post a few days a week."

My smile falters slightly, but from the look on her face, she didn't notice.

Before everything happened with my father, I had asked Nate if he had come back to the bar. He had told me no, because for some reason it felt wrong for him to go without me.

I might have swooned hard at the comment and worshiped his cock in the shower that night.

But that was weeks ago. Six weeks have gone by with me not speaking to him, so maybe he threw that sentiment away and has been coming here with Ava regularly.

"That's nice."

"Yeah." Her fake smile grows even more. "Did he tell you that he was meeting me here tonight? Is that why you're here, you're crashing?"

He's meeting her here.

He's meeting her *here.*

This time, my smile does go away. I guess a part of me thought that since he knew what today was, he would at the very least not hang out with Ava.

"He didn't tell you?" She asks, shocked.

I shake my head. "Nate and I aren't on speaking terms at the moment."

"Oh, he didn't tell me that." Of course, he didn't, because she's probably lying about him coming here tonight. "Let me guess, your age got in the way? Or maybe it was the fact that you lied about your identity? Maybe it was both?"

A cold rushes through me, something that I haven't felt before.

You lied about your identity.

She knows who I am.

How? Did Nate tell her?

"My age had nothing to do with it and I have no idea what you are talking with the lying about my identity."

I try to convey strength as much as I can, trying to give her nothing. To make her believe that she's just talking out of her ass.

"So, you aren't Camila Morales, daughter of Ronaldo Morales, the head of the Muertos Cartel? The same man that was killed only a few weeks ago?"

The way she raises her eyebrows at me and how her smile goes into a smirk gives me chills, like she's silently telling me that she has me all figured out.

"I don't know what you are talking about," I say again. My voice wants to shake at the words, but I keep it at bay.

I can't break down in the middle of a bar.

"Of course, you do. I'm guessing that's why you aren't talking to Nate, because he killed your father?"

If we weren't in public, I would be slapping her right now.

I need to get away from her.

This bitch is after something, and I need to walk away before something is said and all my family history is out for all of New York to know.

Ignoring her, I reach into my purse and take out a few twenties to pay for my drinks. I place the cash on the bar and stand up from the stool.

"Bye Ava, I hope that your sadistic lying ass gets what it's looking for."

I leave the bar without a second look in her direction. Not bothering to get a cab, I walk to my apartment.

Pissed off, tears streaming down my face.

I want to go back to where I was before all of this started. I want to be able to go home to Nate and just forget about everything happening around me and just be. If only I could go back to the day he left to go on his mission.

Then maybe I wouldn't be living in this nightmare.

I make it to my building and once I'm inside, I beeline to my place.

I'm about to take out my keys from my bag when I notice something in front of my door.

Flowers and something else.

I look over my shoulder and down the hall hoping to see who might have dropped it off, but the only person in the hallway is me.

Approaching the door slowly, I see that the bouquet of flowers is sitting on top of a white box. Both items have a card with my name on it.

I recognize the writing right away.

Swallowing down the lump in my throat, I pick up the stuff and open the door. Once inside, I place my things on the floor and the flowers and white box on my table.

I look at the white box, and everything in me is telling me to open it. But I know the second I do, I'm going to break.

And I don't want that to happen.

I'll open it second.

Grabbing the note on the flowers, I open the small envelope and take out the card.

. . .

Happy birthday, beautiful girl.
You said you needed time, and I'm going to respect that as long
as you want me to. Just know that there isn't a day that goes by
that I don't think of you. That I don't regret my actions that led
us here. I do. I regret them, every last one of them.
I hope that one day, maybe not anytime in the near future, but
one day I hope you forgive me for what I did to you and your
family.

I love you, Camila.
Detective.

WHY? Why did he have to write this and make me more of a blubbering mess? Why?

Wiping the tears away, I put the card down and pick up the one laying on top of the box. Might as well become a bigger mess.

I open the letter and read it.

I found your surprise. I love everything about it. Hopefully you
like what I did with it. I hope you use what's in this box to make
something more amazing.

. . .

MY SURPRISE.

He found it.

I had an idea around Valentine's Day to stretch the canvas we had sex on all those months ago and had painted with our bodies.

I wanted to see the art that we made together on the wall and have only the two of us know how it was created.

It was going to be a surprise from when he got back from his two-week trip. When I stormed out, I forgot all about it.

Opening the box, I'm met with so much white tissue I have to dig through it to find the contents.

At the top are paints and a folded cloth canvas. Seeing this, I now know what he meant by using the contents to make something amazing.

Putting the supplies to the side, I take out the last item in the box.

It's a picture frame.

Unwrapping it from the tissue, I turn it over and see what exactly is in the frame.

It's a picture of Nate's bedroom, of the bed that we shared, but the bed isn't what catches my attention.

It's the canvas that is hung above the headboard.

His surprise.

He hung it up.

I look at the picture frame for a little while longer before I put it down.

Not wanting to wallow in sadness, I grab the paint

supplies and set them up much like I did that night when Nate was over.

Once everything is to my liking, I start to undress.

Then I make something amazing with just paint on and my body.

The whole time I'm thinking about Nate and how I so badly want to reach out and thank him.

And to tell him I love him.

I may not be ready to forgive him, but I still love him.

30

NATHANIEL

Sleeping in a bed alone after spending months sharing it with a person, sucks ass.

As a grown man and not having shared a bed with someone for years, you would think that this thing going on with Camila would be an easy transition, but it's not. Every single night I go to sleep wishing that her gray hair was spread out against the pillow, and that she was telling me about her school projects. And every single morning I wish that she was sleeping next to me with her pouty lips begging to be kissed.

I miss Camila and I fucking hate all this distance shit, but it will stay that way until she is ready.

No amount of calls, text messages, or sending gifts is going to send us back to where we once were.

But everything with Cami is just an added bonus to everything that is happening in the Muertos case.

After that lovely press conference, we had for the raid and Ronaldo, the DEA started receiving backlash. Not for killing Ronaldo, no, we've been getting backlash for letting Leo and Santos free. The press has been having a field day with that little tidbit.

There even have been conspiracy theories popping up on social media about why they were let free. None of them are even close to the truth, but to each their own, I guess.

Gotta love getting praise for one part of the mission and getting dragged through the mud for the other.

Putting all thought of Cami and the press backlash out of my head, I walk into the DEA building and head straight to my office.

The sooner I get started with my day, the sooner I get to go home.

Home where I'm just going to spend the night staring at my girlfriend's paintings and hoping she walks through the door.

Is she even still your girlfriend?

Fuck if I know, but since we didn't officially have a conversation to end this, I'm going with yes, Camila is still my girlfriend.

God, girlfriend sounds so fucking childish.

I step foot in my office, and as soon as I'm about to take a seat in my chair, a knock sounds on the door.

I sigh, it's too early for this shit. "Come in."

The door opens and a junior agent pops his head in. "Sir, Agent Williams wants to see you."

Great. "I'll be right there."

He nods my way and leaves the office.

Grabbing a notepad just in case this is pertaining to a case, I head to Beck's office.

It's a short walk and once I'm there, I knock on the closed door.

"Come in, Madden." I guess he really wanted to see me.

"I was told to come see you," I say as soon as I step in. When I look up, I see that this meeting is not going to be just me and Beck, but also Ava.

"Good morning, Nate," she says, giving me a knowing smirk.

"Morning." I say before giving my attention to my supervisor. "What's going on?"

"Take a seat, Nathaniel."

Nathaniel? Since when does he call me anything but Madden?

I follow orders and take a seat, all the while he and Ava stay standing.

Beck crosses his arms over his chest and looks me dead in the eye. He's pissed off.

About what, I have no idea.

"Is there a bigger reason why Morales and Reyes were let go after the raid at the Morales estate?"

What?

"We had nothing to hold them on. You said so yourself. The evidence we had on them was not sufficient," I repeat his own words to him.

"So, it had nothing to do with the fact that you were screwing the cartel princess? Morales's sister?" he spits out, his words taking me aback.

How in the actual fuck does he know that Camila is Ronaldo's daughter?

Ava.

I turn to the other agent in the room and find her smirking, but not meeting my glare. She told him that Cami was a Morales, she knows her bloodline, but the question is how?

I turn back to Beck. "My relationship has nothing to do with this case whatsoever. Morales and Reyes were let go because there wasn't enough evidence against them."

"I call bullshit," Ava says from where she is standing. Both Beck and I turn to look at her.

"Excuse me?" I'm up from my seat. I'm not going to take whatever the fuck this is, sitting down.

"I said I call bullshit. You and that little trollop probably met and decided that you will kill her father so that she could get all the money that comes with the cartel."

What in the actual fuck?

Am I hearing this correctly?

"Sorry to disappoint you, Agent Hall, but that explanation is what's bullshit. I've been working on this case for fucking years. I've wanted to take down Morales since the start of my career. And if I do my math correctly, my relationship started far after I came across Morales and the Muertos. So, I repeat again, my relationship and this case have nothing to do with each other."

She doesn't back down; she just continues to glare at me. The stare down finally breaks when Beck speaks.

"Whatever the case may be." His voice is like a boom through the room. "We now have sufficient evidence to go after Morales and Reyes. In the next coming week, we will be infiltrating their operation."

"What evidence?" I ask him.

Nothing new has come in since Ronaldo's death, so there shouldn't be any reason to go after Leo and Santos. Not yet at least.

"Not something I can disclose to you. You're officially off this case. Agent Hall will take the lead." He gives me a nod as if to make it final.

"I've been on this case from day fucking one. You can't take me off this case because you think that I've been working with the Morales family in secret."

I have, but it's on the side of the DEA not the other way around.

"Decision has been made. You're off this, Madden."

My blood is boiling right now.

"Both of you are dismissed." He waves for us to leave his office. Without saying anything, Ava leaves first, but I stay behind for a few seconds.

"This is fucking bullshit and you know it." I leave his office, not wanting to hear his response.

I don't care what he has to say, all my attention is on Agent Hall as she walks down the hallway to her office.

She starts to close the door, but I stop it before it hits the latch.

"What are you playing at, Hall?" I say through my gritted teeth, but she doesn't seem fazed one bit.

"I don't know what you're talking about, Madden." She leaves me at the doorway and heads to her desk. "I'm just doing the best for not only this agency, but this country.

And if that means going against one of my own to do it, so be it. The Muertos Cartel will be done with in a matter of time. Something you obviously couldn't do, you know, since you decided to sleep with the enemy. Literally."

She sits back in her chair and gives me a smirk, like she just won the ultimate prize.

"There's more to this. I know there is."

She shrugs. "Maybe you shouldn't have slept with the kingpin's daughter."

"Jealousy doesn't suit you, Agent Hall." I walk into her office and place my hands on her desk. "Whatever shit you have against me, isn't going to help you take the Muertos down. It's taken me over a decade to get to this point, whatever you have planned for next week, isn't going to work out how you hope."

"Are you threatening me, Agent Madden?"

"No, I'm warning you. The Muertos are hard individuals, they don't go down in one swoop."

"I think I'm going to take my chances."

I scoff. "Suit yourself."

I push away from her desk and leave her office, slamming her door behind me.

This is not how I planned my day to fucking go. Kicked off a case that I've worked almost my whole career. I accomplished the major objective. With Leo's help I was able to take down his father.

Now, I probably won't be able to keep my end of the deal and keep him and his men out of prison.

Unless you warn him.

Can I?

My mind goes back to when they were arrested, and I brought Cami to the conference room. I saw in her face how much relief she was feeling at seeing her brother and brother-in-law. I saw the concern she had.

If I don't warn him, Cami will get that taken away. I already took her father away. I can't take her brother too.

Cami being in the picture, even if she isn't speaking to me, is the only reason I would consider doing this.

For her.

Instead of heading to my office, I head to the staircase heading to the parking garage. Given what just happened in Beck's office, what I'm about to do can't be done inside of the agency.

I get into my car and pull out my phone. There is hesitation for a few seconds as I second guess myself. But then I start thinking about a certain gray-haired beauty and I jump. After pressing the contact, I bring the phone to my ear and listen to it ring.

The phone rings three times before it goes silent. I hold my breath, just waiting for a greeting.

"This better be good." Leo's voice comes through.

One beat, two.

Am I going to do this?

Am I going to throw away everything I worked so hard to get, for this?

A pair of brown eyes cloud my mind.

"I'm calling a meeting."

31

NATHANIEL

I ARRIVED in Austin late last night. Given that it was a Friday, there were a few delays, but I was able to make it to my hotel before two in the morning.

Now, I'm sitting in a park in Austin at seven o'clock in the morning, waiting for my meeting partner to show up.

It's a good thing I have coffee.

It's not for another fifteen minutes that there is movement in the park. That movement includes someone that looks a lot like Leo pushing a baby stroller.

As he comes closer, I realize that it is in fact him.

Never thought I would see this known killer covered in head to foot tattoos pushing a baby stroller.

It's times like these, that remind me that Cami talked about her siblings to me, painted them in a normal light than what I'm used to. She told me about her sister's wedding and her brother having a baby. The number of pictures she showed me of her nephew is insane. Seeing the connection now is messing with my mind a bit.

"I didn't know that bringing a baby to this meetup was a requirement," I throw it out when he gets closer.

"Fuck off. Serena was still sleeping so the little man and I decided it was best to let her sleep." He takes a seat on the bench next to me, continuing the motion of moving the stroller back and forth. "His name is Noah."

I nod. When it came to mentioning her family member's names, Cami used generic terms. Brother, sister, sister-in-law, brother-in-law. Never saying anyone's name besides the baby's.

"Yeah, Cami introduced us during a video call when he was born." I give a nod toward the stroller.

She was so excited that he was born that she spent the whole call with me, pointing out everything she loved about him. It was cute.

"I bet that girl also sent you all the damn baby pictures. She bugs me every single morning for a new one. It's annoying."

I snort. It sounds like her.

"But you love it."

"But I fucking love it," he grunts out. Finally, he sighs and faces me. "What am I doing here, Madden?"

"Let me ask you something first. Am I speaking to the kingpin or the second in command?" With his father's death, Leo takes the throne.

Leo looks at me before looking at his son, then answers. "I took over. We took a few weeks to deal with the death and to get re-situated, just started back up. I'm the new head of the Muertos Cartel."

He doesn't sound very happy about the prospect, but he's going to do the work because it's in his blood.

I sigh. Guess I should get to the point. "As you know, the case that the DEA has on the Muertos isn't officially closed."

He nods. "Yes, so?"

"Yesterday, I was removed as the lead agent on the case. I no longer have access to any evidence or will partake in anything involving the cartel."

The words cause Leo to stop moving the stroller and turn fully to face me, not without taking a hand off the stroller.

"Why?"

"Someone told the supervising agent that the reason you and Santos were let go was because I was sleeping with your sister."

"Motherfucker," Leo says, scrubbing a hand over his face. He is silent for a long while, probably digesting what I just said. After about five minutes, he speaks. "Something is happening, isn't it?"

I look at the baby cooing in the stroller, and just think about how his life will change with the words I'm about to say.

"Yes."

"How bad is it?"

Might as well come out and just say it. "Apparently there is new evidence against you and your men, enough to put you away. They are planning a raid next week."

It's as if baby Noah knows what I just said was bad, because he starts crying the second I finish speaking.

Leo stands up from his seat and reaches into the stroller to take out his son. The baby is wrapped around in a blanket with a little hat on and as soon as he's in his father's arms, he calms down.

It's as if he knows he's safe and his father will do anything to protect him.

"I'm guessing you don't know what they are planning on raiding?" Leo asks, his eyes never leaving his son.

"No," I say and Leo nods, accepting my response. Eventually he sits back down with Noah in his arms.

We sit there in silence as he continues to rock the baby. After a few minutes, Noah falls asleep.

"Why did you tell me this?"

I could lie and tell him that I'm holding up my end of the bargain, but what good would that bring.

"You may think that I went after your sister for the wrong intentions, but that is completely wrong. When I met her, I didn't know who she was, she captivated me and I fell hard. So hard that I asked her to move in two months after making it official. So hard that I have her paintings all over my apartment. I'm telling you this because of her. Because I saw the worry in her eyes the morning after the raid when she couldn't see you. I saw the elation radiating off her when she was finally able to wrap her arms around you. The second I found out about the raid they're planning, all I thought about was Camila and how I couldn't take away any more family from her than what I already have. So, I'm telling you. Because I love her and I would rather not be able to hold her in my arms again than have her go through the pain of her losing you."

Never in my life did I think that I would be pouring out my heart to a cartel member in a park at seven in the morning, but here I am.

"And here I thought that you were a cold-hearted bastard with no soul," Leo says, breaking the emotional aspect of the conversation.

"I have my moments, but not when it comes to her."

He gives me a nod and looks down at his son. "Does she know?"

I look at him, my eyebrows raised silently, asking a question.

"Does she know why you went after him?"

I nod in understanding and sigh. "She stormed out of the apartment before I could tell her and well, she hasn't talked to me since then."

"Then maybe you should. Maybe you should tell her everything and then maybe she will give you a second chance." He shrugs. His voice carrying every single ounce of seriousness.

"You want me and your sister to be together?" Are we really having this conversation right now?

"Look," He shifts, Noah moving along with him, "I hate your fucking guts. Both me and Santos do. You're a snarly bastard and a pain in our asses, but I've noticed a shift in Camila ever since she's been in New York.

"She was happy, elated even. It made me not want to get on a plane and drag her ass back here. And I'm guessing that's because of you. Her being with you made her into one of the best versions of Camila I have ever seen. I haven't seen that since Ronaldo died. So, yeah. Maybe I do want you two to be together."

"How the actual fuck did we get here?" This whole conversation is fucking mind blowing.

Leo lets out a chuckle. "Don't get me wrong, I'm still going to punch you in the face for going after my sister, who's fourteen years your junior by the way. But maybe not right now."

I snort at his threat. I'll be ready and I will be punching him back.

"Yeah, well, getting back together with Cam will have to mean that she has to talk to me, and that doesn't seem like it will be happening anytime soon."

Especially if I get her brother killed.

"You doing anything tonight?" Leo asks, standing up and placing Noah back in the stroller.

I'm confused by the sudden change in conversation. "No?"

"Come over tonight. I'll call a family meeting and after that you, me, and Santos will be discussing what we are going to do with the DEA. I'll send you the address."

With a head nod, he walks away.

Did Leo Morales just invite me to be a part of his family meeting?

32

CAMILA

I DECIDED to fly out to Austin this weekend because I didn't feel like being alone for a few days. After spending my birthday alone, it felt like a much-needed trip.

So I called Leo on Friday morning and had him send the family plane to New York and now here I am. Sitting in a room at my brother's compound, trying to figure out what exactly I'm drawing.

I look at every line and every piece of shading, just trying to figure it out.

A knock on the door takes my attention away from my sketchbook. Looking up, I see Leo standing at the doorway. In a way, it reminds me of when I was in Noah's nursery trying to come up with a design.

"¿*Todo está bien?*" I ask him, closing the book.

He nods. "*Si*, I was just wondering if we can talk real quick."

I nod, and he comes in, taking a seat on the corner of the bed.

"What's up?"

"I wanted to talk to you about your relationship with Madden."

That takes me by surprise. Leo is definitely not one to talk about boys with me.

Especially ones that are fourteen years older than me and know how to work my body like they are a gift from God.

Leo raises his eyebrow at me.

I shake my head and answer him. "What about it?"

"You never mentioned—" I stop him before he even finishes his sentence.

"I never told him anything about the cartel. Or anything about what you and Santos do. I swear, Leo, I didn't talk. I swear. I didn't tell him anything." I feel tears running down my face, feeling a tinge of sadness because my brother believes I betrayed our family.

Leo gets up from the bed and comes over to where I'm sitting on the bay window.

When he's in front of me, he takes my face in his hands and looks me right in the eye.

"I know you didn't talk. I know, Camila."

"How? How do you know that?"

"Because I did." He pulls away from me and I see all the seriousness in his face. He's telling the truth.

Leo talked to the *federales*.

"Wh-why would you do that? Our father died because of that."

Leo is shaking his head. "No, our father died because of his own actions. I went to Madden because he had gone after Serena and had put Isabella into an arrangement with the Castros. I had to do something before he did something to you. I had to do what was right to protect the three of you. And I don't have any regrets about it."

I don't say anything. What is there to say? What's done is done. Leo talked and whether he did it or not, the actions of our father, might have led to the same outcome.

"Was it hard?" I ask, my voice low, but he is still able to hear it.

"It was, but it needed to be done. It was the only way."

I nod.

It was the only way.

I guess it's best that Ronaldo Morales was brought down by his own son rather than a complete stranger.

"Back to my original question," he says taking a seat back on the bed. "You never mentioned Madden's name to us, why is that? I mean, you lived with the man, why hide it?"

Okay, this is definitely not the direction that I thought this conversation would go. I seriously thought that he would be lecturing me for dating someone that was almost twice my age.

I think about it.

"I mentioned his name to Isabella a few times, but I think I wanted to keep that part of me to myself. I didn't want what we were building to be tainted by the cartel or what you do on a daily basis. I didn't want him to judge me for it, I guess. A get to know me for me type of thing."

My brother nods like he understands.

"I also didn't want you to fly to New York and cut off his

dick and feed it to him," I add, because let me tell you, that was a legit fear.

Leo laughs. "I wouldn't do that, but I would tie him up to a chair and beat his face in."

I smile. "Please don't."

He nods again with a smile playing on his lips. "You love him then?"

My bottom lip trembles at the thought. "I do, but I don't know if I can forgive him for pulling the trigger."

Pulling the trigger.

For weeks, I've been battling my inner demons just trying to figure out why I'm so mad about this whole situation. Why I'm angry at Nate for killing my father.

In the beginning, it was simple. He killed my last living parent. It was that simple.

But as the weeks went on, I got angrier at the fact that he was even in that room, inside the estate to begin with.

"You will once you know the whole story." He sounds determined.

"The whole story?"

Leo nods, giving me a small smile. "There's more to this, Camila. There is always more."

"He killed our father, Leonardo."

Again, my brother nods. "It was either Ronaldo's death or his. If I was put in that situation, I would have done the same thing that Madden did."

By the look in his eyes, I know he is telling the truth. I can see it in his dark orbs that Leo wouldn't have hesitated. He would have pulled the trigger to save his own life, even if it meant killing the person who made him who he is today.

After looking at him for a few seconds, I give a nod in understanding.

Leo stands back up, putting an end to our conversation, and heads out the door. "*Cambiate.* Put some makeup on. Madden is coming over in a few."

"What?!"

"You're getting the full story, Camila."

————

"STOP BITING YOUR NAILS!" Isabella slaps my hand as I chew on the remainder of my nails.

"I'm sorry, are you the one that has the man she's been in a relationship with, that she's not talking to because he killed her father, coming over in a few minutes? No, you're not, so I can bite my nails all I want." I slap her hand back, going back to my nubs for nails.

"Jesus," Serena mutters from where she sits next to me at the dining room table.

"Do I look okay?" I stand up from my seat and twirl around, showing them my full outfit.

After Leo dropped the bomb that Nate was coming over, I emptied out my whole suitcase to find something at least decent to wear. I settled for one of Isabella's dresses.

Yes, I haven't seen him since the funeral or spoken to him in weeks, but I still want him to think I look pretty.

"Yes, you look okay," Isabella answers.

"Like just okay or like hot okay? Like do you think he will want to jump my bones the second he sees me?"

"Fucking hell. That is not something that I needed to hear." Santos walks into the kitchen, heading straight to the fridge.

"*Callate*. It's not like you don't screw my sister's brains out."

"Camila!" Isabella yells. I should mention there's a smirk on his face and a blush on her cheeks.

"I thought that you weren't speaking to the guy," Santos grumbles as he comes to sit next to my sister.

"I'm not, but him coming here is a big thing." My mood tones down a bit. "And I'm trying to deflect so that I don't have a panic attack."

I give my brother-in-law a sad smile.

He looks at me, not saying a word, and eventually he lets out a sigh.

"I can't believe I'm saying this, but if the man doesn't at the very least check you out, I will beat his ass."

A chuckle leaves my mouth. "I will hold you to it."

The chime of the doorbell sounds through the kitchen and the dining room and right away my heart starts beating in overdrive.

Everyone just looks at me as if I'm going to run to the door, but I don't move an inch. I stay standing in my position, waiting to hear something.

Waiting to hear the door open or for footsteps to approach.

It takes a few seconds but eventually I hear just that

and the second I do, I feel like I'm about to have that panic attack that I talked about.

That feeling goes away though, when I meet the icy blue eyes that I love so much.

I haven't stood this close to him since I walked out of the apartment. I should be angry at the man for doing what he did, but I find myself wanting to run to him.

Wanting to find comfort in him.

"Hi." I breathe out, my eyes not moving from his

"Hi, Cami," he says giving me a small smile, one that doesn't reach his eyes.

We continue to stare at each other until someone clears their throat.

"Should we sit?" Leo says, coming behind Nate.

We all nod, moving to take a seat at the dining room table. Of course, Leo takes the head seat and I end up next to Isabella, right across from Nate.

"Want to tell us why we're here?" Isabella asks our brother before briefly looking at Nate and looking back to Leo.

Nate looks a little uncomfortable being here. I give him a small smile to put him at ease, but I don't get one back.

"We all know that our father has hurt a lot of people in his life. Including everyone at this table."

Everyone at this table?

"What?" I look to my brother back to Nate, trying to figure out what Leo is saying.

Finally, Nate gives me a small nod.

"How?" My voice breaks a bit just trying to come up with some sort of scenario where my father hurt Nate.

Nate sighs and clears his throat before he speaks.

"Before my father died, he was an FBI agent. Before I was born my father got a tip that there was a new cartel climbing up the ranks in Mexico. They started looking into it and found that the cartel was smuggling Colombian coke into the United States. Back then, it was easier to infiltrate something like the cartel, so the FBI sent in a man. That man being my father. He became a part of the cartel and was a part of it for two years, became friends with Ronaldo and Rosa Maria, all while reporting back to the FBI. He was in deep, that is until Ronaldo found out that he was being double-crossed.

"I was two at the time, so I don't remember a thing, but from the research I did, I found that a few months after Ronaldo found out he had a mole, my father went up to Canada to talk to a member of the cartel, which he did. He was able to get even more information to send back to the FBI."

"Canada?" Isabella asks, looking at Santos. "Cristiano?"

Santos nods in confirmation.

Cristiano Reyes was talking to the FBI?

"A few days after arriving in Canada, my father died in a car accident. Someone messed with some of the lines which resulted in faulty brakes and the car spinning out, hitting a tree and going up in flames. It was rumored at the time that the hit was called by Ronaldo himself. That he had found out that my father was an agent, so he had sent his most loyal man after him."

"Cristiano Reyes killed your father?" I have to ask. The

man was like a second father to me, and I can't picture him doing it.

"He was ordered to, yeah. But my anger was never toward Cristiano. It was always toward Ronaldo, because he was the one that ordered the hit. He was the one that wanted my father dead."

Nate continues telling us every detail as to how he came to become an agent and why. He tells us how he found out about the cartel when he was sixteen and wanted Ronaldo to pay for what he took away from him.

He talks about everything he has done since the start of his career to take down the Muertos, but eventually switched courses and concentrated just on my father.

Everything comes up. How he really didn't know who I was when we met, how my father found him when he was twenty-five and had threatened him. How Leo reached out and offered any information to take down our father.

By the time that the end of his explanation is reached, I feel as if my heart hurts. It hurts because I really didn't know who my father was. It hurts for Nate because he was robbed of a father at such a young age. It breaks when I think about how Nate was practically forced into this life because of what happened to his father, all because of mine.

It hurts hearing this story all together. It hurts even more when I hear Nate apologize.

"Why are you apologizing?" I ask.

"Because I took your father away. You said so yourself. He may have been a bad man, but he was still your father. For that, I'm extremely sorry."

That's when I lose it.

Tears stream down my face as I place my hand on the table and hold it out for him to take.

He hesitates for a few seconds, but he puts his palm in mine.

I want to be closer to him, but for right now, I will take this.

"We'll get through it." I know that we will.

"I killed your father."

"And he killed yours. It's a vicious cycle that we live in, but we will get through it."

33

NATHANIEL

I'M in the home of the new cartel kingpin, drinking fucking tequila, trying to come up with a plan to stop a raid. What the fuck has my life come to.

After I gave the Morales family my whole life story, Leo told the girls that we had some business to handle. Of course, that brought on a whole lot of questions on its own, but after Leo agreed to tell them later, they got up and left.

All but Cami.

She continued to sit there, looking at me with worry in her eyes as if she was afraid that something was going to happen to me. I reassured her and after asking her brother to not hurt me and he agreed she left. Not before placing a small kiss on my cheek.

That was the closest we'd been in weeks and I'm man enough to say that I missed it something deadly.

In all honesty, I would much rather be with Cami,

talking about everything she learned and figuring out where we stand, than being here in Leo's office.

"Why am I here?" I ask before taking a sip of the tequila I was handed. Damn, it's smooth. I'm not a tequila drinker but I may have to start.

Leo sits behind his desk, while I sit in a chair in front of him and Santos takes a seat on the couch.

"Because we need to know what we're up against, and you, my friend, are the only one that could tell us that." Leo leans back in his chair, acting like the possibility of getting raided excites him.

I sigh. "I already told you, I don't know anything. I don't even know where this said evidence came from."

"But you know the agent replacing you. What's their deal?" Santos asks, placing an ankle on his knee and getting comfortable.

I'm already throwing my career away by being here, might as well give them everything.

"Her name is Ava Hall. Up until yesterday, I had no idea that she had any interest in working this case. She was never involved."

"What changed?" Leo asks.

I think about it. Think about when I saw the shift in Ava. Maybe she's been wanting to partake in this case for a while and I'm just becoming aware of it.

"Honestly, I have no idea. She must have had a close eye on the case and had looked into all the people involved because she knows who Cami is. Something I didn't know until the morning after the raid."

I've been trying to figure out how she would have found out. She didn't know Cami's full name, or at least the full fake name she uses. So, it doesn't make sense as to how she knew.

Unless...

"Unless she saw Camila come to the prison. Saw her walk into the conference room and then saw you bring us in," Santos voices from his place on the couch.

That's where my mind was heading.

She must have seen when I brought Cami up, and probably started putting the pieces together. Add in the fact that she didn't like seeing me with Cami, her seeing me bring the three of them to the conference room must have fueled the fire.

"That has to be it. And she probably got confirmation when the pictures of the funeral were leaked."

A couple of hours after the funeral, someone leaked pictures of the Morales family standing by the gravesite. They were wearing sunglasses, but if you knew Cami and knew how she wore her hair, you would know it was her.

Ava probably saw the picture, saw Cami and got confirmation.

"But why wait until now to take you off the case?" Leo muses.

I shrug. "Maybe she was waiting for something. She had to be triggered about something."

"But what?"

"You're asking me questions I have no answers to. If I knew why she decided to go behind my back to take me off, I would tell you."

The office goes silent for a few beats, all of us thinking of some way to go about this.

"We need to know what the new evidence is." Leo muses, picking up his phone that lays on his desk.

"And how do you want to do that without breaking a few laws, or me losing my badge?"

At this point, I'm starting to think that there may be more important things outside of holding a badge than to protect and serve.

"We have our ways." He gives me a smirk as he swipes his finger across his phone screen before laying the phone back on the desk. The ringing sounds through the room.

There are five rings before someone answers.

"Your Royal Highness! Or should I say Your Majesty, since you're now the king of the kingdom?" a kid's voice fills the room, causing me to raise an eyebrow at Leo.

"Lane." Leo says in greeting, rolling his eyes at the mention of him being king. "Calm down."

Lane?

As in the Lane family, the wealthiest family in the country?

"Sorry, I got a little excited. What can I help you with?"

"Can you hack into the database of the DEA?"

The kid doesn't answer right away, but the breathing on the other side tells me that the call didn't drop.

"I mean, I can, I did it last time you asked, but what exactly would I be looking for?"

"Any new evidence that they may have on the Muertos, and when and where they are planning to raid," Leo says into the phone.

Again, there is silence from the other side, then the kid speaks. "I will start working on it right away. I will let you know when I have something."

Call ended.

The three of us sit there in silence.

"Now what?" I had to ask.

"Now we wait."

————

CAMERA FOOTAGE.

That's the new evidence that the DEA has on the Muertos. Camera footage of Santos interacting with some street-level dealers and then a video of Leo interacting with a box truck driver as he arrived at one of the warehouses. The second video wouldn't seem like much, but with the right eye, you will be able to see the exchange of money and a weapon hand off.

Both videos were from last week.

As someone that has worked this case for years, I've seen these types of videos before. For me, they don't warrant a raid. A judge could see these videos and have them dismissed because there is no clear evidence of any wrongdoing.

It makes me wonder why Beck is jumping the gun on this one.

There was one more piece of camera footage that's in the hands of the DEA and that's of me at Ronaldo's funeral. Apparently, me standing in the background at a man's funeral, not interacting with anyone, is confirmation enough that I was working with the Morales family.

The only reason I went to it was because of Camila. I had to see her, and I needed to know she was okay. I didn't go for the man that was being put in the ground. I couldn't care less about him. I went for his daughter.

Drake, the Lane family member that Leo called, also found that I've been put on probation without any notification.

Meaning that I will keep my badge and if I do anything bad in the eyes of the DEA, it will be taken away.

I honestly don't know how to feel about that.

As for the raid that they are planning, it will be at one of the warehouses that the Muertos operate out of in Austin. A warehouse that Leo says is functioning as a candy manufacture but now that they know, things will be moved around, just to be prepared.

"While all of this is happening, you need to me in New York. They can't know that you have anything to do with this," Leo says to me as we walk out of the office.

"They are probably already aware that I'm in Austin. No doubt ready to take away my badge the second I step foot in New York."

"Don't let them. We need a man on the inside," Santos voices.

Is he suggesting that I become a double agent like my father? Work both sides for the benefit of the cartel?

"You want me to work on both sides?" I look at both men like they are fucking crazy.

Leo shrugs. "You're part of the family. It would be beneficial to have a DEA agent at the dinner table."

"What the fuck are you talking about?"

Leo sighs at me like I'm missing the bigger picture. "I've seen the way you look at Camila. You were sitting at a table full of people and you only looked at her. That girl has her claws deep in you and there will be no way to get them out. The way I see it, you will be an official member of this family soon enough and it will work for my benefit."

I don't give enough credit. This motherfucker is a lot more observant than people think.

"Or am I wrong?"

I sigh. This is a conversation that I should be having with Cami, not her brother.

"No, you're right."

Leo nods and places a hand on my shoulder. "You hurt her, they won't find a body. It will be cut into tiny pieces and then burned to a crisp."

I look Leo in the eye, not afraid of him. "Did you give him this same talk?" I nod toward Santos, who is smirking as he leans against the wall.

Leo shrugs. "Not really, but he isn't the one in the relationship with my twenty-one-year-old sister while he's in his mid-thirties."

"Fair enough." I can't with this guy but if being with Cami gets me this, then I will deal with it.

"Good. Now go talk to her." He slaps me on my shoulder and starts to walk away, Santos following him.

"Wait." I call after them, having one more question on my tip of my tongue just begging to come out.

Both Leo and Santos stop moving and turn back to face me.

"It may not be my place, but Rosa Maria. Did you ever try to figure out why she was really killed?

The teasing banter that filled the hallway a few minutes ago, is now completely gone and in its place is something somber.

Leo looks at me, probably wondering why I'm bringing up his mother. After a few minutes of staring me down, he lets out a sigh.

"I tried. For years after she died, I tried to find everything I could on why she was killed. I knew he had something to do with it, even at fourteen, but I was never able to find out the whole story. My father stopped me before I went down a hole that would have been too dark to crawl out of."

Leo's facial expression changes. It's as if he's not the new leader of the Muertos cartel but a grieving son.

"Would you ever want to know?" I have no right to ask these questions, but either way Leo answers me.

He nods. "I do, but I don't know if I will ever be ready to discover that information. No matter how many years have passed."

I give him a nod of understanding. Without another word from Leo, he starts walking down the hallway again, with his most loyal man behind him.

Maybe one day, I can help him find that information out.

For now, though, it's time to go find Cami so we can talk.

I just hope that Leo is right and there's still a future for us.

I don't know how she could forgive me, but hopefully I can try and prove to her that I love her with everything I have.

34

CAMILA

THE PICTURE from earlier grabs my attention once again. This time as I draw the line, I see what the paper and pencil is trying to tell me, who or what I'm drawing.

I guess my art really knows what's on my mind.

After Leo had dismissed me, Isabella, and Serena from the table, I came back to the room I'm occupying and picked up my pencil. I needed a distraction from everything that Nate had said, and him being in my brother's office.

I also needed a distraction from my hopes that Nate would stay to talk to me after he was done with Leo and Santos. It could be that he is just going to talk to my brother and he's going to leave. And that's most likely the case if my brother scares him off.

The need to talk to him is there, especially with all that I learned about him today, but I doubt that it will happen. So I keep drawing.

Painting with acrylics may be my favorite medium, but

drawing with just graphite makes me not overthink and be in the moment.

I'm drawing a few lines when I hear a knock on the door. Taking my earbud out, I turn and a small smile forms on my face when I see who it is.

"Hi." I place my pencil down and give him my full attention.

"Hi." Nate hangs close to the door, probably thinking I'm going to kick him out. "Um, Serena told me where I could find you."

"You can come into the room," I say, trying not to laugh at how awkward he looks just standing there,

He nods and comes in, looking around for somewhere to sit, eventually settling for the bed.

I watch as he leans his elbows forward and rests them on his knees, bowing his head before he speaks.

"That morning, I thought that I had accomplished something. For years, I had worked on that case and never thought that I would see the end of it. I was angry at Ronaldo for taking away my father, for taking away my chance to get to know him in person and making me only know him by story. So that morning after I pulled the trigger, I finally thought that I had conquered my biggest obstacle, I had slayed the monster that had haunted my life for so long. My father is one reason why I pulled that trigger, but there's a second."

There's pain in his voice, and I want to go to him, but I stay seated and ask one simple question.

"What was the second reason?"

He looks up at me, sadness swimming in his icy-blue

eyes. "You."

I let out a small gasp when he says his second reason.

"How was I the second reason?" If he didn't know who I was, how was I even a reason for he pulling the trigger?

He lets out a sigh. "I didn't say this at the table earlier, but your father knew things about me. He knew things about me that aren't known to most people. As me and you got closer, the thought of him knowing I had someone in my life that was important, sprouted. If he knew about you, would he send someone to hurt you? Would he kill you to get to me? To hurt me? That night, as I was standing in front of him with my gun up, he mentioned your name. He asked how you were enjoying New York. I told him that he had no right to mention you. He had a gun pulled and pointed in my direction, yelled a few things and that's when triggers were pulled. Both his and mine. If I wasn't wearing a vest, I would have been brought out in a body bag next to him."

Nate talks but my mind started to spiral when he said that my father mentioned my name to him. How did he know that Nate and I were together? Did he have men following me? Following Nate? The only person I mentioned his name to was Isabella, but she hadn't spoken to our father in months.

"My father knew?" I say, dumbfounded by the thought. I can feel the sting in my eyes from the tears that are about to make an appearance.

Nate nods. "He knew. He had eyes and ears everywhere. There is nothing that could be hidden from him."

I should had figured that would be the case. I should

have known that he would find out I was with someone, since he knew about Isabella's secret relationship with Santos when they first started. Of course, he would know about this.

But how long?

Did he know when I went to go see him? Did he know but didn't mention it?

If only I could ask him.

When I don't say anything, he continues talking.

"It makes sense what his last words were. He accused me of infiltrating his family, for crossing the line with his own blood. I just thought that he was talking about Leo, and knowing that his own son was talking. I was angry at his words, and it was anger that I felt when I pulled that trigger. Anger and then pain from being shot at, and then it was comfort because it was all over. I felt that way even the morning after, until I saw you in the lobby. Until I heard you let out a sob for losing your father. Everything you were saying started to click. You were the little girl in the picture I've seen a million times over, and I didn't even know it. But now that I know, I see it. I see the similarities, the birthmarks. I see that little girl as you. When I heard you cry, that feeling of comfort and accomplishment disappeared. In its place was anger, this time directed at myself, and regret. Regret because I had pulled the trigger that took someone out of your life. You might not have had the best relationship, but he was still your father, still your blood, and I took that away. That's why I didn't fight you on walking out. I let it happen because I didn't deserve you anymore."

I let my tears escape. This man took down the most dangerous man in the world, a man that he was hunting for years, and feels regret over it. Because of me.

"I'm sorry, Camila. I'm sorry that I pulled that trigger. I'm sorry that I took away a life that meant something to you. I'm fucking sorry about everything. If I could take it back, I would."

I look at the man in front of me, seeing the caring and loving man I fell so hard for. The man that holds every piece of my heart.

Not the man that was in a room with my father, holding his gun up ready to shoot.

"I'm not going to sugarcoat it," I start, shifting slightly in my seat, facing the man in front of me straight on. "There was anger inside of me too, these last couple of weeks, but unlike you, I didn't know who it was directed toward. Was it at you because you were the one that held the gun that ultimately took my father's life? Was it at him, for choosing this life and not caring about his children enough to think about the repercussions of his actions? And now that I know everything I wonder if the anger was at the both of you for putting the other in that position. In the position where it would be a life or death situation. That anger then turned to hate. Did I hate you? Did I hate him? Was it the situation as a whole?"

I wipe away the tears, my face probably looking all blotchy and red, but I don't care.

"Then I realized it was hate toward this life that I was born into. A life that took away my mother when I was five, the man that was more of a father to me than my own when I was fourteen and then my father when I was twenty. A life that could have taken you away if things had ended differently. I've always hated this life, not because of the drugs or any of the material things but because of the darkness that it brought. As the weeks went by, I realized that I was angry at you less and less, but the anger at my father still stood."

I give him a tearful smile.

Nate sits at the edge of the bed, looking at me with eyes that are full of emotion it's hard to just pinpoint one thing. I want to get lost in them just as much as I want to get lost in him.

But I can't do that. Not yet at least, I have to continue.

"I didn't tell you this, but when I went home back in November, I went to see him. It was the first time that I had seen him in months, and I just wanted to talk to him. To see if maybe, just maybe, I could make him see that what he was doing with me and my siblings was wrong. But I walked in and all I felt was coldness. I felt like the second I stepped foot into that house, I wasn't welcomed. For the first time in my life, I had walked into my childhood home and had hated every last bit of it. And when I left, I had hoped that wasn't the last conversation I had with him. But it was."

I stand up from my seat and walk over to the bed, standing in front of Nate, itching to reach out to him, but I keep my hand to myself. At least for now.

"Hearing you talk earlier made me realize something that I've known all along. My father was a bad man. Always had been, and there wasn't a thing I could have done to change that. No matter how hard I tried. He would have continued to be a bad man for years to come, become a different version of himself if you hadn't stopped him. You killed Ronaldo Morales, a man that for a long time wasn't the father I knew and loved. You killed the Ronaldo who was power hungry and would have destroyed the world to get what he wanted."

Finally, I reach out to touch him. First I brush my finger along his shoulder until it's around his neck and my hand is in his hair. Nate keeps his eyes on me but leans into my touch ever so slightly.

"What are you saying, Camila?"

"I'm saying…" I run my fingers through his hair, living for the closeness between us. "I don't hate you for what you did. Because here's the thing, Nathaniel, I love you. I've loved you even when I was supposed to hate you. I love you even though you're my father's killer. "

I wrap both my arms around his neck, his legs opening so I can settle between them, but he doesn't touch me.

"Even though you did what you did, I still want to be with you. But the question is, do you still want to be with me? Can you look at me and not see me as my father's daughter?"

Please say yes.

I don't know if I can continue living in New York without him at my side. He's the reason why moving to a new state without my family was an easy thing to do. He was the reason why New York felt like home.

After a long minute of just looking at me, he places his hands on my hips, holding me in place.

"I have one question." I nod for him to ask it. "You may not hate me, but can you forgive me for what I did?"

I feel his thumb circling around on my covered skin.

This question is something that I really think about.

Is this an action of forgiveness?

"I don't think that there is anything left to forgive. The way you described the situation, the way my brother has, it was a life and death situation. Your life or his. Am I sad that my father is dead? Yes, but given the circumstance, that call was something that I would always be waiting for. His death was an inevitable thing, one that could have involved anyone, it just so happened to be you. I think that's what was so painful about all of this. That you were involved. It could have been you in that casket and not him. His bullet could have killed you and it would have taken you away from me. If that would have happened, I would have been destroyed beyond repair." Six weeks ago, those words would have never left my mouth. Leo was right, I needed to hear the whole story to know how I was feeling about all of this.

But there is still something else.

I run my fingers through his hair. "I have my own question for you." He nods before I can even finish the sentence. "There may be nothing to forgive but I don't know if this is something that I will ever be okay with. Will you be okay with that? With me possibly never coming back fully from this situation? Never being okay with what happened in that room between you and my father?"

Without warning, Nate stands up, his hands that were on my waist coming to my face, and he leans down.

"If I get to have you, wake up next to you, fall asleep with you at my side, I will be okay with everything and anything. As long as you're mine." He places a chaste kiss on my lips before he pulls back. "Are you mine, Cam?"

I don't hesitate. "I'm yours."

Our lips collide, but this time it's a lot more than just the chaste kiss from a few seconds ago. There is passion behind this one, passion that I hadn't felt since the last time he kissed me this way.

We kiss until we are both breathless, and our hands are all over the place, pulling at each other's clothes.

"Nate, I need you to touch me," I say against his lips.

I say I need him to touch me, and you know what he does, he chuckles. The man chuckles.

"I'm not going to touch you." He says against my lips

I pull back from him. The audacity of this man. "Why not?"

"I like my dick too much and me touching you under your brother's roof is a sure-fire way to get it cut off."

I let out a whine. "You're older than him and bigger. You can take him."

I hate Leo right about now. I wonder how he would like me interfering with his sex life with Serena.

Nate just smiles at me, taking my face between his hands again. "We have time, Camila. We have plenty of time. However long you want."

"I'll take everything."

Nate gives me another kiss. "I'll give it to you, but first there are a few obstacles we have to take care of."

"What obstacles?"

35

NATHANIEL

I PLACE my gun in my holster and attach my badge to my waist, preparing for just a normal day at work.

But it won't be a normal day, not by a long shot. Not with everything that is going to happen in only a few hours.

Things will happen, and all I will be doing is sitting back and watching it do down, like the actions of today won't affect me one bit.

Adjusting my tie, I look at myself in the mirror and see a different man than who I was a year ago. The man looking back at me is no longer one that is putting the badge before anything else. The man looking back at me has gone against everything that he believes in because he fell in love with the wrong woman.

As I keep looking in the mirror, I know I will forever be that man, and I will never let that man become something else.

With one final look, I leave the bathroom and head

into the bedroom. I take a quick look at the canvas that hangs above the headboard before leaving the room and heading out of the apartment.

It's when I'm halfway to the office when the Bluetooth in the car starts to ring. I don't even look at who's calling before answering it.

"Madden."

"Hey." Camila's voice fills the car and for the first time today I feel a sense of reassurance.

"Hey," I say back to her.

"Are you on your way to work?" she asks. I hear scratching in the background, meaning that she's probably is drawing something.

I nod, even though she can't see it. "Yeah, I should be there in a few minutes. Are you doing okay?"

I left Austin on Sunday morning, but Camila didn't come with me. After we somewhat figured out where we stood with our relationship, I told her what was happening and why I was in Austin in the first place.

At the mention of the raid, she started to get worried, asking what was going to happen. I told her that I wasn't sure, but that I was going to try my hardest to protect her family.

When it was time to leave, she said she was going to stay behind until the raid was over, just in case anything happened. I was a little worried, but after Leo said that he was sending the three girls and Noah away to a place where they were safe, the worry subsided.

Now Cami, Serena, and Isabella are in an unknown location and I'm on my way to watch all of this unfold.

"Yeah, I'm doing okay. The three of us are hanging in there, but Noah has been getting a little fussy, like he knows something is going on, so Serena is slightly on edge. But we are fine."

I nod even though she can't see.

"That's good, and I'm taking a wild guess that you have been drawing nonstop since you arrived."

She laughs a little, telling me that I made the correct assumption. "I have, just like Isabella has been drawing new designs left and right."

"It's good to keep yourself occupied," I throw out there.

"Yeah, oh, and guess what? Isabella is branching out. She said that someone put the idea into her head last year, and she's finally taking the leap." I smile at the happiness in her voice as she tells me about her sister's plans.

Months ago, I didn't think that I would be finding out every detail about the Morales family like this, but here I am.

"She should. The dresses she's made for you, are my favorite," I say adding to the conversation. It's not a lie. Every dress that she wears that was created by her sister, is form fitting and clings to her body in the most perfect way. All I want to do is slide the material off and have my way with her.

"Easy now, Detective. You're on your way to work," she teases.

That's the first time she's called me detective since everything went down with her father. I won't tell her how much I've missed it.

"Speaking of work," I say, pulling away from the

conversation at hand. "I just pulled into the parking garage."

Camila goes silent. She knows that me being at work means something is going to happen soon.

"Okay, be careful, okay?"

"Cam, I'm not leaving the office."

She sighs. "I know, but this whole thing could turn into a dangerous situation. Just watch your back. Especially from Ava."

She scoffs at Ava's name, and I don't blame her. Ava basically threw me under the bus to take the lead on this and for some reason, is out to take me down.

"I will."

"Okay. I'll see you in a few days?" I can picture her eyebrows bunching up and her teeth nibbling on her lip with worry.

"I will see you in a few days."

"I love you, Detective."

"I love you too, beautiful girl. I will call you as soon as this is all over," I promise her. This won't be over though, not by a long shot.

"Okay." The call ends and I take a second to collect myself.

The second I walk into that office and into the viewing room, I will be working both sides.

"Here goes nothing." I push the door open, and I make my way to the elevator and up to my floor.

As soon as I step off the elevator, there are agents all around, but nobody is talking. Everyone is just mentally preparing for what will happen today.

They are probably wondering if this is the day that the Muertos will finally be taken down.

If this is the day that the Morales family will be no more?

What they don't know is that things will change today, but not in the way that they think. Not in the way that they hope.

I walk through all the people and the desks until I reach my door. I don't even bother starting up my computer, I just place my stuff down, put my gun in my drawer and head to the viewing room.

Got to get front row seats to this.

Walking into the viewing room, all eyes turn to me. Including Beck's and Ava's.

"What are you doing here?" Ava asks. Her facial expression tells me that she's angry at me being here.

"I should be asking you the same question. Shouldn't you be in Texas making sure everything is running smoothly?" I raise an eyebrow at her.

"That could be done from here," she throws back.

She's afraid of failing, that's why she's here. So that if something goes wrong in Texas, she's safe from any retaliation from the cartel. She's safe from getting hurt.

"I would have been there, but to each his own, right? You don't mind if I sit in and watch?"

"Why?" Ava questions, crossing her arms at her chest, squaring her shoulders back. "So you can go back to your little harpy's family and talk shit if I fail at this?"

"No, like I said before, my girlfriend isn't connected to this," I say, keeping my tone even. "The reason I'm here is because I've been on this case for over a decade, and just like every single other agent in this room, I want to see you take down the cartel. I want to see you succeed."

The lie falls easily off my lips and by the way that Ava looks at me, she believes every last word.

She gives me a nod. "Okay then. Just don't interfere."

I hold up my hands. "I wouldn't dream of it."

Walking away, I head over to one of the chairs in the room and take a seat.

The whole room buzzes with excitement for what's about to happen, all the while I try to keep my composure as best as I can. I sit there as Ava and Beck talk about the logistics and what agents are on site.

Conspicuously, I take out my phone and send out a quick text to Leo, telling him everything he needs to know. Preparing him for what's to come.

Soon, a call comes in and the mood in the room shifts. Beck and Ava situate themselves in front of the screen that is projecting body cam footage and the lead agent's voice fills the room with descriptions of what's going on.

The scene is similar to how we were when we stormed Ronaldo's warehouse in Nuevo Leon. Except this time, I know how this ends.

I watch as the body cam footage shifts and the warehouse comes into view.

"Sensors detect movement inside. Permission to enter, Agent Hall?" The lead agent's voice fills the room, all eyes shifting to Ava.

"Permission granted. Storm the place and bring them down."

Orders fill the room and within seconds, our men are storming the warehouse that is just outside of Austin in broad daylight.

As soon as the door is kicked in there are screams that ring through from the warehouse as orders are yelled out.

From what Leo told me, this warehouse in particular serves as a candy factory. The Morales rent out a portion of it to a candy company all while the other portion is part of the Muertos operation. Actual people work there, some that are here in this country illegally trying to make a living to support their families. So, the fact that Ava is doing this in the middle of the day is a little cold-hearted. She's putting innocent people at risk.

A little hypocritical for me to think that, in all honesty. Given the way I had agents stormed the warehouse months ago.

The whole room watches as the agents go through the place trying to find something, anything, that points to illegal substances on the property.

It takes a whole hour to clear the whole building and another to get confirmation that the building is clear of our suspects and of any contraband.

"No, check again! There has to be something there!" Ava yells out to the agent in Texas.

"Sorry, ma'am but the building is clear. There is no evidence of contraband anywhere that we can see."

"Then take down every inch of it and look again, we have them on video. The contraband is there!" Ava says, sounding angrier by the second.

I turn slightly and look over at her. Her expression is

filled with anger and stance tells me that if she could strangle the man through the phone, she would.

For a quick second, Ava turns and catches me looking at her. At first, she looks at me a little defeated and then anger replaces it the longer she looks.

She starts to grind her teeth before she marches over to me.

"What the fuck did you do?" she says through her teeth, anger radiating off every inch of her.

"I didn't do anything," I answer her. That might have been the wrong thing to say because she swings back her arm and strikes my face.

The room is filled with dead silence.

"Like hell, you didn't. We had everything to take those bastards down and magically it all disappeared? You did something, I know you did. What was it?" she says through her teeth

I rub at my cheek, standing up to my full height. "What was I going to do, Ava? I didn't know you when you were doing this until last night. I didn't even know what you were going to raid or what evidence you found. How the fuck was I supposed to do anything?"

Ava is fuming, her face is even red from all the anger. "You did something to mess this up for me. I know you did."

"I didn't. I was telling you the truth when I said that I wanted to succeed." I give her one final nod and start to leave the room. "Maybe you should think about the things that you didn't do to accomplish this mission. Look at all sides, don't point fingers just because you can't close a case."

Opening the door, I leave the room and head back to my office.

The second that my phone is in my hand, I dial the new kingpin.

As soon as the ringing stops, I speak.

"It's done. For now."

He's silent for a few seconds until he speaks.

"Thank you, Nathaniel," he says, gratitude filling his voice.

"We're on first names now?"

"Seems fitting, since you're family now."

I guess being with Cami makes me that. "You're welcome, Leo."

The call ends and I spend a few minutes just sitting there.

What I told Leo is true. Everything that has to do with the Muertos, is done, for now.

This war for the time being will stop, but the second that someone finds more evidence, it will start back up again.

It might never end.

But for right now, the Morales family is safe and I will try my damn hardest to keep it that way.

Because Camila Morales means the fucking world to me, and I won't take another member of her family from her ever again.

36

CAMILA

I'M ALMOST FINISHED STRETCHING the canvas onto the frame when I hear the apartment door open and close. Sitting up, I wait for the sound of footsteps to follow and within seconds, they do.

His shoes hit the ceramic tile until they get closer and finally come to a stop.

I smile as the door to the spare bedroom, the one that I took over and made into my studio, opens. The second I see him, I want to jump up and wrap my whole body around him.

"*Hola mi amor*, you made it home." My smile grows even more when his face morphs into a smile I love so much, and his blue eyes brighten.

"I did." He comes into the room, stopping in front of me, crouching down and placing a sweet kiss on my lips. "I thought you were at work."

He pulls away, giving me another smile before he sits

336 | JOCELYNE SOTO

on the ground next to me, in his Tom Ford suit and all. I love it when he's just in slacks and a button-up shirt, especially when the sleeves are rolled up.

"I was, but it was a little slow, so I was able to leave early. And while I was leaving, I got an idea." I pat the canvas that's on the ground, thankfully it's turned upside down so he can't see what it is.

"Oh really? And does this idea match the idea that's hanging above our bed?" He gives me a smirk, probably remembering what it took to make that canvas.

I throw a wink at him. "Maybe, and I will show you, but first tell me how it went in Austin."

It's been three months since Nate sat at my brother's compound and told us why he was after my father, and since the second raid by the DEA. In those few months a few things have shifted.

The biggest of them being that Nate is becoming more and more involved with cartel business. He's not moving drugs around or getting rid of bodies, but he is working with my brother and Santos to keep the Muertos out of the eyes of the FBI and DEA.

At first, I freaked out when Nate told me that he was going to work both sides. Still be a part of the DEA, but give the Muertos intel when they needed it, especially when it was on them or other crime families. The first thing I thought of was that it was going to get him killed. I even called my brother to yell at him for it and convinced his wife to withhold sex for a whole week because of it. Eventually, I calmed down and Nate explained that the reason he was doing it was because of me.

Which, by the way is a shit reason. Any normally sane person would stop fucking the cartel princess and keep his damn badge and his ass in line.

But not this man apparently. I guess my pussy is so hypnotizing that it's worth risking everything he has ever built. There may have been a point when I wanted to slap him across the head to knock some sense into him.

After a few months, I accepted it and I told him that as long as he doesn't get killed, he can do whatever he thinks is right. But I swear if I find a bullet hole in him or he comes home with blood on his expensive suits, I'm flying to Austin and strapping Leo to a chair and doing to him what he does to others.

Last night, Leo called and said he needed Nate in Austin for something. What that something was, he didn't say. All he told him was that he was sending the plane, to be ready by six in the morning and only plan to be away from me for a few hours.

So, he left this morning for Austin and now he's back and I want to know what was so urgent that he had to fly to Austin. Surely it was something he could have done over the phone.

Nate sighs. "Your brother wanted me to look into some people that have been hanging around a few of the warehouses. Just wanted to see if I recognized any of them."

"He made you fly all the way to Austin for that?" I swear Leo is the most extra son of the bitch there is.

"He also wanted to show me what happens when you cross the cartel. Like I already didn't know that part."

Oh my god. "He didn't."

"Yup. Tongue severed and everything."

I'm going to puke. "Leo should not have that kind of power."

"And who should? You?" Nate gives me a smirk, raising an eyebrow at me.

"Um, excuse me, I would be an excellent kingpin. Or would it be queenpin? Either way, I would be a lot more terrifying than my brother. All he has going on is his broody face and that he is covered in tattoos."

Nate snorts. "Baby, your brother is not only the most powerful man in all of Mexico but also the most feared."

"Are you saying I'm not scary?" I narrow my eyes at him, challenging him to laugh.

"Not at all what I'm saying." He leans in and places a quick kiss on my lips, making me forget. "Now, show me what you got here."

He pats the canvas, and if he wasn't so cute, I would be pressing the issue of me being scary more, but I drop it.

"For my twenty-first birthday, I had this plan. Me and you were going to take a trip and just be us for a few days, not worry about work or school. Then everything happened and I ended up spending my birthday by myself. I even went back to the bar we met at to get my first legal drink. Well, my first one here in the States. But of course, even that was ruined when Ava showed up and started saying how you were meeting her there."

"Wait, Ava? You saw her on your birthday?" Nate asks.

I nod. "She said a few things to me. I just got up and left, but that's beside the point. I was angry and sad, so I just went home. When I walked up to my door, there was a box and a bouquet of flowers set on the floor. Do you remember what you got me?" I look at him, giving him a small smile.

"Art supplies. It was the same acrylics that we got when we went to the paint store and then a canvas. And at the bottom was a picture of the hung canvas."

I nod. "And in your note, you said that you hope that I created something amazing. So, I did."

I grab the canvas and flip it over for him to see.

The different colors are all mixed together, and it looks very similar to the one that we painted together.

"I took inspiration from the one that we did and it kind of looks the same, but the major difference is that this one is all me."

Nate takes the canvas and inspects every inch of it. For a second, I'm back sitting at the bar the first time we met and he's looking at my portfolio and I'm scared he's going to see something he doesn't like.

"You did this? With your body?" he asks, not taking his eyes off it.

I bite my bottom lip. "I did. And I thought about you the whole time. Even when we weren't talking, even when I was supposed to hate you, I thought about you the whole time."

My eyes stay on him. I watch as he places the canvas on the floor and shifts his whole body to face me. Before I know it, I'm straddling his lap, his hands are on my ass and our lips are smashed together.

I let out a moan when I feel his tongue lick my bottom lip, asking for access, and I gladly give it to him.

His fingers dig deeper into my ass cheeks, and it causes me to grind against him, looking for more friction. I'm about to rip off my leggings just so I can feel it.

"I need you, Detective." I say against his lips, grinding my body some more.

I pull away from him and place my lips against his jaw that is covered in stubble and then move it down to his neck. I suck on his pulse point, like he has done to me time and time again.

"How much do you need me, beautiful?"

"With everything that I have. I need to feel you inside of me. I need to feel your weight on me. I need to feel your mouth on my pussy, on my breasts, I need everything," I say against his neck.

"You'll get everything you want." His hand clamps down on my ass and he shifts us so that he can stand up with me in his hands and legs wrapped around his waist.

Nate walks us to the bedroom, kicks open the door and as soon as he can, he drops me on the bed.

"Scoot all the way back to the headboard. Head on the pillow. Arms above your head."

"What are you planning on doing, Detective?" I ask as I do what I was ordered. The man is hot when the boss comes out.

"Handcuffing you," he says a smirk playing on his lips.

"Seriously?" I can feel my eyes go wide with excitement. I've been waiting for this day for months.

"Yup." He grabs his cuffs from where they lay on the

bedside table and climbs on the bed, straddling my body. "Got to try out this new railing I installed."

"Railing?" I sit up slightly and look over my shoulder to the headboard, and sure enough, there is a black bar that is only visible at certain angles. "When did you do that?"

"A few weeks ago." Nate's hands land on my stomach and he slides up my shirt until it's fully off and on the floor. My bra is next and as soon as my tits are free, he leans forward and takes both into his mouth.

I let out a moan when I feel his mouth on me, marveling at his sucking motions and at how he grips me.

"I fucking love your tits," he says before he bites down on my nipple.

Instead of responding, I just let out a moan and place a hand on his head, holding him to me.

"I think it's time that you don't have access to those hands." He pulls away from my chest, and I pout when I no longer feel his mouth on me.

"Hurry," I groan out, which turns into a moan when he rubs against me and I feel his hard cock through the material of his pants.

Nate just chuckles, grabbing the handcuffs and getting me situated on the rail.

I like this.

Once I'm put in place, Nate climbs off me and off the bed and starts to undress.

His eyes don't leave mine as he takes off his belt and then unbuttons his shirt. One button at a time and I'm fucking needy.

Rubbing my legs together isn't enough.

"Nate," I whine. Needing him to touch me again. Needing to not only feel his mouth on me but also his hands.

But he doesn't say anything, he just continues to smirk at me as he gets rid of his clothes. There is wetness pooling between my legs and all I'm getting is a sexy, dumb smirk.

Once there isn't a piece of material covering his body, the pooling starts in my mouth. This man has a glorious body, especially for being in his midthirties. No doubt that he will get hotter with age, and I will be able to enjoy every single moment of it.

"What was it you wanted again, baby?" Nate comes closer to the bed, grabbing me by the legs and pulling off my leggings.

"Everything," I breathe out.

"You're going to have to be more specific."

"I need you."

"Need me where?" Once my leggings are on the floor, he spreads my legs open, settling between them.

"Inside me," I pant out when he runs a finger along my slit, barely touching my clit. "On me."

"Do you want my finger in you?" He continues to slide his finger in my wetness before inserting it.

"Yes," I moan.

"Or do you want my cock?" His finger slides out causing me to squirm.

"Your cock. I want your cock."

He gives me a smirk again as he settles on his knees between my open legs. His girthy, heavy cock standing up and asking for attention, if only my arms weren't tied back.

"By the look in your eyes, you want to swallow it."

I take my bottom lip between my teeth. "Maybe I do."

"Is that your answer then? You want my cock in your mouth? So you can feel it sliding down your throat, choking you?"

I twist my lower half, trying to give myself friction at the thought of taking him in my mouth.

"Or do you want it in your needy pussy?" He grabs his cock and slaps it a few times against my wetness.

"Pussy. I want it in my pussy."

This time, instead of a smirk, I get a grin as he slides into me. "Good girl."

I will never get tired of this man's cock in me. It's like fucking heaven every single time.

Nate fucks me until I'm panting. He fucks me until I'm thrashing against the bed, begging for him to release the cuffs so that I could touch him. He fucks me until I scream his name out, as he tells me to give it to him again and again.

My orgasm comes fast and hard and before I could even come down from it, the second one is already on its way.

"Count like the good girl that you are, Cam. Count."

"Two," I breathe out, black spots clouding every line of sight.

"Such a good girl. I fucking love how your pussy feels around me. Fuck, baby," he grunts, continuing to fuck me like there's no tomorrow.

I'm on the brink of three when he places his thumb on my clit and starts to rub at it.

"Don't hold back, baby. Let go. Give me everything that you have," Nate grunts out, thrusting into me faster as the seconds tick by.

"Three!" I scream out, my legs shaking in the process.

I'm still panting, trying to catch my breath when Nate lets out a loud grunt a few minutes later, releasing everything he has into me.

He is still inside me as he uncuffs my hands and when my hands are free, I grab him by the hair and bring his mouth to mine.

We kiss for a few minutes before he finally pulls away from me and heads to the bathroom to get a washcloth. Once we are both clean and settled, we lie in bed, wrapped up in each other.

We lie there for a few minutes, the only sound in the room, being our breathing.

"Nate?" I say, cuddling deeper into his chest.

"Yeah, beautiful?"

"Thank you for loving all my crazy." Because I am crazy, and any other man would have said I was too much.

He lets out a chuckle. "Thank you for giving me all the crazy to love and for not hating me for my actions."

I smile at his words, and we go back to lying in silence.

"Nate?" I tap his stomach this time.

He chuckles. "Yeah, baby?"

"I'm ready for round two." I lift up my head and give him a smile.

This time, he laughs and brings my head closer to him. "You're going to kill me, beautiful girl."

"Well, that's what you get for being with a twenty-one-year-old."

He continues to laugh, but this time he adds a head shake. "Then I better make the most of it, shouldn't I?"

And make the most of it, he does.

37

NATHANIEL

I LOOK at my watch and see that if we don't do this a little faster, we're going to be late. And if we're late, none of us will be alive to see tomorrow morning.

"Can we hurry this up, please?" I ask, slightly annoyed with how long this is fucking taking.

"You have to have patience, *hermano*. We're almost done." Santos gives me a smirk, shaking his head in the process, all the while he wipes at his blade.

"Yeah, you said that two hours ago. Now you two are cutting it a little too close." I look around the room, shaking my head at the amount of cleaning it will take to clear it of any evidence.

"We're almost finished, don't worry your pretty little head. We'll make it on time," Leo voices as he walks around the chair that's in the middle of the room.

I sigh, rubbing a hand across my face. "I still have no idea why I'm here."

A call came in this morning as I was having breakfast

with Cami, that I needed to come down to an abandoned building by the river in the next hour.

I've learned in the last two years not to ask questions when it comes to Leo's requests.

It's better to agree with the man than to fight him on shit.

This though, this, I should have fought him on. When I got the call and then the text message, I thought that I was going to be looking at a damn building so that the Muertos could operate out of, but no. Instead of it being a damn building walk-through, it was a damn interrogation.

An interrogation that included a bloodied body tied down to a chair, hanging on by a thread. A few more punches and the guy at the middle of it won't be able to hold up his head.

"So you won't be blindsided when his body shows up and the *federales* start asking questions." Santos gives me a shrug from where he stands in the corner of the room, waiting for Leo to give him the go-ahead to end the guy.

I sigh.

For the past two years, ever since I agreed to work both sides and the raid that Ava orchestrated didn't go as planned, Leo has been making an effort to include me in things. And by things, I mean his versions of "interrogations" or overseeing the operation that take place.

I usually stand back and watch. There has been the very rare occasion where I have participated in said interrogations and spilled blood on my hands. But mostly I'm standing back.

And today, especially today, I'm standing back. If I

show up with even a speck of blood on me, I will be sleeping on the couch. Can't have that.

As for today's lovely victim, he's supposed to be a dealer here in Manhattan, that decided that it was best to keep the coke for himself. Not very smart on his end.

Sometime in the last year, the Muertos expanded their operations a bit here in New York. It's not a big operation since the DEA are still watching, but enough to bring in a good chunk of cash in.

And before you ask, I do get a cut. Since Leo and Santos aren't here to keep an eye on things, and when I'm not working or with Camila, I'm dealing with the mother-fuckers that move the merchandise around.

It's an easy gig, but sometimes, things hit a snag. Take the guy sitting in the chair, for example.

"Tell me, Duffy, what did you do with the coke?" Leo grabs the man by the hair, tilting his swollen face back, and looking him straight in the eye.

"I lost it," the kid cries out. His legs are shaking meaning that he's probably pissing his pants.

"It was nine kilos, Duffy. How can you lose that much coke?" Leo spits out, his voice raising a bit, which causes Duffy to cringe.

"I don't know. It just happened." His voice trembles and a part of me feels bad for the kid, but he brought this on himself. You don't steal from the cartel.

Great, now I'm including myself in that.

What has my life come to?

"You see, Duffy, I don't believe you. Why don't you just tell us where the merchandise is and we will let you go,"

Leo offers, but the four of us know that Duffy won't be let go that easy.

Instead of answering, Duffy cries. His eyes are probably burning from the swelling and the tears mixing in.

"*Ya matalo*," Santos says, sounding annoyed.

The last couple of years, I've picked up a lot more Spanish than what I knew before even meeting Cami. So I understand when Santos says to just kill Duffy.

At this point I'm with Santos. If it gets me out of here faster, just pull the trigger.

"*Esperate*," Leo tells Santos before going back to Duffy. "Last chance, Duff. Where are the drugs?" Leo asks through his gritted teeth.

Duffy cries out louder, but this time after a few sniffles, he talks.

"In my apartment, under the floorboard in the closet of my living room. It's all there."

"See, was that so hard? Thank you, Duffy. I appreciate your honesty." Leo places his hand on the kid's shoulder, before looking over his shoulder at Santos and nodding.

"About time."

Duffy doesn't see it coming. The shot just rings through the room and then Duffy's screams overshadow it. Eventually the screams subside, and all that fills the room is silence.

It's an eerie feeling, one that I don't know if I would be getting used to anytime soon. It still shocks me just how unaffected Leo and Santos are about this.

Now it's time to dispose of the body, but when I look at my watch, I see that we are now in fact going to be late.

"We have legit twenty minutes to get to the stadium. Are we done here?"

Leo nods, turning to face me. "Yeah, let's go before we get our asses chewed."

I swear if I'm late and have to sleep on the damn couch, I'm going to shoot him myself.

Fucking bastard.

———

WE TAKE our seats seconds before the music starts to play throughout the whole stadium and the graduates start to walk out.

Of course, us arriving wasn't without a few narrowed looks from Isabella and Serena and I swear Noah was looking at us the same way and he's only two.

It's Camila's graduation day. After countless hours of drowning herself in art materials and passing all her classes, Cami is finally graduating from NYU. She added an extra year to her undergrad, but she is finally going to be walking across the stage and get her degree.

In the almost three years since we met, Cami has not only grown with her art, but as a whole individual. Don't get me wrong, the girl still eats her chicken strips every chance that she gets, but ever since her dad passed away, she's changed in a way. More caring, more loving toward everyone, has become more of a light to me.

My life before was one that I don't want to go back to. I was missing something during that time, and I didn't know it until I sat down at a bar and started talking to her. It was this pull that she had that would make the wrong man run away and ungrateful for it. That pull captivated me and made me an addict for her.

Sitting down on that day and spending time with a complete stranger was the best decision that I ever made.

Sure, it brought me closer to the cartel in a way that I didn't expect, and going against the oath I said years ago, but if it means having Camila in my life, I would do it over again. Because she's it.

She is everything to me.

She's the light of my day.

She's the chaos in my life.

She is the woman that I will spend the rest of my life with.

Yes, she's only twenty-three and has her whole life ahead of her, but I will be there right next to her the whole damn way.

That's why I talked to Leo and Santos when they arrived last night.

"I need your permission to propose to Cami," I say and the small office that we currently occupy which feels a little smaller, tighter.

I just asked a kingpin for permission to marry his baby sister and I seriously don't know if it's a death wish or a spectacular move.

Leo turns to me, his eyes twitching a bit and his lips are pressed together as if he doesn't like what I just said.

I don't give a shit.

I'm asking out of respect and since these two are important figures in Camila's life, they get the pleasure of suffering a bit.

Leaning back in my chair, I continue to drink out of the tumbler in my hand, acting like I'm not shitting my pants right about now waiting for an answer.

"She's too young," Leo throws out.

I nod. "I know that. She has her whole life to live, and I'm not going to stop her from going on whatever adventure she wants to take."

"What if she wants to travel for months on end to see every art museum she wants?" Santos asks.

She does, so I have an answer for that. "Then she will go and when the distance becomes too much, I use all my time off or I quit and go to her."

Cami told me a few weeks ago that she wants to spend at least one summer on the other side of the world just seeing every piece of art that she can. I told her to do it and as a graduation present, I'm surprising her with plane tickets for a few weeks from now.

Santos and Leo both look at each other, not saying a word. I hate when they do that, it's annoying. Actually, they're both fucking annoying, and even with how much time I spend with them they still make me want to pull each strand of my hair out.

"When?" Leo asks, breaking whatever silent conversation he's having with his brother-in-law.

"When what?"

"When are you thinking of proposing?"

I give him a smirk. "Does tonight in bed count?"

Leo lets out a growl, his eyes becoming murderous. If I didn't have a desk in front of me, he would probably be strangling me right now.

I shake my head. "After she turns twenty-five. Like you said, she's young, I want her to enjoy her life a little more before she's tied down to me. Don't get me wrong, I want that ring on her finger right this second and officially claim her as mine, but it will happen in due time."

"Why come to us now?" Santos asks, standing up from his seat and coming to stand next to Leo.

"Because I wanted you two to know that I wasn't going anywhere. Ever. I love her with everything that I am and if waiting another two years for her is what I need to do, so be it."

That and Camila specifically told me to not do anything stupid like get down on one knee until her twenty-fifth birthday. She said she at least wanted to rent a car legally before getting married. Fine by me.

Again, Leo and Santos look at each other and have a silent conversation.

Eventually Leo sighs and gives me a nod. "You have my permission and my blessing." He holds out a hand for me to take, which I do, making this official.

"And here I thought we were going to get rid of the bastard at some point," Santos throws out when he too offers me his hand.

"There's still time." Leo says to him.

Now it's me growling. "Not going to fucking happen."

Both of them laugh. "Well, good luck, hermano. You're going to need it with that one. She's a fucking handful."

"Only the best kind."

After that conversation ended, I went to find Isabella. I had to ask her permission too, since she has a big part in who Cami is today.

The conversation with her was a lot more emotional than the one between her brother and husband.

She asked just one question and one question only.

Did I really love her sister?

At first, I was just going to say of course I did, but then I decided that it was best to put it all out there.

I told Isabella that I couldn't see a life without Camila. That had we not met, that I would be searching the world for her. That I loved her, and I had loved her before I even realized it. That I would kill for her every chance that I had if it meant she was safe.

My life started and ended with Camila Morales.

My words caused tears to spring in Isabella's eyes and after she gave me a tight hug and thanked me for giving Camila the world that she deserved, she gave me her blessing and permission.

She then got excited about making a wedding dress and spewing off ideas to me. That's when I got up and left.

Now here we all sit, waiting for Cami's name to be called.

"It's hot as shit out here," Santos grumbles from a few seats away.

"Stop cursing in front of the baby," Serena reprimands him, as she looks at the bouncing two-year-old on her lap.

"I'm sure he's heard worse, especially with who he has as a father," he retorts and I'm sure Isabella slapped him across the head because his next word is "Ow".

"*Ya calmate* and stop complaining," Isabella tells him.

I can't help but chuckle at this family. They do some of the darkest shit in the world, and in everyday life, they're so fucking normal. It trips me out a bit sometimes.

"And now the New York University Department of Art and Art Professions," the person on stage announces and everyone with an art student cheers, including the five of us.

Name after name is called until they reach the one that I want to hear.

"Camila Morales Diaz."

The second the announcer says her name and she starts crossing that stage, the five of us jump up and cheer for her as loud as we can until she steps off.

The ceremony continues until all the names are said, and once that is all said and done with, we are all able to go down to the field at Yankee Stadium and grab our graduate.

It takes me a while to find her, but soon I catch sight of the gray-haired beauty that has captivated my whole world.

I stand in place and wait for her to see me, and when she does, a smile spreads across her face and she charges over to me.

Cami jumps into my arms, wrapping her whole body around me, not caring that there are thousands of people around us.

Eventually I detangle her from my body and I place her on her feet, taking her face between my hands and placing a chaste kiss on her lips. Again, people all around us.

"I'm so proud of you, baby. So fucking proud."

"Thank you because I wouldn't have done it without you," she says, peppering my face with kisses.

"Yeah, you would have." I smile down at her.

Cami shakes her head. "When I had my interview, I was freaking out. Thinking that I wasn't good enough. Then some random guy showed up, looked at my portfolio and said that I would get in, that NYU would be stupid not to take me. And that man has encouraged me, has encouraged my art ever since then. So thank you. Thank you for everything."

I take her face again and this time give her a deep kiss that is definitely not suitable for being in public.

"You are welcome for everything."

"I love you, Detective."

"I love you too, beautiful girl."

CAMILA

THE LIGHTS and the music are surrounding me. The flowers are everywhere and seeing all the families come together is showing me exactly why I love this celebration so much.

This year feels a lot more different from years past. I think because this year, there isn't a dark cloud hanging over our head like it has been for the past four years.

Things started to shift during this celebration the year that Serena and Leo got married. It was dark that year, especially when Serena was taken the morning after. That same year was when everything was going on with Isabella and her marriage arrangement. There was strain between her and Santos, and it threw off the celebration even more.

Then the year after, was when I came by myself to see and speak to my father, and it was the last time I spoke to him.

The year he died, it felt slightly wrong to come to San Pedro and be a part of all the celebrations. Especially with our childhood home sitting empty for months and standing like the aftermath of a war. So I flew to Texas and me and my family had a small little celebration there.

Then when it came to last year, I was so swamped with finishing my last year of school, so the celebrations were put on pause.

This year though, I decided that I needed to do something big and the only way that I would be able to do that was to come to San Pedro.

Because this was going to be a big ask, I went to Leo a few months ago to ask him to make it possible. He told me that going back to San Pedro might be dangerous. I'd asked him why, and he told me that the people of San Pedro were used to being under the protection of the cartel. After my father's death, the last of his men that were living at the compound moved to different parts of the country. It's been two years since there's been cartel presence in the town and if we step foot within town lines, they could come after us.

Even if it was dangerous, I wanted to go. I wanted to be able to spend time at my mother's grave.

Leo wasn't happy, but he made it possible.

The Muertos started making their presence known in San Pedro again. Leo even hired someone to clean up the estate, as it sat untouched for years, so we can stay there.

It was an eerie feeling walking the doors this morning. Like time sat still, but it felt like a different home. All of our stuff was still there. My room was filled with my art. Isabella's studio stood untouched, but my mother's garden was completely gone.

Every last flower was dead. I think seeing the garden out of its glory hurt more than actually being inside of the house.

But I didn't let the state of my mother's garden ruin this celebration for me. No, as soon as everyone was settled, I got everyone together and got to work.

And by work, I mean I got to painting. Every single member of my family was going to be partaking in the celebration, no matter how much they complained.

That means that both Leo and Santos sat in chairs and let me paint at least a little design on them. For how much they complained, they sure did tell me to add more to give it more of an effect.

I even got to paint something on Noah's face and Nate's.

Nate.

He's part of my family.

He is part of my life, and it means the world to me that he is here in San Pedro with me. And when I asked him if I could paint his face, he let me do anything I wanted. So I did.

Now, we're walking in the town square, seeing all the people interact and seeing everyone honor their loved ones.

Like years before, I have flowers in my arms and placed them at the gravesites that have no family around them.

Because every single person should be honored.

At the end, I have three bouquets left. One for each gravesite that means something to me.

"Are you okay?" Nate asks from next to me as we walk through the cemetery.

I nod. "Yeah, I just realized that this will be the first time I will be visiting my father's grave since his funeral."

It hasn't been without wanting, it just hasn't happened.

"If you need anything. I will be here for you." Nate tells me, giving my hand a squeeze.

This is why I love the man. He's caring even when visiting this gravesite might be hard for him too.

I give him a smile and continue to walk to the place where my parents are buried.

My first stop, as always, is Cristiano. I place the flowers around the grave and make room for the ones that Santos and Isabella will be bringing later tonight. When it's to my liking, I stand at full height, place a kiss on my fingertips before placing it on the stone.

"*Vas a ser abuelo, Cristiano.* Isabella's pregnant and both she and Santos are so happy. They even said that if it was a boy, they were going to name him after you. I really hope it is a boy, that way we have another Cristiano running around. They will probably come tell you later, so act surprised." I smile, just picturing him standing in front of me and smirking and telling me, 'I told you so.' He knew this was going to happen eventually. "Keep watching over them, okay? Keep protecting them. *Sigue descansando, Cristiano.*"

With one final fingertip kiss to the grave, I move to the next one. My mother.

I walk a few steps, holding Nate's hand the whole time. When we reach the grave, Nate takes a step back and I get on the ground and arrange her flowers much like I did with Cristiano's. Instead of standing up, I stay on the ground, not caring about the mud.

"*Hola, Mamí. Disculpame por no visitarte.* There's a lot that has happened since the last time I was here. Leo made you an abuela, and you would love Noah with all your heart. He looks just like Serena but acts like Leo. And his little laugh just makes you smile every single time you hear it. And Isabella. She did it, *Mamí.* Her designs are making it big. People are starting to know her and soon, everyone will be wanting their hands on one of her dresses. *Y otra cosa*, she's pregnant. She and Santos are having a baby. Now that she's pregnant, she reminds me so much of you. She has your hair, your same facial expressions. Everything. You would be so happy."

I dab at the tears that are falling down my cheeks. Taking a deep breath, I look over my shoulder to Nate, who gives me a smile of reassurance, letting me know that he's there for me.

"And for me, I met someone. He's older, a special agent, and really cares about me and loves me. He encourages me to follow my dreams and gets excited every time I paint something new. He opened up his life for me and he's everything that you could have asked for in a man for your daughter. I love him, *Mamí.* I love him and I really wish you could have met him, because you would have loved him too. Don't worry about us, *Mamá.* The three of us are okay. We are loved, we have each other and our family is growing every single day. You would be proud of everything that we have accomplished."

I sit there for a few minutes, just wanting to be with my

mom for a little while longer. I want to feel her near, especially given where I'm going to head after I leave her grave.

Giving her gravestone a kiss, I stand up with the help of Nate and we make our way over to my father.

"You don't have to do this. You don't have to go to his gravesite with me," I offer, letting him walk away while I visit my father might be a good idea. I don't want him to regret what he did any more than what he already does.

Nate stops walking and takes my hands in his.

"I said I will always be there for you, and I meant it. And I will be there for you, even in this. No matter the part I played in putting the man in the ground."

I don't deserve this man.

Squeezing his hands, we continued walking the last remaining steps to my father's site.

Unlike my mother, his site hasn't been visited and looks a little dirty.

Letting go of Nate's hand, I get to work on putting the flowers in their place, but unlike my mother, I don't sit on the ground to talk to him. I stand fully and look down at what is left of a man that was once my whole world.

"*Hola Papá.* I don't know why, but I expected to feel different coming here tonight. I thought that I would be heartbroken or that I would be wishing that you were here next to me like I am with *Mamá.* The reality is though, I'm not. Do I want you back? Yes, but I don't want the man that you were when you died. I want the man that was there for me when I was five or checked on me during my teenage years when Leo and Isabella weren't around. I want the father that would walk the garden with me and tell me the most mundane part of his day. But you hadn't been that man in a very long time. I hope that you're resting. I hope that a part of you is with *Mamá* and you are both looking down at us, proud of what we have become. I hope that in death you have found calm to the storm of a life that you lived." I place my fingers to my lips and then to the stone. "I love you, *Papá*, and I always will, and hopefully I can forgive you for how you treated your children."

I look at his grave for a minute or two, tears running down my cheeks.

Nate steps next to me and wraps an arm around me, and that's when I lose it completely. The tears come out like a pipe is broken and there is no way to stop it.

I'm not crying because my father is dead, I'm crying because all the words that I just said should have been told to his face, but I never got the chance.

Not because Nate took that chance away from me, but because my father did, and I hate him for it.

I hate my father.

The hate won't be forever, but even two years after his death, it's still there and it will take some time to dissipate.

There is one thing that has disappeared, though.

Finally, I calm down and I turn in Nate's arms and look into the bluest eyes that I have ever seen and bring my hand up to his cheek.

"I'm fully okay with what you did," I say to him.

"Camila."

"No, let me finish. I'm okay with it, fully. You did what you had to do and if he was still alive, I have no idea what other bad things he would have done. You stopped him, and I'm okay with it."

I stand on my tiptoes and place my lips on his.

"Are you sure?" he asks, his eyebrows bunching up a bit.

I nod. "I'm absolutely sure." I give him one more kiss. And when I pull back, I get a smile.

Once again, he takes my hand and we make our way out of the cemetery.

As we head back to the compound, I think about how much my life has changed from one simple trip to New York.

On that trip, I was utterly terrified of my father. I was scared of what he could do with me if I didn't fall in line. If it wasn't for my sister and brother, I would have been there until his death, if it even came.

That one trip changed my life.

I was accepted into one of the best art programs in the country and I met the love of my life.

Now years later, the fear of my father is gone, but the cartel is still intact, yet I don't fear it like I once did. The only fear that I have is that someone will take my family away from me, and I won't let it.

Now, I'm a lot stronger than what I once was and feel like I can take on everything that comes my way.

I have my family.

I have a man that loves me and brings a light to the darkness that surrounds me. And I love him, with every inch of my being.

We might have been brought together as strangers who

had chicken strips together, fell in love as friends, pulled apart by a vendetta and brought back together with honesty, understanding and love.

I may be a cartel princess that fell in love with the federal agent that killed her father, but I wouldn't change a thing.

Not now, not ever.

I guess even members of the cartel family get happily ever afters too.

Even if they are a bitch to get to.

THE END.

PLAYLIST

Six Feet Under - Oshins, Leslie Powell
Into it - Chase Atlantic
Watch me Burn - Michele Morrone
Daddy Issues - Sophia Gonzon
Dangerous Woman - Rosenfeld
Bad Girls - M.I.A
Bad Bitch - Bebe Rexha, Ty Dolla $ign
Fuck Up The Friendship - Leah Kate
Chains - Nick Jonas
Saturday - Jaime Lorente
Give Em Hell - Everybody Loves an Outlaw
Do it for Me - Rosenfled
Heaven - Julia Michaels

ACKNOWLEDGMENTS

Camila's and Nate's story is finally here and there is something about this story that feels a little bittersweet. It has nothing to do with the story itself, but the fact that this is the last book in the series. It makes me a little sad just thinking about it.

With this story, I wanted to take it in a slightly different direction. This book still has the dark elements to it but still has light hearted moments. I wanted to give Cami a relationship that wasn't centered the cartel and hopefully I was able to achieve that.

For now this is the end of the Morales Family but do not worry, you might see more of them in due time. I'm not ready to give up this family just yet.

Now onto the thank yous!

Ellie, thank you for being a rock star editor. Especially with my chaotic writing. You are awesome!

Shauna and Wildfire Marketing Solutions, Thank you, thank you, thank you! Thank you for helping me promote not only this book but also this whole series. I have no idea what I would have done with out your team.

Readers, thank you for falling in love with these characters and giving me happiness that you want to read something that I write. It's because of you that I was able to push through some dark times when it came to this series and I can't thank you enough.

Thank you to everyone that has shown me love and support on this series and this family.

Now onto the next writing adventure!

A college romance anyone?

BOOKS BY JOCELYNE SOTO

One Series

One Life

One Love

One Day

One Chance

One for Me

One Marriage

Flor De Muertos Series

Vicious Union

Violent Attraction

Vindictive Blood

Standalones

Beautifully Broken

Worth Every Second

Powerful Deception

ABOUT THE AUTHOR

Jocelyne Soto is a writer born and raised in California. She started her writing journey in 2015 and in 2019 she published her first book. She is an independent author who loves discovering new authors on Goodreads and instagram. She comes from a big Mexican family, and with it comes a love for all things family and food.

Jocelyne has a love for her mom's coffee and writing. In her free time, she can be found reading a romance novel off her iPad or somewhere in the black hole of YouTube.

Follow her website and on social media!
www.jocelynesoto.com

facebook.com/authorjocelynesoto

twitter.com/authorjocelynes

instagram.com/authorjocelynesoto

bookbub.com/authors/jocelyne-soto

goodreads.com/jocelynesotobooks

pinterest.com/authorjocelynesoto

tiktok.com/@authorjocelynesoto

JOIN MY READER GROUP

Join my ever-growing Facebook Group.

https://www.facebook.com/groups/jocelynesotobooks

NEWSLETTER

Sign up for my Newsletter!
You will get notified when there are new
releases to look out for, giveaways and more!

https://www.subscribepage.com/
authorjocelynesotonewsletter

Made in the USA
Middletown, DE
18 September 2023

38632874R00216